THE WIND FARM

Alexander Godhelping read law and has worked as a solicitor and journalist, and as an entrepreneur in natural resources in the Russian-speaking world and in China, learning those and other languages. He and his wife and their cat have a flat in Notting Hill in London. The Wind Farm is his first novel.

ALEXANDER GODHELPING

THE WIND FARM

First published in paperback in Great Britain in 2016 by Wind Farm Publishing.

Paperback ISBN: 978-0-9954635-0-9
E-book ISBN: 978-0-9954635-1-6

A CIP catalogue record for this book is available from the British Library.

For Susanne with my love

Acknowledgements

I am very grateful to those who helped with this book, both in
the energy industry and others, including individuals in both
major parties and in both houses of Parliament.
Special thanks go to Jane Underwood, Roger Taylor,
Paul Simpson and Taki Kiometzis.

1

ONSET

Hearing about something is not the same as seeing it with your own eyes. I had heard on the ship's radio about the rising sea levels and flooding but this did not prepare me for the sight of Dover. Even the web videos failed to match the reality.

The port of Dover had disappeared – the breakwaters, the piers, the row of hotels along the quay, all gone. The sea lapped at the hill on which Dover Castle sits. The ferries which carried tourists to France had all gone, to where I couldn't say. They'd probably been evacuated by their owners as the sea level rose. Evacuated – the word probably applied also to most of the people who used to live in Dover. The famous white cliffs looked unformidable.

I had been at sea for nearly seven weeks, and my young colleague Frank for almost nine weeks. This was much longer than the rules of our company allowed. Four weeks on, four weeks off was the rule. Our workplace was like an offshore oil rig, except we were concerned with offshore wind turbines. We maintained them from a station fixed in the sea bed which we reached on a ship built specially for that purpose, the *Windsail III*. And however wonderful the station was – with all the comforts of home, so to speak – there was nothing I wanted more than to get off it. And Frank likewise. Of course there was no smoking on station and I was dying for a smoke. I wouldn't say no to a drink to go with it. Our immediate supervisor had refused let us off until our 'big' boss,

Phil Burnley, had radioed his OK. Health and safety regulations forbade lowering the bunker boat in seas above one metre, and the seas were higher.

To hell with health and safety regulations was our argument. England's under water, or so they say, and we want to get home to see for ourselves. Besides, those same regulations forbade us to spend more than four weeks at sea.

But what really drove me was my determination to see Nessa. I'd spent my time at sea working up the nerve to ask her to marry me and stay in England. She was in London and I was worried about her. We'd been together for nearly a year, and our anniversary was coming up soon – the target date for my proposal. I was trying to work out exactly what to say.

None of that would have mattered to our supervisor – everyone was worried about someone ashore. We kept our arguments strictly to the regulations. Phil overrode all the supervisor's objections, as I expected he would.

'Let Jack Mason and Frank Cross go,' he said. 'There's no work for them to do on the sea turbs in this weather. They're due for a little "R and R." And they'll need it, because there's a special mission coming up.'

The bright orange bunker was a match for the waves – even if she capsized we could right it – but she was too short for the swell, with the result that her screws were as often out of the water as in it. The speed was therefore reduced and we crawled toward the coast of Kent.

The water had risen so high that the pilot was able to bring the boat among the houses just below the castle and we were able to disembark at the water's edge. Dry land. Well, not exactly dry, but land beneath our feet. We scrambled up the hill and surveyed the scene – we could just make out the roundabout leading to the A20. There was nothing to do but walk. Here and there we saw small groups of emergency workers wearing bright yellow waistcoats, but they paid no attention to us and we avoided them. They might tell us what we were doing was forbidden, that we should get away from the area. That was exactly our purpose. As soon as we put some distance between us and them, Frank and I reached for our smartphones.

No signal appeared in my screen.

'Blast!' I shouted. 'Frank, do you –?'

'Useless,' he said.

We walked in the rain to the motorway junction. Fortunately our gear was right for the weather – the best rain jackets that our employer, England's biggest wind energy company, could afford.

There was hardly any traffic and most of it seemed to be vehicles of the Kent constabulary and the Territorial Army. We had a vague notion of using public transport but reality on the ground made that a nonsense. There was nothing to do but walk and see how far we could get. We had different objectives. Frank lived in Ramsgate and I had a flat in London. At the junction we split up. Walking from Dover to Ramsgate was in theory possible, but it was about sixty miles to London and that didn't seem like much fun in the rain. There wasn't any alternative.

'Well, mate, this is it,' I said. 'I'll see you when I see you.'

'Jack, in a few weeks we'll be back on station and this flood will seem like a bad dream,' said Frank.

We shook hands and I turned to walk on, up the A20. The rain was in my face and after a bit I turned for a moment's relief. The figure of Frank was gone in the mist.

I walked on. The A20 became the M20. I was alone on one of England's major motorways. On an ordinary afternoon the road would be full of cars and lorries. Lorries there were, but they were all parked up on the shoulder. I didn't see any drivers in the cabs. Cars were much fewer. And the traffic – if I can use that word for motionless vehicles – was all going one way. All were on the side of the motorway *from* London, hardly any on the side *to* London. That could easily be explained by the fact that the Eurotunnel had been flooded – we'd heard that news on station – so it was logical there would be no traffic coming from Europe. The ones coming from London must have begun their journeys before the flooding.

After a couple of hours, the Eurotunnel entrance came into view and I could not resist the urge to see what it looked like. I'd seen it a thousand times in normal circumstances. I walked up the entrance ramp for lorries. There at the top I could see the train yard. It was a strange sight. The train cars looked like they were sinking – maybe they were – here and there the big sliding doors were open and the water filled them like bottles half submerged in a bathtub. There was no movement and no people to be seen.

On the top of the hill stood a row of wind turbines, their red tower lights visible through the mist. The lowering giants seemed impervious to the chaos imposed by nature. Despite a stiff wind, their blades were perfectly still, pointing away from the wind direction. To my trained eye, that seemed odd.

I walked on along the M20 towards London. My thoughts, like those of millions of others, were on what people had begun to call 'the Great Flood.'

The danger of rising sea levels had been noticed for years, of course, even decades. Back then, scientists had spoken of annual sea level rises in terms of millimetres – three or four millimetres per year. It didn't sound too serious. But now, in the middle of the twenty-first century, these estimates had been upped to centimetres and then metres. The phenomenon of rising sea levels was evidently accelerating, according to the experts.

Widespread flooding was the result. Lowlands all over the world were inundated. Some small islands in the Pacific and elsewhere simply disappeared. It made for some pretty dramatic internet videos but once you'd seen a couple they all began to look the same. Some small faraway place had ceased to exist, so what?

It struck closer to home in Kent. Parts of the southeast coast had been seriously flooded by the rising sea. Bad, but not unprecedented, and – everyone assumed – the waters were likely to recede. But they didn't. It only got worse.

The experts explained the rising sea levels in terms of global warming. That, again, was nothing new. I'd been hearing about global warming since as long as I could remember. Although I considered myself a 'green' my eyes would glaze over reading dire predictions on the web. I visited climate change web sites more often than most people, I think. To my way of thinking, they got more and more 'doom and gloom' all the time whereas, for me, it was more in my nature to look for practical solutions than to focus on the worst case. Doom and gloom turned me off.

Then there were the winters. Warmer and wetter, in England at least, than anyone could remember, but with sharp cold spells and storms that shut the country down for days at a time.

I will never forget the day, last winter, when I saw the first web video on the polar meltdowns. A stream of videos taken from aeroplanes and helicopters soon appeared. Spectacular shots of huge mountains of ice and snow sliding into the sea. There was no sound in the videos, but you could just imagine the roar as these gargantuan blocks broke away and crashed into the water.

The sight of the poles melting caused a general panic and demands for governments to do something. Oceans of virtual ink were spilled in online blogs. Some people became, simply put, obsessed. One film star, convinced the world would end, killed herself online – with her last words ('for the earth') tweeted to her followers. After a second such celebrity suicide, this quickly became known as a 'celebrity death tweet' – breeding a mood of panic.

But there really wasn't anything anyone could do, save for dealing with the immediate effects of the flooding.

One school of thought called for a ban on fossil fuels. Some said all forms should be banned while some said just the more harmful forms like coal-fired power plants. Gradual measures like these were already included in the climate change policy of the richer nations. But how could an immediate ban be enforced? Experts, anyway, said it was too late for that. Other schools of thought focused on ways to cool the earth's temperature at the poles. But the technological means for quickly achieving that end were doubtful.

In the end, a few governments closed coal-fired power plants that were deemed inefficient and took other half measures like limiting vehicle use. The wealthier countries declared the formation of an emergency organisation to stop the polar meltdowns but that meant, in the short term, setting up such an organisation, defining its authority and studying the means to achieve its objectives. This alone would take time.

In England the prime minister appointed a Royal Commission to tackle the crisis, and she named as its head Toby Lang, the deputy prime minister, a rising young politician. I liked the bloke. He seemed different from other politicians, more open. But I was sceptical about government in general.

Wind energy had, of course, been a major part of the new 'energy mix' to reduce dependence on fossil fuels. Millions of wind turbines – both on and offshore – had been built and brought into service. But not enough, soon enough.

Meanwhile, disasters mounted. An oil tanker struck an ice block in the sea north of Alaska, producing an environmental catastrophe. A ferry sank off the coast of the Philippines, and then a cruise ship sank in the Adriatic Sea off the Croatian port of Split, drowning a hundred British holiday makers. Lost ships became too commonplace to command media interest.

All this was only a prelude. It soon got much worse, but I was already at sea by then. We followed the situation aboard ship as best we could, via the web, spending our time exchanging news and debating the cause of the flooding.

England, as an island nation, was hard hit. Without ports, everything that moved by sea ceased to move. That included things that people can do without for a while, like steel for construction. But it also included things that we can't do without, like biofuel for vehicles and uranium for our nuclear power plants. Our reliance on wind energy, that is, on the turbs, grew.

The coastal flooding meant refugees, lots of them, from Kent, Essex, Suffolk, all over England. And London, too, after the Thames Barrier failed to perform as promised. Flooding brought a lot of road and rail traffic to a halt. As for the airports, the one in the Thames estuary was, of course, shut down almost immediately. Later the other major airports closed for lack of aviation fuel. Besides, pilots and passengers couldn't get to them.

Was it a natural event or made by man? That, essentially, was the debate. Phil had helicoptered out to the station only a week before Frank and I went ashore, and we had had another of our endless discussions in the station galley during a meal.

The seas had been too rough that day for maintenance work on the floating wind turbines – sea turbs, as we called them. The station, resting on pylons, was impervious to rough seas. It was our 'home away from home,' with computer work stations and sleeping areas that we'd personalised.

The station served two purposes. It was a maintenance base for storing tools, equipment and spare parts, and it was also an electrical transformer. Cables brought current from the turbs to the station, where it was transformed into a higher voltage and thence carried ashore via a single large cable. I liked the idea that somewhere under my bed was enough electricity to light London.

With twenty odd thousand sea turbs over two hundred square kilometres, the Thames Array was the largest offshore wind project in the world, and I was immensely proud to be a part of it.

'It's a historical fact,' argued Frank, 'that extreme climatic conditions occur in nature at intervals, even if those intervals are counted in the thousands or millions of years.'

'True but not the point,' said Phil. 'This crisis is man-made, and it's been predicted for donkeys' years.'

'And what if it's both? A combination of factors is the most likely explanation,' I put in. 'Nothing as complex as nature can be explained simply.'

'You're probably right about that,' said Phil.

I admired Phil greatly. Sir Philip he was actually – knighted for his work in developing offshore mobile turbs, as I will explain – though I never called him that. I wasn't afraid to disagree with him, and he didn't mind. He was a huge, genial man with a lifetime's experience in wind energy. Phil hid his steely determination to get the job done – whatever it might be – behind a jovial manner and an ever expanding paunch made, I think, from English ale. His eyes sparkled when he got excited and he was always excited when talking about wind tech.

Frank Cross, six years my junior – I was then thirty-three – was the most promising wind engineer I'd seen in a while. He was smart, almost precocious, but with an honest, straightforward manner.

I saw in him my younger self, but with a difference. Whereas Frank was open and trusting – oblivious to what others thought about him – I had learned the value of listening rather than talking. I had learned to move quietly, but not to hesitate when opportunity arose.

I didn't consider either Phil or Frank to be experts on climate change, but they probably knew more about it than most people. I certainly wasn't an expert, but then again training and experience in wind energy had taught me something about how the planet works.

'It's the lack of preparation that amazes me,' said Phil. 'What is happening now was foreseen but ignored. Perhaps "ignored" isn't the right word, but it was foreseen and not tackled continuously over long periods of time. It's a defect of democracy. Governments come and go, and there is no consistent policy over the long term.'

'Are you saying a global dictatorship could have done better?' I asked.

'A new world order for the environment? Not my cup of tea,' said Phil. 'Better the devil you know.'

'Let's change the subject,' he said after a pause. 'What have you found out? Are the mobile sea turbs disobeying instructions from their control computers? And are they breaking their tethers? Because if they are, it's a hell of a mystery that we've got to solve.'

'Yes, they are,' I said. 'We checked a sample population, two hundred turbs in the southeast quadrant. There are discrepancies between where the turbs have been told to go, and where they have actually gone. And not only about that, but also about other things like blade angle and directional facing. And, yes, they're breaking their tethers to the power grid, so we're not getting electricity from them.'

Phil rubbed his chin.

'Any idea why?' he asked.

'No,' I said. 'Not yet.'

'Well, check another sample in a different quadrant, say, the northwest. Take another week, and then I'll get you two off station. I'd like you to be involved in continuing this investigation onshore. That's the special mission I'll mention to your supervisor.'

'Phil, I've got a hunch I can find the answer onshore, at the wind farm near my family's house in Oxfordshire,' I said. 'There is no wind project I know better than that one.'

'All right, you're on,' he said. 'But first finish the mission here. I'm sorry to keep you here at sea for so long – you probably want to get back to that Chinese wind engineer you're so fond of – what's her name again?'

'Nessa Chao,' I said.

'That's right,' said Phil, smiling. 'By the way, I just heard that her delegation leader wants to take them all home because of the flood crisis – so maybe you need to see her. And Frank, what about all your girlfriends?'

Frank blushed but soon recovered.

'Sir Philip, they've chartered a boat to come out to the station,' he said.

'Well,' said Phil, laughing, 'you don't have to go ashore then!'

But we did. And I slogged on along the M20 in the rain. The landscape before me suggested the worst. Parked cars and lorries with no people and rain that would not let up. I began to calculate how long it would take me to reach London – that is, unless a coach or a friendly driver might pass. But they didn't. My calculation, at a rate of three or four miles per hour, was a twenty hour stroll. It was already late afternoon. Clearly, I would have to find someplace to sleep along the way.

Then came a bit of luck. A parked car with two bicycles hanging onto its rear. At first I thought, no, they'll be locked up. But as I approached the car I saw that they were merely strapped on tightly, not locked. I paused to consider the moral aspect of what I knew I would do anyway. It wasn't stealing, I told myself. I found a pen in my pocket and wrote down the registration number of the car and, on a separate paper, my name and smartphone number, which I then wedged under one of the bike straps leading into the boot. Later, I told myself, when all this was over I would track down the owner through the DVLA and return the bike or pay for it.

I untied the bike and looked it over. It looked fit for purpose. There was air in the tyres.

'Hey, mate,' came a voice.

I turned and saw a man approaching. He was sopping wet and dishevelled.

'Awful weather isn't it?' I said, for lack of anything else to say.

'It surely is,' he replied, coming closer to me than I would have liked. 'But you've got the best thing next to a car – and you've got two. Can I buy one of your push bikes? I'm serious. I've run out of biofuel. You as well by the look of it.'

The first thought that ran through my mind was: then money still had value. The man was offering me money. Of course money had value. I relaxed.

'Have you come from London? What's it like there?' I asked.

'Chaos,' he replied.

I waited for something more but nothing came.

'Never mind about the money,' I said. 'You can take the other bike. Bring it back here if you can.'

I rode off, not waiting to be thanked. I felt uneasy about the man, or about the situation. Helping myself, with a stranger, to someone's property on a deserted motorway.

Even with the new mode of transport it was clear that I would not make it to London before dark. I cycled past Ashford. If I could make it to Maidstone I could find a hotel. But even Maidstone began to look too far. Then I saw a sign for Leeds Castle. Junction 8. I knew the castle – my mother had taken me there when I was young and I'd returned a few times. The castle had rooms for the night and it was only a short distance from the motorway.

When I got there I saw at once that something was out of the ordinary. I rode right up to the gate and found it shut. Leeds Castle isn't very high, but it is surrounded by a moat, and the only way into the castle yard is across the bridge over the moat.

Behind the gate stood a couple of men who made no move to welcome me.

'Good afternoon,' I said. 'Is there a room available? I'd like to stay the night.'

The two men looked at each other.

'Full,' one of them said.

I didn't accept that as being an accurate description of things, but the way the man spoke communicated to me that, one, he was a foreigner and, two, he and his mate weren't the soul of hospitality.

'Are you lorry drivers? Is your lorry out on the motorway?' I asked. They looked to be from eastern Europe.

'No room here,' the man replied. 'Full with refugees.'

That confused me. Were they lorry drivers or refugees? I remembered the refugee camp on the French side of the Channel.

They walked away from the gate, leaving me to make the only decision I could make. I rode away, deciding to see if I could break into the castle ticket office and spend the night there. That was exactly what I did, only I didn't have to break in. Others had already done that. There was a family from Romney inside and a couple of men travelling alone who'd had the same idea. One of them explained to me about the 'refugees' in the castle.

'Apart from the foreign drivers, who seem to be in control, they're mostly from London' he said. 'They're English refugees.'

English refugees?

I found it hard to get used to the idea of English refugees. English people weren't refugees – refugees were people who came to England from somewhere else.

He didn't volunteer any more information, if he had it. And what did he mean about the drivers who 'seemed to be in control'? I was too tired to try to get more out of him. I unrolled my bedroll – our company truly provided well for its employees – and staked out a broom closet as my royal suite, with just enough room to squeeze my bike in. Otherwise it might not be there in the morning.

The next morning the weather was no better and still I had no signal in my smartphone. I avoided contact with the others and got back on my bike. I continued towards London along an empty motorway, past the junction with the M25, through Swanley then Sidcup and then that point where the traveller is treated to a view of Canary Wharf in the distance. I stopped and dismounted. It was not a particularly pretty skyline, nor one that was very familiar to me – I had never worked in those skyscrapers and I didn't care for Canary Wharf – too sterile for my taste. Nevertheless it was there and the fact of its presence suggested things weren't so bad. That impression would change soon enough.

On reaching Lewisham, along the Old Kent Road, I saw the first signs of chaos. I wouldn't have thought there was anything of value to steal in Lewisham but evidently others held a different view. The windows of supermarkets and discount clothing shops were smashed and broken glass strewn across the pavement. Here and there I could see men and women inside, picking through the merchandise. In front of one supermarket lay crates of produce which, though rotten, had attracted some takers.

I saw a Chinese restaurant that was totally gutted, with tables overturned and crockery smashed. Inside a Chinese woman scurried around trying to right the tables. Nearby the window of a local car service had been shattered. Why a car service? What was there to steal – or had someone done it just for the fun of it? Beside the window a black man pushed a wet broom over the pile of glass.

Here and there I saw dead animals in the gutters, now a dog, now a couple of cats, small feasts for London's eager rats.

Many on the street carried luggage – were they refugees or looters? Probably looters. No police were to be seen. Nor was there any of the usual traffic – no cars or buses.

I thought I might get a signal in my smartphone when I entered London but there wasn't one and then it didn't matter much – the battery was almost out.

I wanted to know what was going on, that is, besides what I

could see for myself. How bad was the flooding? What were the government doing? When would things get back to normal? Would they get worse before they got better? Would they get better?

Even an old-fashioned newspaper would do, but I didn't see a single newsagent open for business. I scanned the people I passed for someone who might know something.

I spotted a man wearing a bright yellow waistcoat. When I got in front of him I saw he wasn't wearing a uniform. I stopped anyway.

'Sorry, do you know anything about – uh – what's going on? Is central London flooded? Is the Tube running?'

He eyed me wearily.

'I don't know anything about central London,' he replied. 'I don't think the Tube is running.'

'Thank you,' I said.

The man turned away.

'If I were you, I'd head the other way,' he said. 'Get out of London.'

'But I've just come – .' The man was walking away. I let him go. I stopped two others in Lewisham High Street but got no more information.

I cycled on. Deptford was no better than Lewisham. The same scene of devastation, the same cheerless brown brick Victorian buildings. It looked like a good old fashioned London riot had taken place the night before. What especially struck me was the burned out hulk of the Deptford Library. Why had anyone burnt the library? What was the attraction of burning books? It wasn't the only burnt out building I passed. It struck me as odd that buildings had burnt in such a downpour.

In all this I did not feel any sense of danger. I did not imagine that any of these looters – or refugees – would be interested in a lone cyclist. No one bothered me.

I badly wanted a coffee but I saw no open café, not even a fast food place. I badly wanted a smoke, too. This bothered me. There might be some cigarettes overlooked by the looters but I could not bring myself to enter a looted shop to hunt for them – with the other looters. I was not a looter – not at that stage – and if I went into a shop with them, I would become one of them. Borrowing an abandoned bicycle on a motorway was different.

It was still raining buckets so with the wet streets I failed to notice the rising level of water. Whereas the gutters in Lewisham had little rivulets running by the pavement curbs, in Deptford the entire Old Kent Road was covered by a couple of centimetres of water and by the time I reached Elephant & Castle the water depth in the street was up to the spokes on my bike. The elaborate pedestrian tunnel system under the roundabout was completely filled with water. I saw rats swimming among the trash in the flooded stairwells.

The big shopping centre on the west side of the roundabout appeared to have been looted four ways from Sunday. On one wall, a sign for the *London Bingo Palace* hung precariously.

I reckoned I was less than half a mile from the Thames.

Yet at Elephant & Castle there was some sign of organised activity. Several large tents stood in the centre of the big roundabout but as I looked closer I saw only a few people standing about. One of the tents was in the process of being dismantled.

I walked over to it. One side of the tent hadn't yet been removed and it flapped in the wind. With each flap I caught a brief glimpse of what was inside. It seemed like an emergency shelter – I saw a row of sleeping people.

I took a few steps closer. The side of the tent kept flapping, making a snapping sound. I was curious – how could people sleep in this chaos?

Then I saw what was inside the tent. The people weren't sleeping. They were dead. There were rows of human corpses.

I froze. I had never seen such a thing before. I averted my eyes but after a moment, I felt compelled to look. My heart went out to these people. I struggled to compose myself. Details caught my attention. The bodies had an odd colour. Some of them were naked or had only scraps of clothing. They were of all ages, even some children.

What struck me most was that they all had big smiles on their faces. I shuddered.

'You there,' said a voice. 'Come away from there. Get over there with the others.' It was a policeman. He poked me in the side with his rubber truncheon.

I turned and saw a large group of people moving away from the roundabout past the Tabernacle and south towards Camberwell Green. There were police cars with lights flashing ahead of and behind them.

'Go on, move with the others,' said the policeman. 'What're you staring at?'

'They're smiling,' I said.

'They've drowned in the flood. Didn't you know that people who drown always look that way – sort of happy?' replied the policeman.

'No, I didn't know that,' I said. I found it difficult to speak. I looked again at the row of bodies and noticed a small child among them. I felt nauseous.

I moved as if to join the group. I thought to ask him what was going on, but it was clear what was going on: the water was rising and people were being moved away from the Thames, that is, the live ones. If I started a conversation he might insist that I join the group heading south and I didn't want that. I wanted to get across the Thames to Notting Hill.

Just then a young couple tried to break free of the group and the policeman showed surprising agility as he sprinted over to them, his raised arm waving the rubber joystick which he brought down freely on both the man and the woman.

I seized the chance to get to the main Tube entrance on the far side of the roundabout, but it was gated and locked. A handwritten cardboard sign hung from the gate: 'No Tube today.' The cardboard was soaked through. 'Today' was probably several days ago.

I would have to continue by bike. The authorities didn't want me to do that. A yellow band reading 'Police Line – Do Not Cross' was strung across the side of the roundabout leading toward Westminster Bridge. One end had fallen to the pavement. There were no police nearby.

I cycled up St George's Road past the cathedral. The water was deeper now, covering about a quarter of my tyres. As I reached Waterloo Station I saw that the underpass beneath the rail lines was seriously flooded. I went round the other side of the station, via Lower Marsh, to the taxi rank on the raised level. The doors of the station were padlocked. There was no one in sight. Coming round the other side into York Street I saw that the roundabout between the station and the bridge was also under deep water. But the bridge, I could see, was not submerged. I could cross.

I managed to pass through the square in front of the old County Hall to a spot where I could make it onto the bridge. From the middle of the bridge the sight took my breath away. The Thames had become as wide as the Rhine. It was no longer possible to say where the river left off and London began. A pane of water covered everything. The buildings stuck up out of the water as though that was the most normal thing in the world. I could see the pillars of Waterloo Bridge but the bridge itself wasn't there.

Water filled the road between the Houses of Parliament and Portcullis House. I couldn't see it, but the warren of tunnels and offices beneath Westminster was filled with water, including of course the Tube station, one of London's deepest.

But on the surface it did not appear to be deeper than on the south side. I could see that the water covered the riverside terrace cafes of both the Lords and the Commons – the flood was no respecter of party or class – but it did not appear to be deeper than my knees. I went on.

On the other side, the further I got from the river the dryer it became. Bird Cage Walk was submerged but the Mall on higher ground was still traversable. I crossed St James's Park near the Old Admiralty Building. At the far end of the Mall by Buckingham Palace I saw a couple of emergency vehicles but I avoided them by slipping through the side streets in St James's. I crossed an empty Piccadilly and turned into Bond Street.

All the jewellers' windows were gated and emptied of their treasures. Here and there people had tried to break the windows by throwing things at the glass and through the holes I could see the rocks and pieces of trash which had replaced diamonds.

A couple of men hadn't given up so easily, and were wielding huge metal bars to pry open the gates of one shop. I watched as they had some success. The gate yielded and one of the men was able to reach inside the window.

'Got something!' he cried.

Then the other man brought the bar down on the head of the first man, who crumpled to the ground.

'I saw it first,' he sniffed, giving a good kick to the man whose head he'd bashed open.

I was shocked – my first impulse was to move toward the fallen man – but the one with the bar had seen me and took a menacing step in my direction.

I stood my ground.

'All right, help him,' I said. 'Help the man you hit.'

'F– off!' he shouted, raising his weapon.

I didn't move, and gradually the man lowered the thing. Then he took a step toward the fallen man. I thought for a moment he would hit him again but he didn't. He reached down and pulled the man's head up. I'd seen enough. It wasn't my fight and I turned to go on.

At Berkeley Square I saw another collection of tents and emergency workers. I had by then no curiosity to look inside the tents.

I made my way along Mount Street toward Hyde Park – this was higher ground and although there was water everywhere, it was not flooded. Hyde Park was merely soggy, a pleasure.

Through the whole bizarre journey from Dover I felt that if I could just get back to my own flat and find Nessa everything would be all right.

My street seemed normal. But the curious thing was, it didn't *feel* normal. I couldn't say why. I put my key into the lock praying Nessa would be there.

2

THE RISE OF
THE TURBS

One of my earliest memories is watching the coronation of George VII as King of England and Wales – Scotland had long before travelled its own path – memories that may be completely irrelevant, now that that world has been swept away by the Great Flood and all that came with it, but it's comforting to recall that ordered world and it takes me back to the beginning of this story, my story.

When I was born my parents lived in a small flat in Cranbourne Villas in London. It had much less space than my parents and I required, but still it would have cost more than what they had then. My father was a petroleum engineer, a dying breed but a well-paid one – though few could be well paid enough to afford a flat smack in the middle of Notting Hill. We lived there only because my mother had inherited the property from her parents, who bought it back when London property was within reach of ordinary mortals. Then it had cost a song.

My father travelled constantly as part of his job. Early in his career he spent time on offshore rigs near Brazil, Indonesia, West Africa and other places. At one point when I was still young we relocated to the USA for a time, which left my English somewhere in the middle of the Atlantic. As he became more senior he worked only on land at jobs of his choosing. Later he became a director of several of the smaller oil and gas companies.

I learned a lot from him. I learned, first of all, that fossil fuels would not disappear despite the emergence of other sources of energy. Technology was the key to this. Energy that could not be developed in the past due to technological limitations became increasingly available. The world never ran out of oil, instead it kept producing more of it in new ways. I use the term 'oil' loosely of course to describe the energy that comes from various forms of fossil fuels – oil, gas, condensate, oil sands, oil shale, tars, etc.

Everything depended, he would say, on the technology and tools for finding energy and extracting it from the ground. In my lifetime, these have improved continuously.

Still, my father was more in awe of the financiers behind the oil projects he worked on than of his own technical skills.

'Those chaps are the smart ones,' he told me. 'They don't get their hands dirty and they don't risk their own money.'

Much as he tried to push me in that direction, it was not where I instinctively wanted to go. Finance, the world of suits and offices, did not appeal to me.

My mother, on the other hand, put no pressure on me. She herself had spent her entire career working in one of England's largest charities, gradually working her way to the top, or near the top. I suppose I learned from her the self-confidence that comes from unconditional love – I learned it from somewhere, because people seemed to think I was always sure of myself.

I was an only child, and I imagine that meant I was spoilt. My parents poured everything they had into me: their love, their expectations and their time. Being the centre of the universe left me oddly lonely. I had no brother or sister to share secrets with or to fight with. In our house there was no mob in the kitchen, no queue for the loo and no pile of laundry in the hamper. There was just me. When I thought back on those I knew in school and at university, I felt jealous of those who came from big families.

As a child I was physically fearless. That everyone saw. I would throw myself off anything high, a playground swing or a tree branch. My Mum told me about one time she thought I'd broken my back. I was trying to climb one of the small turbs Dad had installed on the hill above our house, but I couldn't keep my grip and fell. She shivered with the memory.

'I was terrified,' she said. 'I ran to call the ambulance, but then you got up!'

I felt guilty that I was at sea when she died last year. I sort of knew, but didn't want to know, that the end of her life was coming. Dad had died only a year before, and Mum seemed to have lost the will to go on. I saw how she was during a visit home a few months before she died. I didn't like it at all, and I urged her to eat more, to be more active. She nodded, but did nothing.

When I was six we moved to a house which my parents bought in Oxfordshire. It was just outside of a small village, sort of in between village and country. Strange as may seem, that house determined the future course of my life. Or rather, not the house but the land around it. A fair bit of land came with the house, some of it sloping away below the house toward the main road and the rest of consisting of several hills ringing the house in a semi-circle.

On these hills my father installed the first home wind turbines in the area – the site of my ill-fated climbing adventure. Wind turbines were not new, of course, huge numbers of them had been built, but those were 'industrial' so to speak, much too large for the home consumer. My father was one of the early backers of small scale wind turbines designed for homes.

When I say 'backer' I mean he tried to emulate the oil financiers by investing in wind turbine companies, only he made the mistake of putting his own money at risk. At that time the value of small scale wind turbines was still open to question, both in terms of their ability to produce significant energy and their cost effectiveness. Several different types of small scale turbines existed then, and as technology improved some models succeeded and others didn't. My father didn't always back the winners.

He was also an enthusiastic supporter of the first wind farm in

Oxfordshire, which was built not far from our house, on the Ferguson farm near the big Chinese shopping centre on the A40.

Called the *Hope and Glory Wind Farm*, the project was bitterly opposed by some local residents, but, as my father put it, 'reason prevailed.' He stood proudly by the leader of the local council and people from the wind industry as a cousin of the King declared the farm 'open for energy from the wind.'

I was eight years old at the time. I remember thinking the turbs looked like trees. It seemed to me all these grown-ups were dedicating a new forest.

My father did not see any conflict or contradiction between his work as a petroleum engineer and as a dabbler in wind and other forms of renewable energy (he also invested in wave energy schemes). Energy is energy, he would say. He did not value one form of energy above another. In this sense he was part of the older generation. He found it incomprehensible that some proponents of renewables viewed different types of energy through the lens of morality, regarding energy derived from fossil fuels as somehow 'bad' or 'wrong.'

My father was of the view that all energy produced by man, by whatever means, involved essentially the same process: man's genius applied to the resources available.

Besides, he said, even a wind turbine – as an example of 'good' renewable energy – was made from steel (that was before the plastic ones came along) and to produce the steel you needed coking coal and iron ore as ingredients, high temperatures for the process and numerous other old-fashioned, 'politically incorrect' inputs.

So, we had small turbines mounted on the hills around the house – and they fascinated me. Some would turn faster than others, some would not turn at all under conditions that made others spin crazily, and some were plainly useless for want of good design or reliable parts. It was still early days for home wind turbines.

I went through the usual period of indecision in my teens. Looking back, I don't think I was different from most. But when I made up my mind and told my father one day that I wanted to study engineering, he was pleased. I suppose he felt flattered. But my decision had less to do with imitating my father and more to do with finding any alternative to work that required a suit and tie.

'I mean wind engineering,' I explained. 'I want to design and build wind turbines. I mean to be a wind engineer.'

He accepted my wishes but he did not conceal his view that I was making a mistake. Despite his enthusiasm for it, he believed that wind energy would never provide more than a small part of the so-called 'energy mix' upon which human civilisation depends.

*

In the event he was mistaken. Technology drove the development of wind energy just as it did oil and gas in the past – and the key innovation was mobility. Wind turbines became mobile.

With giant wheels at the base, they began to roam the land like techno dinosaurs.

Mobile turbs were the brainchild of a Danish wind expert named Rosenborg. He realised that more energy could be harvested from the wind if turbs could change their location as the wind direction changed. As a renowned professor of renewable energy at the University of Copenhagen, Rosenborg was well known. The leading Danish wind turbine manufacturer took his ideas seriously and offered him a contract to turn his ideas into reality.

He'd been experimenting with 'leaning' turbines – that is, fixed turbines with an axle at the base that enabled them to 'lean' to change their angle to the wind – but these models had problems with stability and there were some ghastly accidents. Then it hit him. Why not put wheels on the things?

The earliest mobile turbs conceived by Rosenborg had four wheels at the base, arranged at right angles to each other, so that the turb could execute very slight turns to adjust to changes in the direction of the wind. This was a big improvement over the older generation of turbs, which could only move their nacelles, or heads, to adjust to changes in wind direction.

At first, some in the wind community laughed at Rosenborg's innovation. If all four wheels turned rapidly, they said, the turb would spin round and round in a circle. No one could conceive of a situation where that might be useful, but it was theoretically possible.

Rosenborg went further. He then designed two-wheeled mobile turbs. These were less precise than the four-wheeled models in their ability to capture the wind by sideways movement, but then the two-wheeled models could move faster, and they could lean forwards and backwards, whereas the four-wheeled models couldn't.

Rosenborg solved the problem of how to capture the energy generated by a mobile turb by means of a tether connected to the electricity grid. The tethers were an added cost, of course, but as mobile turbs generated so much more electricity than their fixed ancestors, it was deemed worth the extra cost.

The tethers, generally made of tough plastic or fiberglass composites, allowed turbs to wander up to several hundred metres. The control computers could recall them to their original location, or another location, as desired.

The result was that two-wheeled mobile turbs became the industry standard, and the technology was licenced, or simply copied, by turb makers everywhere. Millions of mobile turbs were made and installed all over the world. Rosenborg became a rich man.

It was an English company, our company, I'm proud to say, that made offshore turbs mobile. Phil Burnley played a key role in this.

Sea-based turbs had for a long time been expensive affairs resting on concrete pilings driven into the sea bed. Phil had the idea to base them instead on floating, semi-submersible platforms, using water as ballast. The floating turbs would prove to be much cheaper to build than their fixed foundation predecessors. There was no need for expensive seabed pile-driving and no need to design foundations capable of supporting the huge weight involved. Moreover, they could be positioned almost anywhere in even shallow water depths.

To capture electricity from the mobile sea turbs, Phil and his team used the same device that Rosenborg had used for land-based mobile turbs – a tether. The tethers were connected to underwater cables that led to transformer stations. This allowed the sea turbs to roam with the changing wind direction and yet enabled man to harvest their energy.

Initially, they were built with petrol or diesel-fuelled motors that enabled the turb to move and relocate itself back to the desired location after currents had moved it. But this solution required fuel, and that meant the time-consuming process of refilling fuel tanks. Later, the fuel-powered motors were replaced by lithium battery-powered motors, which could be re-charged *in situ*.

To control the direction of the sea turbs, Phil invented the equivalent of fish fins – metal fins attached to the base of the floating platforms. This, in my mind, as I studied the emergence of the modern sea turb years later, was Phil's real genius.

Inevitably, the floating sea turbs were not as stable as land-based turbs or indeed the earlier offshore turbs implanted in the seabed. They gave rise to their own unanticipated problems. In rough seas they tended to 'lean' up to ninety degrees. The blades sometimes struck the water. There were incidents of fishing nets being sliced right through, with the catch cut up into a bloody mess. In several well publicised incidents, fishing boats were struck and sank. *Sea turb sinks trawler!* screamed one tabloid, referring to a particularly serious incident off the Norfolk coast that left two fishermen dead. Fishermen swelled the anti-turb ranks.

Notwithstanding such rare incidents, the mobile floating turb was a tremendous success, both engineering and financial. Like the land-based two-wheeled turbs, millions were built and launched in the seas. Phil Burnley became Sir Philip Burnley – and, like Rosenborg, a rich man.

I witnessed these changes, though I was still at university when the mobile turbs made their appearance. I remember their effect on the popular imagination.

They were soon dubbed 'Segway Turbs' by the press. People likened them to dinosaurs and monsters. A film featuring a turb-like monster called 'turbzilla' led to a line of children's toys, including battery-powered turbs that scurried around people's lounges with the turb rotor blades spinning. They were quickly recalled when, predictably, children's fingers were sliced off by the blades. A group of parents issued proceedings against the manufacturer in the High Court, which they easily won. The tabloids carried a heart-wrenching photo of tots with stumpy fingers, lined up before the Royal Courts of Justice in the Strand.

So, mobility hadn't made turbs a more popular form of energy. For the countryside, they were still considered a blight. Farmers wanted the extra income offered by giving up land for their construction, but no one wanted to live near them. Land values were adversely affected. The occasional decimation of bird flocks put animal rights activists squarely in the anti-turb camp.

'Turb' became a frequently used term in the popular press. It had a negative connotation.

The term 'turb' was useful for creating various short hand references such as 'pro-turb' or 'anti-turb' or 'turb free zone' and a dozen other terms. It was taken up internationally. In Germany the gentle-sounding 'wind wheels' (*die Windraeder*) became *die Turben*. France had *les tourbes* and the Spanish speaking world *los turbos*. Even Russia – which because of its abundant oil and natural gas had many fewer turbs than most other countries – had *TYPBEN* which sounds similar to the Russian word for 'pole' (*TPYB*).

Yet there was one aspect of mobile turbs that few commented on. It was this: the invention of mobile turbs was made possible – like all of the improvements in turb tech – by computers. The smartchips installed in the nacelles of the mobile turbs controlled not only the movement of the turbs from place to place, but every other aspect of their behaviour – the direction of the head, the angle of the blades, the 'leaning' of the turb mast, down to the centimetre.

Nobody marvelled at the emergence of 'smart turbs.' After all, there were many other 'smart' things, beginning with smartphones and smartcars. Everything used by humans was becoming smart, though not the humans themselves.

*

I got my engineering degree and then an advanced degree in wind energy. I went to work for a large Danish turb manufacturer, and then a Spanish one. Though I was well versed in onshore wind energy, I gravitated toward a specialty in the offshore field – that was the future, everyone said, and it was true. When the flood came, Europe alone had over four hundred offshore turb packs, ten times as many as a few decades ago. The seas were thick with them.

And England led the way. England had more than the rest of Europe put together – countless thousands of shiny, sharp creatures bobbing in the waves around our islands.

I found myself more involved in practical issues of maintenance of wind turbines, rather than their design and construction, which I'd dreamt of as an engineering student. Eventually I came home, landing a job in the maintenance unit of England's largest wind energy utility. There I met Phil. Under his tutelage, I began working my way up the ladder, and eventually got my own staff with responsibility for the whole of the Thames Array.

I had the authority to hire the people I wanted, and I wanted Frank. I'd first met him when I was working at the Danish company, where he was a very junior engineer. I saw immediately that somehow he – how shall I put it? – Frank had a knack for the power of the wind. Some people do. That's didn't mean he didn't have a lot to learn.

Just before he joined me at the Thames Array, when the flood came, we'd spent time together on a consulting assignment for a big Danish turb maker, in the far north of Denmark, the Jutland Peninsula, endless flat land, ideal for wind energy. If once trees had grown there, they had disappeared – dense turb forests now covered the landscape.

One evening after work Frank launched into a critique of the latest eighteen blade horizontal-axis turb – known in the trade as a 'HAWT' – being developed by the Danish company. His discourse on the design's shortcomings was beyond anything a junior engineer could be expected to understand. He was a sharp kid, that was for sure.

The sun was setting and we had begun to sample the excellent Danish beer. Before us stood a vast expanse of turbs.

'Listen,' I said. 'Do you hear them howling in the wind? It sounds like they're complaining about something.'

'Sure,' said Frank, grinning.

'Don't humour me – and don't get the idea you know everything, not just yet,' I said. 'I think the turbs can communicate.'

'Of course they communicate,' he replied. 'They're networked. The smartchip in each one is connected to the control computer.'

'That's not what I meant,' I said. 'I meant they communicate amongst themselves – and they have intelligence.'

'What do you mean by "have intelligence"?' said Frank. 'They're things, they're not alive.'

'Something doesn't have to be alive to have intelligence. Look at just about every "smart" gadget you have,' I said. 'It's a form of intelligence that we gave them. You know what I'm talking about, Frank. You've seen the latest research.'

'Yes, I have,' he replied. 'I saw that article in *Wind Tech Times* – it's about, now what did they call it?'

'The "deviation factor",' I said.

'Something to do with the movement of the turbs,' he said. 'Without being told.'

'That's right. It's the difference between what a turb is told to do by the control computer and what it actually does,' I said.

In theory, there should have been no deviation. But there was.

'Let me play devil's advocate,' I said. 'You know that some experts say the deviation factor is related to changes in wind direction. In other words, the turbs aren't disobeying instructions, only the constantly changing wind direction, which is difficult to measure precisely, gives that impression,' I said.

'I read that,' said Frank. 'But it doesn't strike me as correct. The instruments we have now are very precise.'

'All right,' I said. 'Other experts claim the turbs make small movements to compensate when *they* sense a change in wind direction.'

'I've heard that, too,' said Frank. 'But I don't buy it. Only the very latest models are programmed to that level of sophistication, and the deviation factor seems to be more widespread.'

'Fine. How about this,' I said. 'Some say the use of plastic and epoxy composites in turb heads and blades explains the deviation factor. These materials, they say, yield more than metal to the wind, which gives a false impression of independent movement.'

'Bollocks,' said Frank. 'These materials are extremely hard and will not bend in the wind. So, what's your take, Jack? What do you think?'

'What I think is that the deviation factor has nothing to do with changes in wind direction or the use of flexible materials,' I replied. 'It has to do with artificial intelligence. The smartchips in the turbs have taken over control – they make their own decisions on blade motion, blade direction and, of course, movement of the turb from one location to another.'

'But always subject to the control computer,' observed Frank.

'No,' I said. 'Suppose the smartchips are overriding the control. They have the capacity to do that and I think that's exactly what they're doing – that's causing the deviation factor. The question is why. What's driving the chips to cause the turbs to act independently?'

'Do you have an answer?' he asked.

I opened a bottle of beer and then another and handed one to Frank.

'No, not yet,' I said. 'But I've discussed it with Phil. He wants us to investigate this phenomenon at the Thames Array – soon as we're back in England. It will mean spending some extra time offshore.'

'I don't mind that,' said Frank. 'In fact, I'd be keen. Extra pay.'

I sipped my beer, gathering my thoughts.

'It seems to me – it's possible – that the turbs, acting independent of control by man, are like a new species,' I said. 'With their own drives, but what are they?'

Frank chuckled.

'What kind of a species?' he asked. 'Plant or animal?'

'Does it matter what *we* call it?' I asked, a bit frustrated by my own inability to grasp the problem. Irritation showed in my voice.

'Jack, your imagination is as strong as this Danish beer,' said Frank, laughing.

'Sorry, I didn't mean to be – it's just driving me a little nuts, this deviation factor,' I said.

'I can understand that,' said Frank. 'But we humans are animals, and this animal wants something to eat.'

We left our musings that night, but returned to them again a few nights later. There wasn't much else to do in the remoter parts of Jutland. I think he never knew how much of my banter was serious and how much was intended to provoke a reaction. I think he was also a little afraid of looking crazy. As a young wind engineer, he naturally wanted to project an image of seriousness.

But there it was: the deviation factor. It hadn't been explained. Now Phil had asked us to look into its appearance in the Thames Array. If he didn't know how to explain it, then no one did.

3

NOTTING HILL

I pushed open the door of my flat.

'Nessa!' I called out.

There was no reply and I knew at once, in such a small flat, that no one was there. I looked around for a note, but found none. It seemed as though she hadn't been there for a while. The flat looked exactly the same as I had left it.

I sat down on the sofa, dejected, soaked from the rain but not totally surprised. After all, I'd been at sea for weeks and she didn't know I was coming. At least part of that time, I knew she'd been up north touring wind farms in Yorkshire with her Chinese delegation.

There was only one other place where she could be – in the service flat at Imperial College where her group were staying. She was living there when we met and hadn't given up her flat.

I reached for my smartphone. *No signal* still appeared in the screen. How could that be, I wondered, in the heart of London?

My flat was on the first floor of an early Victorian conversion, with the characteristic high ceilings and large draughty windows. As always in wintertime, it was freezing. The pressure in my pre-historic boiler had dropped whilst I was away. Of course, my smartphone was programmed to tell the thermostat I was coming and switch the boiler on, but that depended on battery power. No battery, no smart heating. I tinkered with the pressure valve and felt the radiators getting warmer.

I didn't fancy going out into the wet streets again, but there was no alternative. I knew I wouldn't be able to sleep without finding her. Besides, I told myself, it wasn't far, just on the other side of Hyde Park.

Still in the same clothes I'd been wearing since landing at Dover, I came downstairs and stood for a moment on the front steps, looking up and down the street. It was just past dusk. Now I saw what had struck me as I'd come home. There were hardly any lights in the windows. Practically every house was dark. And only a few of the street lights were working.

Then I noticed something else. Two of the dark houses across the street showed signs of a break-in. In contrast to our house, these were not broken up into flats, or, if they had been in the distant past, they had been turned back into single family homes in the less distant past. They were worth many millions. And they looked to be abandoned.

At the house directly opposite mine, the sliding forecourt gate appeared to have been rammed. The gate was bent in the middle and the force of whatever rammed it had pulled the gate off its hinges. The smart Italian sports car that was once parked in the forecourt was gone. The windows on the ground floor were all smashed and the door was wide open. At the house next to it, the garden level window that gave light to the underground swimming pool had been broken into jagged edges. I imagined I could see the water in the pool but it was probably something else that I saw. On the top floor a window was open and a wet curtain flagged in the wind.

Of course, sympathy had limits with people as wealthy as my neighbours. Cranbourne Villas was characterised by large homes whose gated forecourts boasted expensive motors and whose cellars had been converted into swimming pools and home cinemas. Houses like mine, the ones broken up into flats, were less common, but nonetheless even the small flats cost a fortune in Cranbourne Villas.

I headed for Hyde Park on foot. After a few minutes I came to the gate I usually used to enter the park, but it was padlocked. I grabbed a tree branch and pulled myself up, swinging my feet up to the top of the fence, then reaching further up the branch to bring my body up to a position where I could jump to the other side. Then I was in the park.

I'd never been in Hyde Park at night before. In other circumstances I might have found it beautiful or even a bit magical. As it was, I trudged through the freezing rain past the Round Pond, heading towards the Albert Hall, keeping a keen watch for strangers. Fortunately I saw no one.

I found Nessa's block of flats soon enough but the sight of it was not reassuring. It had a glass door flanked by glass panels that opened onto the lobby, and much of the glass was either cracked or smashed. A chair stood propped against one of the cracked panels. Inside, at the reception, sat a portly security guard with a torch and a taser gun lying on the table in front of him.

'Good evening,' I said, sopping wet and a bit breathless. 'My name is Jack Mason. I'm looking for Nessa Chao. She's one of the Chinese wind engineers staying here.'

'They left this afternoon,' he replied.

'It can't be!' I muttered.

'Please, I'll just check her room,' I said. 'Don't worry – I know where it is.'

'You can't – ' he began, but made no move to follow me.

Nessa opened her door.

'Jack!' she cried. 'I didn't expect you!'

We embraced and kissed, and then kissed again and again.

'I'm so glad to see you. But what are you doing here?' she asked. 'I thought you were out at the Thames Array.'

'I was. I came off station day before yesterday,' I said. 'And I'm glad to see you. What are you doing here? Why weren't you in the flat?'

'I had to be here – the others left today,' she said. 'I had to explain why I didn't want to join them, and to ask permission to stay. I work for a Chinese wind company, not an English one. We're not so free. My boss Mr Zhong – you met him – gave his permission, but only after an argument. He has some crazy idea they can go back home.'

'I know – Phil told me,' I said.

'I don't know how – there aren't any flights, are there?' said Nessa. 'Oh, Jack, part of me wanted to go with them. I'm worried about my parents. They live in Shanghai, and it's under water. The whole south coast of China is flooded, from Guangdong right up to Zhejiang.'

'But I decided to stay,' she said. 'To be with you.'

I kissed her again.

'I tried to call you and text you a thousand times but there was no signal,' I said.

'Jack, you're wet from head to toe,' she said, looking me over.

'I had to cycle up the motorway from Dover,' I said. 'There was no other way to get to London. I spent the night along the way. The worst part was seeing dead bodies in London – people who'd drowned.'

'Oh, my God, that's terrible,' she said. 'It hasn't been so bad here, but we've had nothing to do. We've been in these flats for two or three weeks – I've lost track of time – our minders from the English Energy Department stopped turning up. They basically abandoned us here. Mr Zhong sent a couple of us out to look for food, but there wasn't much. Fortunately, like all Chinese delegations, we travel with our own rice and noodles.'

'All right,' I said. 'Let's get away from here. I'll take you home.'

We packed her things and headed out into the wilds of Knightsbridge.

'Let's not try to go through the park,' I said. 'We'll go up the street that passes in front of Kensington Palace – it might be more secure.'

It was. Before the palace were several police cars with lights flashing. But the safety they offered disappeared as their lights receded behind us. It was pitch dark and none of the streetlights were working. We saw no passers-by.

'Nessa, I think we should to get out of London,' I said as we walked. 'I told you about my house in Oxfordshire – we should go there.'

'You think it will be safer than London?' she asked. 'The way you describe it, it sounds a bit isolated.'

'No, it will be safer,' I said. 'But that's not the only reason to go there. I told you about the wind farm my father helped found there. I need to visit that wind farm.'

'Why?' she asked.

'Because I want to find out what's going on with the turbs. The turbs in the Thames Array project – and elsewhere – are disobeying instructions from their control computers. They're behaving independently. We don't understand why. When I say we, I mean Phil and Frank and the other engineers in our company. I've a hunch I might find something useful. After all, it's the project that I know best.'

'That's funny,' she said. 'We've encountered the same phenomenon in China and we don't understand it either. I'm not supposed to be telling you this – it's a secret. Mr Zhong would be angry if he knew.'

'Tell me,' I said.

'Have you heard of the *Fortune Wind* project?' she asked. 'It's an offshore project south of Shanghai.'

'I think so,' I said. 'It's the largest offshore project in China, isn't it? Something like fifty thousand sea turbs?'

'More like a hundred thousand,' she replied. 'And they're not doing as they are told.'

Out of the corner of my eye, I saw a dark shape move at the far end of the street. I turned and saw a group of young men approaching. One of them saw us and elbowed another. They broke into a run in our direction.

I saw at once they were *drivs* – descendants of *chavs*. With nearly every inch of skin covered by tattoos, and with metal rings in their ears and noses, the thickly bearded male *drivs* had a reputation for violence.

'Quick, we're near the house, run!' I said.

We bolted to the house and I pushed Nessa up the half dozen steps to our door, feeling for my keys. My last look round saw the first *driv* nearing the bottom of the steps. The door was open now, Nessa inside. The sound of footsteps was close by, and shouting voices. I slid into the hall and threw my weight back at the door. I heard the latch close and then banging on the door. Quickly I turned the upper lock. My heart was pounding and my hands shaking.

Nessa was leaning against the wall, breathing heavily.

'Quiet,' I whispered. 'They're still out there. Let's get inside the flat.'

We sat in the lounge, now and then peeking out the window. The *drivs* lingered for a while below the window but then their attention was drawn to the ransacked houses across the street. A little while later a fire appeared in one of them. Still later we saw a pair of torches in the street and I could make out two soldiers. The fire had sparked their curiosity. They went inside the house and the fire went out soon after. The *drivs* had gone.

It was a while before we were able to sleep.

*

Over coffee the next morning we returned to the subject of the deviation factor.

'Tell me again what you've discovered in China,' I said.

'Well, not much really,' said Nessa. 'It was first noticed at the *Fortune Wind* project. The project wasn't generating as much electricity as it should have. We looked into it – I actually went out there myself – and we found the sea turbs were not where the computer had told them to go. Apart from that – '

'You went out there?' I asked. 'How?'

'Well, first to the offshore station, then I visited a couple of sea turbs – winched down from a helicopter,' said Nessa. I nodded.

'Apart from the location, the blade angles were off, and the turb heads weren't facing into the wind. We're talking about thousands of sea turbs. It was statistically significant,' she continued.

'What else?'

'We noticed the same phenomenon onshore, at the *Black Dragon* wind project in the far north of China, in Heilongjiang Province, near the town of Qitahe. Only this time, the turbs had wandered so far from their programmed positions that many of the tethers had been snapped. Power output was way down,' Nessa said.

'What happened?'

'We re-connected the tethers. But within a fortnight, many were broken again,' she said.

'Anything else?'

'Yes, at the *Black Dragon* project there were an unusually large number of bird strikes. I mean, once or twice a year was within the normal range, but we were seeing two or three per month. What does it all mean, Jack?'

'I don't know yet, and we're not going to find out sitting here in Notting Hill.'

Just then I looked out the window and saw the neighbours next door loading things into their car. Theirs was a single house like the ransacked houses across the street, but much more modest looking and their car an older, ordinary model. Neither had been touched by looters.

'Nessa, the neighbours are outside – I want to talk to them.'

Hungry for information, we hurried down the stairs with our coffee mugs.

'We're getting out,' said the neighbour as soon as he saw us. I knew his name was Ned and that he was a barrister, but I didn't know anything more about him. His wife soon appeared.

'Jack, what on earth have you come to London for?' she said by way of greeting.

'This is Nessa,' I said.

'Oh, pleased to meet you,' she said. 'I'm Eve.'

'We've decided to get out,' said Ned. 'It's not been pleasant here. There have been a lot of houses broken into. Pillaged, basically, with no sign of the police. Sewage backing up in the streets. Bodies floating in the Thames. The government moved out of London last week. Gone to Cheltenham – to that big snooping centre they've got there.'

'If you're thinking of going to the shops, don't bother,' Eve chimed in. 'Only the supermarket is open and the shelves are pretty bare.'

'What about the local restaurants?' I asked.

'All closed,' said Eve.

'No,' said Ned. 'The Star of Madras in Westbourne Grove is still open. I saw it.'

'Well, if you fancy eating a curry every night till the flood comes to this part of London,' said Eve.

'And the pubs?' I asked. 'What's the chance of a pub meal?'

'The pubs were closed by police order a fortnight ago,' said Ned.

'We've decided to get away while we still can,' said Eve. 'We don't know what it's going to be like here in a week's time.'

We left them and decided to venture round the neighbourhood. It looked eerily like Notting Hill at carnival time, with few local residents and many boarded up shop windows. Except instead of carnival revellers there were roaming gangs, *drivs* and others, from Willesden and Neasden and other parts north, I imagined. Many more properties were damaged than the two I saw the night before.

It was true what Eve had said about the shops. Only one supermarket was open and it had little to offer. The man at the till wore a tie and seemed to be the only employee in the place.

All the stalls in the antique market in Portobello Road were shut, as well as the fruit and vegetable stands down at the bottom of the road.

As we returned home, we came upon Edna, the upstairs neighbour and the only other resident of the house. She belonged to my parents' generation. Like them, she had bought her flat in the forgotten age when ordinary people could afford flats in central London. She was sweeping the steps.

'We have to be clean when the flood comes,' she announced when she saw us.

I thought she might be joking, but she put the broom down and sort of wilted onto the landing.

'Really I don't know what else to do,' she said. 'I haven't anywhere to go. I'm alone.'

'It's not likely to reach here,' I said. 'It's likely to subside soon.'

She did not seem convinced.

'I'm afraid,' she said slowly. 'Very afraid.'

Then she asked suddenly: 'Have you got any food? I haven't eaten today.'

Nessa took her arm and brought her into the flat, and we shared with her what we had, which wasn't much.

*

The signal returned briefly in our smartphones, so we had news.

The flood waters from the Thames had reached Cromwell Road, less than a mile from Notting Hill.

'Nessa, did you see the news?' I asked. We were both absorbed in our screens.

'What news?'

'The flat by Imperial College where you were staying is now part of the flood area,' I said.

'Didn't see that. I was looking at the news from China,' she said. 'It's not good. More flooding. Airports closed. I'm sure Zhong and the rest of them are stuck somewhere.'

'Hang on, there's more,' I said. The face of Toby Lang appeared in my screen. He wore a grim expression.

'The government are advising anyone who can leave London to do so without delay. For those who can't, transport will be organised by neighbourhood,' Lang was saying. 'The fact is that our ability to maintain order is spotty. We're stretched too thin with the flooding. We might have to impose a curfew in London and other cities. For the time being, we're asking people to stay off the streets at night.'

It was bad news but at least Lang gave the news straight. And there was more. Electricity in London, he said, would be limited to two hours in the morning and four hours in the evening. Nothing was said about the gas supply, but I'd noticed the flame in our hob had become much weaker.

The signal also brought an SMS from Frank.

'Alone here in Ramsgate - family already evacuated to the north. London OK?'

'No and getting worse all the time.' I replied.

'I've been thinking, if turbs break their tethers, we won't have any power – no tether, no electricity. So it is critical to understand the deviation factor,' Frank wrote.

'Nessa,' I said. 'In China, what do you and your colleagues call the phenomenon we've been talking about – the turbs behaving independently.'

'It's a combination of two Chinese characters, one is *dao* meaning "road" and the other *li* means "leaving" or "going away from." The two together mean "leaving the road",' she replied.

'So it's the same,' I said. 'That's interesting.'

'What's the same?' she asked.

'It's the same name we've given it – "deviation" – it's from Latin, and it also means "to leave the road".'

'Glad we settled that,' said Nessa. 'Jack, I'm hungry. We haven't anything to eat. And that poor lady upstairs, I imagine she's starving.'

'All right,' I said. 'Let's find something to eat.'

The local supermarket now had a soldier standing guard by the door, which was reassuring, but there wasn't much to be had.

We walked and walked in search of food and eventually found ourselves in Queens Park, more than a mile north of Notting Hill.

'Look, that butcher shop looks open,' I said. 'Let's go in.'

The shop's sign – obviously made a long time ago, before Scotland had turned heel – had a Union Jack on either end and in between were drawings of dancing pigs, sheep and cows. The door stood open.

'Hello,' I called as we entered.

There was no one in the shop. The counters, empty of meat, had traces of blood and bits of entrails.

'Hello,' I called again.

'Maybe they're in the back,' I muttered, moving behind the counter through an open door.

In the back of the shop was another door, which also stood open. A waft of cold air came my way – this was the freezer. I peeked inside – through the mist I saw rows of metal rods suspended from the ceiling, but no animal carcasses hung there. But from one hook hung something large. I stepped closer. It was the body of a man, the butcher presumably, hanging from a meat hook, his white apron streaked red.

'Bloody hell,' I shouted.

'Nessa, stay out there,' I shouted. 'We're going, now.'

I grabbed her arm and we left the shop as quickly as our feet could carry us.

'What was it Jack?' she asked.

'A dead man,' I said. 'Let's go home.'

There was rubbish everywhere. Collection had stopped some time ago. Piles of bin liners lay around the overflowing bins, many torn open by scavengers. Here and there vermin feasted on the spoiled food that seeped out.

The quantity of rubbish in London seemed to be increasing, just as the human population was decreasing. The rat population, on the other hand, seemed to be growing.

We crossed the Harrow Road, into the top end of Portobello Road.

Under the Westway we began to see signs of fresh looting. Smashed windows, clothes and other wares were strewn about the famous market road. The Spanish *groceria* just below the Westway was completely gutted. It seemed a lot of the food hadn't been easy for the looters to carry away – olives and chunks of cheese and broken bottles littered the pavement. The small bar directly across the road had been relieved of all its alcohol. The looters had paid special attention to the Electric Cinema. I couldn't understand why till

I saw the remains of chocolate bars and popcorn on the pavement.

We saw the *drivs* when we reached Talbot Road – mostly young men but many women, too. The female *drivs*, like the males, were covered in tattoos, but instead of rings in their ears and noses, they sported metals implants in their cheeks, lips and chins.

They were in the part of the market where the antique dealers had their stalls, breaking windows and hacking open doors with axes and metal rods. There wasn't a policeman in sight.

'That's the same gang that attacked us last night, isn't it?' said Nessa.

'I think so,' I said. 'Nessa, we can't fight against so many. But I know a place where we can hide till they're gone.'

I lead her into a small road off the market and then under an archway into a mews. I knew what I was looking for and I soon found it. The wooden doors were padlocked but someone had already had a go at the lock and I had no trouble knocking it off, using a rock from a nearby garden.

I led her into a dark space, almost as long as a barn, but not so high.

'This is the storage hall for all the fruit and veg traders in the Portobello market,' I explained. 'It's hidden away in this little mews. Nobody knows this place except them – and me,' I smiled.

Nessa looked around.

The hall was filled with wheeled carts and crates, mostly empty, but some still holding bits of produce gone rotten.

'It stinks in here,' she said.

I shut the doors.

'Let's find a spot where no one will see us,' I said, gesturing towards a cart. 'Over here.'

I pushed a crate against the wall, behind the cart, and we sat down.

'My Mum brought me here when I was very young.' I said. 'She was friendly with some of the traders. She said it was amazing that in the twenty-first century English people still made their living selling things in a market – that in a generation it would all disappear, like all the great London markets of the past.'

'But it's still here,' I added. 'I guess it took this flood to end the Portobello market.'

'Sometimes I wonder if this flood crisis will end,' said Nessa. 'Or if it does, whether everything will be the same as it was before.'

'That sounds pessimistic,' I said.

'Oh I'm not pessimistic, not usually,' she smiled. 'It's just that nothing like this has ever happened before. I guess I'm scared. Is it OK to be scared?'

'Absolutely it's OK to be scared,' I said. 'I'm scared, too, sometimes.'

'We may be here for a while,' I said.

'I never really told you about my parents,' she said. 'I miss them and I'm worried about them, but there's nothing I can do. I tried calling several times – no luck.'

'My mother was very strict with me and my sister. It was difficult, but in Chinese families, you obey. She is very traditional. I don't suppose you know what that means in China. For instance, there is a holiday called *sau mou* – it means *sweeping day*. The whole family goes to the cemetery to sweep clean the graves of ancestors. Then, at the graves, we burn money for them because they will need it. Not real money, of course, play money. It is a symbolic act. My mother always does this and she made us do it, too.'

'My father observes all the traditions, too, but I don't think they're so important to him,' she continued. 'He's a typical businessman. What's important to him is making money. He doesn't say that, but I can see. Once I imagined what he would say if we burned real money for our ancestors!'

She began to laugh and put her hand over her mouth. Abruptly she stopped.

'Your turn now,' said Nessa. 'Tell me something about you I don't know – something personal. You told me before that you've never been married. But you didn't say why.'

The question – and it was a question – threw me. Why, why had she asked that now? Now, after she'd cut her ties to the delegation that brought her to England – because she wanted to stay with me. I wished she hadn't asked that, because I wasn't ready to 'pop the question' – I was still rehearsing in my mind exactly what I wanted to say. Besides, I didn't want to do it in the market shed.

'I guess I wanted to keep my freedom,' I said lamely.

'You make marriage sound like a prison!' she laughed.

'I didn't mean it that way,' I said. 'I meant only that if you do one thing, you can't then do something else. I suppose I wanted to keep my options open, though I never thought of it that way.'

I mentioned my job and how often I was away travelling.

'Jack, don't kid me. My job is the same as yours. I travel a lot, too. We're wind engineers. But if I found the right person, I wouldn't let the chance go,' said Nessa. 'At least, that's the way I look at it.'

Just then came the creak of a door and the sound of footsteps.

'Anybody in here?' came a voice.

I looked at Nessa and put a finger over my lips.

The footsteps came nearer.

'Come on, I saw you come in here. Don't play with me,' came a voice.

'All right, mate,' I said, standing up. 'What do you want with us?'

The figure of a man approached.

'To help you,' he said.

I looked him up and down. He was a *driv*. His thick, black beard and shaved skull were hard to miss, and even in the darkness, I could see the faint glint of metal rings in his nostrils.

'I don't get it,' I said. 'Last night, some of you tried to mug us.'

Nessa stood up beside me.

'Jack, give him a chance,' she whispered.

'What's your name?' she asked.

'Tony.'

'My name's Nessa and this is Jack,' she said. 'Do you live near-by?'

'Me and my mates, we live in Willesden. We got a squat, know what I mean?'

'Yes, I think so,' said Nessa.

'Look, I saw what happened to you last night,' he said. 'It don't seem right to hurt you. If you come with me, I'll get you home safe.'

I smelled a trap but yielded to Nessa's instinct.

'Tony, you're not what I expected,' she said. 'A lot of the English aren't so friendly, but you are.'

He appeared to blush.

'Come on,' he said. 'Got to move.'

We followed him out of the market hall. He led us out the far end of the mews, in the direction of the flat. As we turned into Ledbury Road, we came smack into a pack of *drivs* intent on smashing their way into one of Notting Hill's wildly expensive eateries.

'Hey, Tony,' one of them called out. 'Them your friends? Bet they've got something.'

'They haven't got nothing,' he replied. 'Just keep walking,' he said to us.

We turned into Cranbourne Villas.

'Thank you, Tony,' said Nessa. 'I would be happy to see you again.'

'Thanks, mate,' I said.

Tony appeared to blush again, and turned away.

'What was that all about?' I said as we went upstairs. 'A friendly *driv*, I can't believe it.'

'He was nice,' said Nessa. 'I'll make us something to eat. Jack, why don't you go upstairs and invite the neighbour, Edna.'

'I will, but Nessa, we've got to go to Oxfordshire. Tomorrow. I'm eager to get to that wind farm. Do you agree?'

'Yes. But there's a problem, isn't there?' she said. 'How will we get there?'

I laughed.

'Did I forget to tell you? I have a car,' I said. 'It's down there in the street. I've been keeping an eye on it. No one's touched it. No one would – it's just an old clunker.'

'Does it have biofuel?' she asked.

'Yes, full, I never use it.'

'Look,' I went on. 'I'll go to the supermarket and get whatever I can. You pack up all the clothes and anything else you think we need.'

I went upstairs to knock on Edna's door, but she didn't answer. Then I went to see what I could find in the supermarket, pausing outside the house to look up and down the street.

Near the entrance to the supermarket a small crowd attracted my attention. They were standing in a circle around what I saw was the body of a woman.

An old man in the crowd noticed me approaching and blurted excitedly, 'She's dead. An elderly lady – knocked down because she wouldn't give up a tin of beans. That's what that man over there says. He saw it. There was a whole gang of them – *drivs*, they're called. What's London coming to? I ask you.'

I moved closed and saw that it was our neighbour, Edna. Her head was bloodied. The sight of it made me feel sick.

Another man in the crowd said wasn't it a pity? Because in the next day or two, he'd heard, the army was going to remove everyone in Notting Hill to a refugee camp outside of London – even all the celebs, if any were still there – whether they wanted to go or not.

I'd lost my appetite, but I forced myself into the supermarket and wandered the narrow aisles with a basket. I found the beans, and took three tins. I also found some other tinned vegetables, carrots and peas, I think. I couldn't concentrate. Edna had been our neighbour since I was very young, and it shocked me that she'd been murdered in the street a hundred metres from our house.

Coming home, I told Nessa we'd be only two for dinner and the reason why.

'Jack, that's awful,' she said. 'You're right – we ought to get out of London as soon as we can.'

As we had our tea, we heard windows breaking up and down the street.

'That must be Tony's mates,' I said. 'We'll go tomorrow, before dawn.'

4

ESCAPE FROM
LONDON

Groggy with sleep, we carried our things to the car, piled in and locked the doors. Then we set out through the silent streets, passing under the Westway and up the Harrow Road, which stank from the backed up sewers.

It was still dark. I used smaller roads to make our way to the North Circular. From there my objective was to join the M40, near the junction with the M25.

Everywhere we saw signs of looting. I fancied I saw corpses in one street. I was sure I saw, under a dim streetlamp, a group of Territorial Army soldiers falling down drunk. I saw a pack of animals I imagined to be stray dogs. No matter what we saw, or thought we saw, we didn't stop to look closer. I thought it wiser not to stop at red lights, just to reduce the speed slightly. Thankfully we met no roadblocks or checkpoints.

And so, I thought, there I was – in the unusual position of being a refugee in my own country. Well, not a refugee actually, since our destination was the house I grew up in. But I felt like a little like a refugee, I suppose because the journey was partly occasioned by fear of what might happen in London.

Still, fear wasn't really driving me. I wanted to get to the bottom of the turb deviation factor, and that wasn't going to happen in London. The place to begin was in Oxfordshire, at our 'own' wind farm.

And I wanted Nessa to be safe, and London obviously wasn't safe anymore. I believed that Oxfordshire, particularly, our small village and its tightly-knit community of people who knew each other well, would be safer.

'Nothing works in my car, by the way,' I warned Nessa as we set off. 'Not the Auto Drive, not the GPS, not the Anti-Collision Radar – nor the Video System, the Voice-Activated CS, or the Touch Finger Lift Control.'

'A wonder that it can still move,' she said.

'Here,' I added, tossing her a book.

'What's that?' she asked.

'It's called an "A to Z" – it's a map of all the streets in London from A to Z. I found it in a used book bin.'

She positioned herself in the front passenger seat with the book on her lap, which she never once opened – not necessary, since I knew London.

As we joined the M40 outside of Denham it began to rain. Dawn came but it only made the thick clouds slightly lighter. Here and there were a few other vehicles, all moving out of London. We passed a convoy of army lorries. I imagined they were carrying the population of Notting Hill or some other London neighbourhood.

We drove on in silence. The rain got very heavy now. I kept forgetting the Voice-Activated CS wasn't working, so the car ignored all my voice commands. I switched the headlamps on manually and set the windscreen wipers thumping at the highest setting.

Some miles on we began to pass abandoned vehicles like the ones that I'd seen on the M20, only this time I noticed something odd. Some of them had open doors. First a lorry, then an estate car, then a small van and more cars.

'Let's pull over,' said Nessa. 'The rain's too heavy. You can hardly see twenty metres ahead.'

'Did you notice something about those cars we just passed?' I

53

asked. 'Some of the doors were open,' I paused, 'As though the people in them wanted to get out in a hurry.'

'Maybe they – '

'Forgot? Who would forget to close a car door, especially in this rain?'

'I don't know,' said Nessa. 'Maybe they weren't closed properly and the wind blew them open.'

'So many cars? I don't think – ' I left the thought unfinished.

'Look,' said Nessa. 'The rain is red.'

Our eyes turned to the windscreen. The *thump, thump, thump* of the wipers was the only sound.

The rain *was* red.

'It's blood,' I said. 'Rain mixed with blood.'

Just at that instant something smacked into the windscreen. It was there only a second before being swept away by the wipers.

'It was an eye! A great, big eye!' Nessa cried. 'Jack, it scared me to death!'

'An animal's eye,' I said, scared myself. 'Probably the eye of a horse or a cow.'

Now the road curved to the left, leaving the heaviest rain on the right side of the car. Suddenly came a crack. Something hard had hit a window on that side, cracking the glass. Nessa screamed.

'Jack, it looked like – a hoof! An animal's hoof!'

The few seconds distraction this caused meant that I caught sight of the dark object in the road ahead too late to make any manoeuvre other than a sharp turn, throwing Nessa against the door. 'Control the vehicle,' said the car's computer.

'Sorry,' I muttered. Then I realised what it was: a horse's head.

I was alert now and soon another object appeared. Curiosity got the better of me and I slowed down.

Nessa screamed. 'It's horrible!'

It was a dead animal. It looked to be a cow, or rather, half a cow, sliced clean through along the spine. It lay on its side, with its open guts facing upwards. Its two remaining legs seemed to be twitching.

I sped up. I was in no mood for more such sights.

For a moment the mist cleared slightly and I could make out the red mast lights of turbs high above the motorway.

We drove on. It got darker and then lighter again and finally the sky cleared and the sun appeared. We left the M40 motorway for the smaller A40 just east of Oxford, near to the junction for Upper St John. Lovely country. But the scene was marred. For in the beautiful green field before us lay a flock of dead and dying sheep. Among them a terrified young lamb – apparently unhurt – ran crazily in circles.

'Jack, what was all that?' Nessa asked.

'I've a hunch it was turbs.' I said. 'I saw some over to the right when the mist cleared. Maybe turbs from our project. Did you see them?'

'No, I didn't,' she said.

'Doesn't matter. You see, back when mobile turbs first came into operation in this country, sometimes they would lean over too far, too near the ground, I mean, and there were livestock kills,' I said. 'It didn't happen very often – much less often than bird strikes – but when smartchips were installed in the mobile turbs, the livestock kills stopped. The control computers prevented the turbs from leaning too close to the ground.'

'All this was before my time – I was still a student then,' I added.

Nessa remained silent for a moment.

'It happened in China, too,' she said. 'I've read about it. It was years ago. Before my time, too. And with us, too, the installation of computerised controls solved the problem.'

'So why, my love, did it happen here today?' I asked. I leaned over and tried to kiss her. The car swerved. 'Control the vehicle,' bleated the car's computer.

'I'm not sure that turbs did what we saw,' she said. 'We saw some injured animals – OK, a lot of them. But we didn't see turbs slicing them up.'

'So if it wasn't turbs, what was it? *Drivs*? Refugees? The Territorial Army making food provisions?

'Maybe all of the above,' she said. 'Let's get to your house –

that's home for the moment. I'm hungry.'

*

By mid-afternoon we were approaching Upper St John. We did not have to pass through the village to get to the house, but I was naturally curious to see what the situation was there.

I pulled over at the roundabout leading to the high street. I rolled down the window and leaned my head out. No unusual sounds. The church next to the roundabout had a few cars in its car park but no sign of life.

I got out of the car and walked to the other side of the roundabout. From there I could see part of the way up the high street. A parked van partially blocked my view, but I didn't see anything out of the ordinary.

I drove up the high street, dead slow. First, on the left, came the DIY shop. It was completely gutted. Then came the fast food place. The windows were all boarded up. About a hundred yards on came the petrol station. This was a beehive of activity. Cars pointed in every direction, doors open, people shouting at each other.

'Shall we stop to ask what's going on?' said Nessa.

'No, let's reconnoitre a little more first,' I said.

Before the other big roundabout, which led out of the village toward our house, I turned right to follow the one way system through the village. The familiar chemist's came next. It looked like a hurricane had struck it. Then the *Everything One Euro* shop, also a ruin. A few more small ransacked shops followed.

The rail station came into sight, an ugly flat-roofed creature of glass and steel. Bins in front of the station had been overturned and the contents set alight. Knots of men and women crowded around the bonfires. Faces were lit up by the flames and a raised bottle caught the light.

I saw someone I knew. It was Thom Ferguson, the farmer who'd allowed his land to be used to build the *Hope and Glory* wind project.

'Come on,' I said to Nessa. 'Over there. He's the man we need

56

to see.'

We jumped out of the car and ran over to where he was standing.

'Oh, hullo Jack,' he said. 'Where have you come from?'

'From London,' I replied.

'Oh, what's it like there? Any worse than here?'

'I'm not sure,' I said. 'We've only just got here. How are things here?'

'Take a look around you,' he gestured to the bonfires. 'Things here aren't good. I'm a little worried.'

'Have you got enough to eat here?'

'Yeah,' he said. 'But I wouldn't plan on gaining any weight.'

'Been any flooding?'

'Not yet, it's high ground, you know.'

'So you've decided to stay put then,' I observed.

'Course I have,' said the farmer. 'Haven't anywhere else to go.'

'Thom, I wanted to ask your permission to enter onto your land, to visit the wind farm,' I said. 'Sorry, this is Nessa. She'll come with me. She's a wind engineer like me.'

'Course you can come, both of you,' he said. 'Any day you like. We'll be there.'

'Give my best to June,' I said.

'Come anytime,' he said.

'We'll come tomorrow,' I said. 'But we won't disturb you. We'll just check out some of the turbs in the project.'

'Suit yourselves,' he said, stepping closer to one of the bonfires.

We got back in the car and drove on through the village. As we passed the council building, we saw a sign advertising a town meeting on the flood emergency, to take place the next day.

We finished our circular drive around the village, coming back to the first roundabout and then to the second, again passing the DIY, the fast food place and the petrol station. This time around Nessa noticed a Chinese restaurant across from the petrol station.

'I've always been disappointed by Chinese restaurants in England,' she commented. 'They're sort of foreign.'

I decided we would not investigate the big shopping centre beyond the village. It was too far, and the day was getting on.

We finally arrived at the house late in the afternoon. The drive sloped up from the road to the house. It looked as I had hoped. All the windows were shut and the house was dark. That was a good sign. No looters and no squatters.

The house faced east, which meant at that time of day it cast a shadow across the lawn. This, together with being set higher than the road, gave it a bit of a foreboding look when seen from the drive. But I knew it as home, so it didn't cast any spell over me.

'Come, let me show you the garden,' I said. I took her hand in mine.

The house had the shape of the letter 'L' and I led Nessa around the longer end, peeking into the windows of the lounge. All was intact.

We rounded the end of the house and turned into Mum's flower and herb garden. There in the garden at the inside juncture of the 'L' was a spit where we used to barbeque lamb, flavoured with home-grown rosemary and thyme.

'It's very beautiful,' Nessa said.

The shorter end of the 'L' comprised the kitchen – dating to the eighteenth century – and the dining room. There were no signs that anyone had been in the house.

We unloaded the car and began to take stock of what we had. There was some tinned food in the larder, but not much.

In terms of energy, at least, we were well off. In the kitchen there were two full cans of natural gas. Next to the kitchen stood a large shed that was full of firewood. And on one of the hills above the house, stood the three mini-turbs that Dad had installed years ago. They were tethered to a small generator.

I could see them quite clearly from the house with the telescopes and field glasses which Dad had collected over the years. The field glasses would come in handy.

I also took stock of anything that might be used as a weapon. Into that category fell a hatchet, a couple of hunting knives, a large hammer and a garden hoe. It wasn't much and, needless to say, I doubted I could bring myself to use any of it.

*

The next morning we rose early and trudged through the snow to the Ferguson farm. It was a bright, clear morning and the sun shone across the hills. As we climbed the last hill the tops of turbs came into view over the crest.

'That's it,' I said. 'The *Hope and Glory* project.'

'How old did you say it is?' asked Nessa.

'About twenty-five years,' I said. 'My father was still working when it came online.'

We reached the crest of the hill and stopped to survey the project in the valley below us. Turbs stretched as far as the eye could see.

'It's not a big project by today's standards, but when it began operation it was classed as a major project,' I said.

'By Chinese standards, it's a minnow,' Nessa commented.

'Well, you can see by the height alone, they're not the newest models,' I said, 'Though many of them have been replaced. The original models had a twenty year life span, give or take.'

The highest among them were in the hundred twenty metre range, well short of the two hundred metre plus models that had become common at the time of the flood.

'So, which one are we going to climb?' Nessa asked.

'That one in the middle,' I said. 'It's the tallest one.'

We made our way through the turbs.

'Jack, look,' said Nessa. 'The turbs seem to have moved toward that end of the valley. Which direction is that?'

'South,' I said.

'OK, noted,' she replied. 'They've moved toward the south. Is that significant?'

'Could be,' I said.

We reached our target and I swung my backpack around, fish-

59

ing for a turb wrench. Between the two giant wheels at the base of the turb was a hatch. Turb hatches were generally not locked, but to open them a special tool – which we called a turb wrench – was required. This was done to prevent just anybody from entering and climbing the turbs.

I pulled the hatch open.

'I'll go first,' I said. 'These probably aren't much different than the turbs you have in China, but I'll show you the way, just in case.'

'Jack, I'm sure they're not different from ours – all the earlier turbs in China were copied from Western designs. This one is probably no different.'

It wasn't. We belted up our safety cords, latched them to the vertical wire hanging by the rungs and began working our way up. The climb was easy. Within a few minutes we'd reached the yaw motor drive, located just below the turb head. Above it was a hatch leading into the head, which I opened with the turb wrench.

As I opened the hatch a waft of smelly air hit us. I stuck my head into the nacelle, with Nessa just below me.

'Nessa, please open my backpack and hand me a pair of turb gloves,' I said.

Special gloves had been developed for the insides of turb heads. They were made of thick rubber, with adhesive material on the palms and fingers. Their purpose was to help wind engineers deal with the plants and plant oils that had taken root in turb heads. Surfaces were slippery, and a fall could have dangerous consequences.

I hoisted myself into the nacelle and Nessa followed.

The head of a wind turb appears to be quite small when seen from the ground far below it. It makes a turb look like a praying mantis, a creature with a long, thin body and tiny head. But in fact the head is easily high enough for an adult to stand upright.

'Wow, Jack, this one is really a dinosaur,' said Nessa. 'Look at the double shaft generator.'

She was right. Twin shaft turbs had gone the way of the horse drawn carriage.

In the twin shaft design, the wind turned a low-speed shaft connected to the blades, which then turned a second, high-speed shaft inside the turb head, which was connected to the generator. Between the two shafts were a set of gears, which enabled the second shaft to turn at the much higher speed needed to spark electricity in the copper coils inside the generator.

Many years ago a simpler, single shaft design was invented. The rotor blades turned a single shaft connected directly to the generator. This was possible due to the use of a metal in the generator much more conductive than copper – a rare earth metal called *neodymium*.

'Nessa, you're the botanist. What do you make of the plant life inside this turb?' I said.

'There are hardly any plants,' she said. 'That's unusual. You know, I studied botany as a minor to wind engineering because I kept seeing so much plant life inside turbs. But this one's pretty clean.'

'Let's go up top,' I said. I clambered up a set of rungs leading to the roof of the turb head. I popped open the roof hatch and stuck my head out.

'Ness, this turb hasn't got a platform on top. It's too slippery to go out,' I said. 'We'll take a look in turns.'

The turb's blades were still. Consequently, I was able to look around without the distraction of the blade wake in my face. Many of the turbs had indeed moved toward the south, in the direction of the A40. I'd been away so long I'd forgotten the size of the project. There seemed to be more turbs than I remembered. I made a rough calculation and estimated the current size of the *Hope and Glory* herd at around two thousand turbs.

'You take a look,' I said, coming down. Nessa climbed up.

'Jack, I can see a lot of broken tethers,' she said. 'Looks like they snapped when the turbs moved.'

'Well, forty thousand kilos of moving turb will do the trick,' I said.

'There's something else, Jack,' she said. 'This herd is densely packed – I would say two times rotor diameter.'

That didn't surprise me. When the *Hope and Glory* project was built, the rule was a distance of six to eight times rotor diameter between the turbs. That set them fairly far apart. The reason for this was the 'mast wake' effect – the turb blades created a wake that put a drag on the turning of blades located behind or 'downwind.'

But thanks to the invention of an algorithm by a Norwegian maths professor, the problem of mast wake had been solved. Still, even the 'Oslo algorithm,' as it was called, did not permit such tight spacing.

Nessa came back down into the turb head.

'We should take this turb's smartchip. It might tell us something,' I said.

'You're right,' she said. 'It'll be at the back of the turb head. Can you squeeze yourself back there?'

'I'm sure I can,' I said. 'I've done it many times.'

I made my way toward the rear of the nacelle and squeezed myself past the generator into the conical space at the rear end of the nacelle, a bit like the nose cone of an aeroplane. With my stomach pressed against the generator, I reached into my rucksack.

'Blast,' I said. 'I haven't got a key. Nessa, have you got one?'

Control box keys, like other specialised turb tools, were meant to keep out the curious. Nessa fished in her bag and tossed me a key, which clattered at my feet.

I slid downwards and grasped the key with two fingers. Then I eased my body upright as far as I could and reached up to grope for the box's keyhole. I got the key in and the box popped open. I felt around inside. There it was – the turb's smartchip.

The size of a small external hard drive, the chip had multiple functions – it processed information about the speed and direction of the wind that came into the turb from its wind vane and anemometer, and it received instructions from the herd's control computer. It also served as a memory chip, recording all data relating to the turb's movements.

'Got it,' I called out.

Slowly I eased myself back around the generator and toward

the front of the nacelle.

'All right,' I said. 'Let's get out of this turb.'

Just then my smartphone beeped.

'You have to climb a turb to get a signal around here!' I laughed.

'What is it?' Nessa asked.

'It's a message from Phil,' I said. 'It's about the mission he mentioned while we were at sea. He wrote someone is going to make contact very soon.'

'What's this mission about?' she asked.

'The deviation factor,' I replied.

5

TOWN MEETING

We walked over the hills back to the house, the winter sun slanting behind us.

'The English countryside is beautiful, even in winter,' said Nessa. 'But I'm not sure we learned anything.'

'We need to analyse the smartchip, then we'll know something,' I said. 'What's your take?'

'What we saw was an older model,' she said. 'I'd like to see a newer model, one with a single shaft generator.'

'I agree, and we will,' I said. 'But at the moment, I'd like to get home and change clothes. I'm very curious about this town meeting.'

'Why?' Nessa asked.

'Because I grew up here. But I've been away for years. I'm curious to see what it's like now, whether I recognise anyone,' I said.

I was also curious about the situation in the village, and in particular whether and when the flood might reach us. We changed clothes and drove to the meeting. As the village mosque was the only public space large enough to accommodate so many people, the council decided to hold the meeting there. Even so, it was hard to find a space in the car park.

The space had been filled with folding chairs and we took seats on the aisle toward the rear, trying not to make too much noise. The meeting was already underway. I glanced around. Quickly counting the rows of chairs, I estimated there were about three hundred people present.

I couldn't say what kind of people they were as I'd spent so little time in Upper St John since leaving for university and a career. Judging by their clothes, I would have said that most did not look well off, but then it's hard to judge by clothing. Rich and poor alike wore luxury name brands, both real and fake, and I couldn't tell the difference.

'Hullo, Jack!' came a voice. It was Chris Porter. He ran the best garage in the village, that is to say, the cheapest. 'Value for money' was his way of putting it. I'd known him since I was a boy. He could service any kind of car, but specialised in England's gems, the Rolls Royce and the Bentley. My Dad had had a Bentley for a time.

'Hey, Chris,' I said. 'How are you?'

'I'm fine – or rather, I was fine, till this crisis came along. You've been away a long time.'

'Maybe too long,' I said, introducing Nessa. 'We came late. What have we missed?'

'The copper talking about house break-ins and looting and stray animals, and good old Dr Moore talking about boiling your drinking water. That's the gist of it,' he replied.

'Why, it's Jack Mason,' said a woman, turning around. 'How are you?'

'Fine, Jenny,' I replied. 'Long time, no see. You've brought the whole family.'

Jenny Towton's two daughters smiled and said hello. I introduced Nessa. The younger one, Isadora, was wearing the uniform of the Territorial Army. I hardly recognised either of them as they'd grown so much since I'd last seen them.

The Towton woman was, to her credit, a symbol of England's global service economy. Divorced, she supported herself and her daughters by working from home as a consultant to the energy industry, specialising in the social effects of large-scale energy projects, both traditional and renewables. My father had met her through work. She'd lived in Upper St John for donkeys' years and knew everyone.

'Quiet, please,' said a woman on the podium. It was the leader of the council. She sat in the middle – obviously in charge – with another woman on her left and beside her, old Dr Moore. On her right sat the local policeman, Deputy Chief Superintendent Withers. Next to him was another man, wearing a dark suit and tie, whom I'd never seen before, and who didn't say a word during the meeting.

Listening to the woman, I took an instant dislike to her voice. For lack of a more precise term, it was officious. Her body seemed to match her voice – tall and thin, with short cropped hair, she wore glasses with bright red frames which made it hard to see her eyes.

'I'm asking you to be quiet because I have an important announcement,' she was saying. 'I've just received word that the Thames and other rivers in our area are likely to breach their banks within the next forty-eight to seventy-two hours. This will include the marshland north of us known as Ot Moor. Serious flooding will result.'

The audience gasped.

'When did you say?' cried a man in the first row.

'The day after tomorrow,' said a woman next to him.

'Here? It can't be!' another woman yelled. 'We've never had anything like that before.'

'What's happened to the BBC?' yelled someone else. 'Our screen's been blank for days.'

'What about my smartphone – it hasn't had a signal since I can't remember,' someone else called out.

'Quiet, please,' said the leader. 'We don't know yet how bad it's going to be. It may only be a matter of rivers breaching their banks and the sewers backing up. Or it might be much worse, especially in the marshland north of here. We just don't know.'

'What *do* you know?' called Chris Porter, standing up.

She eyed him icily, but resumed speaking as though he didn't exist.

'As I was saying, the precise parameters of the flooding aren't clear yet,' she continued. 'What is clear is that we must be prepared. We have a plan.'

'Tell us then,' someone shouted.

'Yes, out with it,' came another voice.

'We've a plan, of course. You'll be told,' the leader went on, defensively. 'My assistant, Ms Rhynd-Smythson, will share some of the details with you now,' said the leader. She gestured to the woman sitting beside her.

'Sorry,' said a woman in the first row, rising tentatively. 'What do you mean by *some* of the details? I'd like to hear the whole plan. I'm sure I'm not alone in this.'

'What I meant was that we'll set out the important points that everyone should be aware of,' said the leader, putting on a plastic smile.

'Why not give us all the information?' the woman asked.

'We can't very well read out the whole plan,' said the leader, her smile giving way to a scowl at the corners of her mouth. 'You've no idea how complicated these things are. Let's start with the important points.'

'All right,' said the woman. 'Sorry to be a bother.'

'Not at all,' said the leader, and to her assistant: 'Go ahead, please.'

Ms Rhynd-Smythson, a wavy-haired woman of middling years, gathered some papers before her and began to read them.

'The council's public realm scrutiny committee met on the twenty fifth of the second just past at four o'clock in the council building. Present were – '

'Get on with it,' Jenny Towton called out.

'Perhaps we might dispense with a recitation of the bureaucratic formalities and just read the essence of what has been decided,' interjected the leader.

'Of course,' said Ms Rhynd-Smythson. She brushed back her hair.

'It was decided to evacuate the population of Upper St John – '

'What?' cried several people at once.

Ms Rynd-Smythson struggled to be heard.

' – for their own safety and protection – ' she raised her voice, but was soon drowned out.

There was chaos. People stood up, shouting. It all welled up into a single question: evacuation to where? And that question was joined by a torrent of tributaries – when, exactly? How? What could one bring with?

Withers, the policeman, rose.

'You'll learn more when you quiet down and the leader's able to tell you,' he said sternly. 'We can't give you the information if everyone's shouting.'

The villagers, momentarily cowed by the uniform, dropped their protests to a murmur, but they did not entirely subside.

'That's right,' he said, sitting down.

This meeting was beginning to get on my nerves. I didn't care for being told what to do or to be quiet, and neither, it seemed, did the others from the village.

'Please continue,' said the leader to her assistant, who looked down at the paper in front of her.

'The evacuation will be conducted by stages,' she began. 'People will be assigned numbers and will be called to a transport centre by number. Coaches will – '

'What if we don't want to go?' Chris Porter called out, on his feet again.

The assistant turned to the leader, who said: 'Let's say the council is encouraging all residents – '

'Does "encouraged" mean it's by force?' Chris shouted, his hands cupped around his mouth. 'I'd rather stay here, thank you very much.'

'Encouraged is a much more pleasant word,' said the leader.

'Sounds like we don't have a choice.' Chris went on.

'It is my responsibility, to ensure that the interest of the community is served by the enforcement of council emergency regulations, even during times like these,' she replied. 'And the emergency regulations – '

'Sod the regulations,' said Porter. 'Tell us what's going to happen to us.'

'That's enough,' she declared. 'Emergency regulations permit me to place you under detention.'

'Now Chris, that's something we would want to avoid,' Withers broke in, rising again. He removed his cap, revealing a big, bald head, which suited his large, imposing stomach.

Porter looked at the policeman and sat down, wearing a contrite expression that was, to me at least, as I knew him well, obviously insincere. I knew that Chris did not suffer fools gladly, and I began to feel that the leader of our council fell into that category.

I stood up.

'Say, there's an alternative to evacuation. What about using the shopping centre near the A40?' I said. 'I mean the big centre built by the Chinese a few years ago. I've forgotten what it's called.'

'The Big World,' said a woman near us.

'That's it,' I said. 'It ought to be big enough to hold everyone in the village. And it's on high ground.'

'Young Jack's got an idea,' shouted Chris, waving his arms for calm.

'He's right,' said Jenny. 'The shopping centre's perfect.'

I was encouraged by their support. Evidently the villagers of Upper St John weren't sheep to be herded by the local council.

'We can organise ourselves to use the things in the shopping centre for survival. That means food, clothing, beds, blankets, duvets, what have you. And there's water in the centre's reservoir, isn't there?' I said. 'I remember a pond there.'

'Yes, there's a pond there – for the rain run-off,' said Withers.

'What about power?' said a man's voice.

I recognised the voice as that of Paul Pritchard, who ran the *Oxon Villager's Blog*. My parents had been friendly with him. I remembered him as a spirited character, full of fight and humour. He'd worked for various news outfits, both in England and abroad, specialising in energy.

'We'll be no good in the shopping centre without energy,' he said, answering his own question.

'Paul, good to see you,' I said. 'You're right. We'll need power, if there isn't any. I'll bet we can get it from the mini-turbs.'

'From the *what?*' a man near me asked.

'Mini-turbs,' I said. 'The smaller, home-sized versions of wind turbs. Lots of homes around here have got them. I've got three of them at my house. We'd just need to move them to the shopping centre, and tether them to the generator – I'm sure the centre's got a generator.'

'What about food?' ventured the woman in the first row.

'Everyone should bring what they have, tins especially, things that won't go off,' I said. 'There are lots of restaurants in the centre, so there'll be places to cook. And if there's power, the cold storage might still be working. There might be lots of food there and if there isn't you can use the cold storage for what you cook.'

The leader of the council banged something heavy on the podium.

'We must have quiet if we are to get anywhere,' she said. Turning her gaze toward me, she asked, 'Who are you?'

Chris Porter spoke before I could answer. 'That's Jack Mason. He's from this village, even if he's been away a while. He's a wind engineer. He knows what he's talking about, energy from the small turbs, I mean.'

'Does he?' the leader of the council snorted.

'He knows a hell of a lot more about it than you,' put in Paul Pritchard.

'I see,' said the leader. She leaned back in her chair. Whether it was wounded pride or genuine uncertainty that made her retreat I couldn't say.

'All right, Mr Mason,' she said. 'Tell us your idea.'

'My idea,' I said, 'is to bring as many of the mini-turbs as we can to the shopping centre. Then I'll – we'll, that is, Nessa here is also a wind engineer –' I gestured toward Nessa, who also stood up '– we'll tether them up to the centre's generator. We may have to jigger up a transformer and do a few other things but there's a good

70

chance we'll be able create electricity.'

'The tricky part will be the transformer,' Nessa explained. 'Measuring the voltage may be a problem.'

'I see,' said the leader, although I wasn't sure that she did. 'Well, the council can't evacuate people by force. I'll speak to the shopping centre manager.'

'There isn't any management there anymore,' Withers, the policeman, broke in. 'They buggered off – afraid of the flood.'

'When did that happen?' the leader asked.

'See?' Chris yelled. 'She's doesn't even know what's going on in this village!'

'That's a bit too far, Chris!' Withers shouted.

'Thank you, Deputy Chief Superintendent,' said the leader, trying to restore order. 'I confess to you all that we in the council aren't perfect. We're trying our best under difficult circumstances. Give us a chance!'

But by then it was too late restore the semblance of an orderly meeting. Everyone was on their feet, speaking in small groups.

I turned to Nessa. 'Let's go outside,' I said. 'A bit of fresh air.'

We made our way toward the door.

'Just a minute, Mr Mason,' I heard a voice behind me and turned. It was the fifth man on the podium – the one who hadn't said anything.

'A word, if you don't mind,' he said. 'My name's Patel. I've been sent here by the government. We need your help.'

'With what?' I asked, looking him over. He was a slight man with jet black hair and a smile that seemed genuine.

'The turb deviation factor,' he replied. 'Your boss Sir Philip Burnley proposed your name. That should ring a bell.'

Of course it rang all the bells, as I reckoned he knew it would. So this was the contact Phil had mentioned in his message.

'Phil told me I'd be contacted,' I said. 'How can I help you?'

'It's not me who needs your help. It's your government. We've assembled a working group to deal with the problem of turbs breaking their tethers,' he said. 'But it's short of someone with your skills.'

'You see, we're losing a lot of energy just when we need it most,' he continued. 'We'd like you to lead a group whose job will be to re-attach as many tethers as you can, and to train others to do the same.'

'Mr Patel, I've already thought about that. Re-attaching the turb tethers won't solve the problem,' I said. 'They'll only get broken again. You've got to get to the root of the problem.'

'Mr Mason, the government are asking for your help,' he said. 'Your own boss recommended you. He said Jack Mason can be counted on. We need you.'

'You can twist my arm, but all you're going to be doing is wasting time and energy,' I replied. 'What you're suggesting won't work. You're barking up the wrong turb, if I can use that pun.'

'How do you know?' he spluttered. He seemed genuinely confused.

'We know because we're wind engineers,' said Nessa.

'Sorry,' said Patel. 'Who is this?'

'This is Nessa Chao. She is — or was — part of a delegation from the Chinese Institute of Wind Science and Turbine Design to our energy department. Until the flood turned everything upside down.'

'Pleased to meet you, Ms Chao,' said Patel.

'Look, I don't mean to be difficult,' I said. 'I'm as patriotic as the next man, and if it's for King and Country, as they used to say, you can count on me. But if I go, Ms Chao here comes with. I'll need — we'll need — her expertise.'

Patel remained silent for a moment.

'I was sent here to fetch you,' he said. 'I don't have authorisation to take anyone else — especially not a national of a foreign power, one that hasn't always been entirely friendly. There may be secret information involved, technical information.'

'Well then, no deal,' I said. 'If Ms Chao doesn't come, I don't come. How's that?'

'That's clear enough,' he replied. 'I'll carry the message back, but my boss won't like it. You'll likely be hearing from me again.'

'Just a minute, Patel. I have a question for you,' I said. 'Why did you sit through the meeting? Why didn't you button hole me earlier?'

He smiled.

'I wanted to watch you. See if you'd say anything,' he said.

'Then you knew what I look like?'

'Of course,' he said.

'And what did you think of my suggestion – to use the shopping centre?'

'Don't get in over your head helping the people of this village,' he said. 'The government are still counting on you. I'll be in touch.'

'Nessa and I will be ready,' I said.

As we left the hall I saw Nessa giving me one of her looks.

'Jack, you should have said "yes" to that man regardless of whether I come with you.'

'What, and leave you sitting alone in an isolated house, in the midst of this chaos?'

'I can take care of myself, Jack,' she replied.

'I'm sure you can,' I said. 'The real reason I insisted you come is because I want you with me – I'll need your input.'

'With all the wind engineers you have in England, I doubt you'd need me,' she said.

'That's where you're wrong,' I said.

Just then Chris Porter came up to us.

'Had enough of the council?' he asked. 'The leader's a bit hard to take.'

'No argument,' I said. 'Are you still living alone, above your garage?'

'Haven't moved,' he said.

'Maybe you'd like to come by the house for a Chinese meal,' said Nessa.

Chris' face beamed. 'I'd like that,' he said. But the shadow of a frown crossed it quickly.

'Those turbs way over there,' he said, gesturing toward some turbs in a distant field. 'I could swear I saw them move.'

'You probably did see them move,' I smiled. 'That's exactly what they're programmed to do.'

'Them those wheelie turbs?' Chris asked.

'Sure are. From the *Hope and Glory* project,' I said. 'They're roaming in search of the wind,' I added, not entirely truthfully, but I had no wish to enter into a discussion of the deviation factor with Chris.

Then I noticed something about the turbs in that distant field. They were moving, but it was the way they were leaning that seemed odd to me – like a dog straining at its lead – as though they were intent on breaking their tethers.

6

FIRST KILL

With the next morning's coffee it hit me that we had to go back to *Hope and Glory* project or, more precisely, to the Ferguson farmhouse located at its edge. Ferguson had made a lot of land available for the construction of the project – thus making a tidy sum for himself and his wife – but it left him a few dozen acres for cultivation. Predictably, he retained the acreage near his house.

'We've seen the broken tethers,' I argued to Nessa. 'But we don't know when they were broken. In other words, we've no sense of timing – how long the problem's been brewing. Maybe Ferguson will be able to tell us. Besides that I want to check out a few more turbs – get a better idea of the models.'

'We'll have to swing by the petrol station to get some biofuel,' I said in the car, after the fuel gauge announced its thirst.

'Low fuel. Buy fuel now,' it droned. I punched the override button and it fell silent.

People still called it a petrol station, but of course the evolving 'energy mix' meant that it had several types of energy used in cars. Traditional petrol was still on sale, but so were petrol and biofuel mixtures, pure biofuels, electric battery chargers, solar energizers and the like. Since the onset of the flood there were shortages in almost every type of fuel, so people were happy to get whatever they could find. My 'clunker' ran on a particular biofuel mixture that was not always obtainable. I considered myself lucky whenever

I found it, each time wondering if it would be the last.

The station was a madhouse of cars and people, all trying to fill up before the flood waters hit.

But, we soon learned, people came not only for fuel – they came, too, for news. The town meeting had made everyone abuzz as to whether the situation was really all that serious, whether they should move at once to the shopping centre for safety and, if they didn't, whether the council would try to evacuate people by force.

The site for all this talk was the village's petrol station or, more precisely, the little café next to it called, for some reason I'd never been able to discover, the 'F Café.' The formal town meeting reverberated in exchanges of fact and rumour in the F.

As soon as we entered the café – you had to pay for fuel in the café, so there was no way to avoid hearing what people were saying – we picked up snippets of the ongoing talk.

'Refugees. Swarms of 'em, covered with lice they were, and eating dandelions,' one man was saying. 'Me neighbour saw 'em just outside Chipping Sunbury.'

'That's nothing,' said another man. 'They've drowned like rats up in London – I tell you there were bodies floating in Trafalgar Square. My brother's wife's nephew saw it with his own eyes.'

'We need the army to take control straightaway,' said the man at the till, and others nodded in agreement. 'But where are they?'

We heard that and much other nonsense.

'Let's get over to the Fergusons' farm before I go mad listening to all this,' I said.

We pulled up the long drive from the road. Before getting out of the car, I lowered the window and stuck my head out.

'Thom, hello!' I called out. 'June!'

There was no reply.

I opened the car door and put one foot on the gravel with a crunch.

Then I noticed the front door of the house was wide open.

'Look at the door,' I said.

Someone had to be there. We got out of the car and stood for a moment, wondering which way to turn. Perhaps Ferguson was in the fields. There was no sound.

I took a few steps toward the house, cocking my head to look at the windows. One was open, on the first floor.

'Hello Thom! June!' I called out again, now at the door. I tried to peer inside the house but in the foyer, what with all the raincoats, umbrellas and Wellington boots, I couldn't see further.

I went inside. Nessa stood in the drive.

'Hello again!' I called out. I went into the dining room – no one there and everything in its place. Then the kitchen – the same. I wondered if I should go upstairs. No, I thought, what if they are up there and it proves embarrassing? I tried to picture Mr and Mrs Ferguson making love. The picture was difficult to form. No sound came from the upstairs and I gave up the idea of going there.

'There's no one in the house,' I said, coming outside.

'Jack, I don't like this,' said Nessa. 'It's creepy.'

The garage, I thought, we should check the garage.

'Their garage is behind the house. I'll just see if their car is there,' I said.

A barn partially blocked the path to the garage and I circled it, hearing only the crunch of my footsteps in the gravel. When I rounded the barn, I saw at once that the garage door was open, but it was too dark inside to see if a car was there. I strode up to the open door. There was a car inside. So they were here, *somewhere*, I thought. I paused to consider where to go next. Something caught my attention in the sky, and I looked up at a flock of birds.

'Nessa,' I called out. 'Their car is here.' I wondered if she heard me.

I turned to leave and there, on the gravel drive, I saw the head-less corpse of June Ferguson.

I took a step towards the crumpled body and gave a start. I hadn't noticed the head, only a few inches from my shoe. June's long, grey hair lay flat out on the gravel, as though she were going to brush it. Her face, lying on its side, had a horrific expression, her eyes open wide and glowing. Her mouth was open, too, as though she were singing in a church choir. Just below her chin lay a tangle of flesh, veins, arteries and blood.

I had never before seen a severed human head and it shocked me. I stared at it for how long I don't know, transfixed and repelled at the same time. I felt a sense of horror at whoever had done this to June Ferguson. It was obviously not the work of an animal, a human had done this – to another human. It made me sick.

Then I moved to examine the corpse. I saw at once that the arms were missing. They were bloody stumps at the shoulder. I looked back toward the head and then I saw the arms. Funny, how I had missed them at first. They lay near the head, the three body parts like a set of bowling pins all knocked down together.

Then Nessa came round the barn. As soon as she saw me she followed my gaze and screamed.

'Oh, my God, Jack, it's – I've never – what happened to her?' Nessa stood with her palm over her mouth.

'I reckon June raised her arms to defend herself,' I said. 'Whoever attacked her cut off her head and both her arms, perhaps with a single blow, if her arms were raised like this.' I held up my arms.

'But what kind of person could have done that?' I went on. 'He must have been tall, and extremely strong. And what weapon had he used – an axe?'

'Jack, I don't know and it's no use us guessing,' said Nessa. 'We'd better get the police here.'

'No, wait a moment,' I said. I was breathing heavily now, with one thought in my mind: to find Thom Ferguson.

I went back to their house and put on a pair of wellies I found by the door.

'Stay near the car,' I warned Nessa.

Then I went into the fields and there I soon saw Thom's farm combine.

Strange, that it should be in the middle of a field. At some distance I could see a dark shape caught in the blades. I walked toward the combine. Some birds were evidently interested in the shape and this drew my attention to the sky. In the distance, I saw the red mast lights of turbs – the *Hope and Glory* project was just over the hill.

Around fifty metres from the combine I could see that the dark shape was a man's body. No doubt it would be Ferguson, and it was. He was hanging upside down in the combine blades. He hung face up from his legs, which were bent at the knee over a combine blade. His arms dangled below his head. As I got nearer, I saw the expression on his face. It was one of sheer terror. Like his wife, the eyes and mouth were wide open.

I felt momentarily sick and looked down at the ground to steady myself. Then I walked under the combine. I saw that the contents of Ferguson's pockets had spilled into the mud. As I looked up, I saw a wound in his back, a blotch of blood and, for lack of a more precise medical term, goo.

Walking out from under the combine, I saw another wound – in Thom's stomach. It occurred to me that he must have been run through by a sword or something similar – probably the same weapon that was used to kill his wife.

I wanted to get away. There was nothing we could do to help Thom or June, who had obviously been dead for some time. I just wanted us to get away.

'What is it, Jack? What did you see?' Nessa asked as I came, ashen-faced, from the field.

'Thom's dead, too. All tangled up in his combine,' I said. 'It's odd, but it seems to me that he tried to use the combine as a defence tool. Looks like he seized on the idea in a hurry, and rushed from his house, perhaps before, perhaps after, his wife died. He seized on the only tool he thought might work. His combine.'

'But why the combine?' Nessa asked.

'I've no idea,' I said, sweating despite the cold.

'Was he also –?'

'No,' I said. 'But he wasn't a pretty sight.'

Only later, as we were on our way to the police station, did it strike me that both bodies seemed mutilated or strangely decomposed, with just bits of lacerated flesh hanging on the bones. Odd given the cold weather. But I was too tired and too shocked to talk more about it just then.

*

At first I was in two minds whether to say anything to the police about what we'd seen at the Fergusons' farm.

'You never know with the English police,' I said. 'They're capable of accusing anybody of anything – or simply ignoring a crime – if it fits their politics.'

'Jack, we've got to tell the police,' said Nessa. 'If we don't, we might even be at risk as suspects.'

I mulled that over.

'You're right,' I said. 'It's better to get it off our chests.'

I told the car to turn towards the police station, and soon we were shown into the presence of DCS Withers. I introduced myself and Nessa, but of course he already knew my name from the town meeting. I hadn't met him before, as he'd come to Upper St John after I'd left.

'Constable Bartle here tells me you've seen something horrible,' he said.

'Yes we have, a farmer and his wife, Thom and June Ferguson,' I said.

'The lady had 'er head chopped clean off. And 'er arms, too,' said Bartle. 'And the man – '

'Thank you, constable,' said Withers, turning to me. 'Did you see anyone else at the Ferguson farm? Hear anything – like a car engine?'

'No, nothing,' I replied. 'The farm was quiet as the grave. Sorry, that's not the best analogy.'

'I'll send some men over there straightaway,' said Withers. 'Bartle, do you know where this farm is?'

'Yes, Deputy Chief Superintendent.'

'Then get over there, if you please,' said Withers. 'And arrange for an ambulance.'

'You needn't hurry on that score,' I said. 'They're both quite dead.'

The Deputy Chief Superintendent frowned.

'Lots of refugees, looters and drifters about these days, because of the flood crisis,' he said. 'Could've been a surprised thief.'

'Deputy Chief Superintendent, the Fergusons didn't surprise anyone on coming home – they *were* home. We found their car in their garage,' I said.

'Look, I'm not a novice at this. You can turn any crime scene this way and that,' he said. 'No matter how you look at it, you can't always make sense of what you see on the first go.'

'I'm sure you know your business,' I said. 'But we're sure there were no other people at the farm.'

He heaved his large body out of his chair.

'I'll wait till Bartle reports on what he saw,' he said.

The interview was over.

Later, at home, I connected the turb smartchip to my computer. My expertise was in mechanics, design and their interaction with the wind. I had only a basic understanding of the programming languages used in turbs.

'Nessa, can you help with this? I'd like to identify the programming language, for a start. I think it's Emerald. I knew that the turb computer networks, in England at least, ran on software with that name.

'I can't help you, Jack, I'm a wind engineer with a minor in botany, not a computer programmer. Why don't you ask your boss Phil to get you some help?'

'I will – as soon as I get a signal in my smartphone,' I said. 'In the meantime, I'll give it a try myself.'

Nessa stared at the screen.

'I give up,' she said. 'Jack, maybe there's someone here in your village who can help, if there's a computer shop.'

'There is,' I said. 'I mean, there was, in the Big World shopping centre. I'll bet it's still there.'

'I'm a little curious about this shopping centre,' said Nessa. 'You said it's a Chinese shopping centre. I wonder what that means.'

'It was built by Chinese,' I said. 'That doesn't mean you'll find your favourite noodles there. To tell you the truth, I'm curious, too. I wonder if people are taking shelter there. Even if we don't find a computer geek, we may find something else useful.'

7

THE BIG WORLD

The Big World shopping centre lay about three miles from my house, by the junction with the A40.

'Let's walk there,' I suggested to Nessa. 'On the way back I want to see the southern side of the *Hope and Glory* project, and the road doesn't reach there. The only way in is by foot. I'll take the camping gear just in case.'

We walked over the hill behind the house and then over the next one. Just before we came to the Big World, before the last hill, was an estate of semi-detached houses that had as street names Stuart Way, Tudor Way, Warwick Way and other similar evocations of lost English grandeur. We circled round it to the crest of the last hill. There, below us, was the Big World, or *Da Shi*, to use its Chinese name – which no one ever did.

I should describe it because so many people – both the villagers of Upper St John and the refugees who'd made their way to Oxfordshire – will never forget what happened there. That is, those who survived.

The Big World shopping centre was the largest in England and among the largest in Europe. It consisted of a single rectangular building surrounded by car parks on three sides. On the fourth side was an artificial reservoir created for rain water drainage.

It had been built by a consortium of Chinese companies as a showcase for Chinese goods. Every conceivable variety of consumer product could be had there. Everything for the home was there: furniture, kitchens, bathrooms, bedrooms and even billiard rooms, music rooms, sport rooms and home cinemas. No man, woman or child could fail to find any item of clothing or accessory necessary or desirable for any season or activity. The variety of appliances and electronic goods could enable any shopper to enjoy infinite leisure and convenience in his or her own home. The array of tools and materials in the home centre could facilitate the building of a small town. The children's toy department could keep a whole school occupied. The travel department had enough luggage to enable the entire population of Upper St John to go on holiday at the same time. And the pet department could have filled Noah's Ark. As for sporting equipment, the FA and rugby union could have added a dozen clubs each.

Then there were the eateries – twenty six of them, offering the cuisine of the world to rural Oxfordshire. To wash it all down, the Big World had six pubs strategically placed around the centre. Whilst Dad enjoyed his pint, the kids could gorge themselves with enough sweets to ruin the teeth of a generation.

Such was the Big World – a showcase for Chinese goods but a subtle one: most of the brands had English-sounding names intended to reassure and blunt any sense of foreignness. Thus, for example, *The Lake District* kitchenware line was made in a place very far from Kendall and *Mrs Winchester's Jam* was made from fruit (partially) that never grew in England. All of this was available at low prices that anyone could easily afford, with the result that the shops in the village withered and died.

Yet, even from our hilltop, we could see that something was not right in the shopping centre.

'Here, take a look,' I said, handing a pair of field glasses to Nessa. 'It seems to be abandoned. A lot of the windows are broken and the main entrance door is wide open.'

'You're right,' she said. 'No cars in the car park. No people. Wait a minute, there is someone – that man you introduced me to at the town meeting. The man with the garage.'

'Chris?'

'Yes, that's him. He's coming across the car park with some others,' she said.

'Ah, so they've taken up my idea – the shopping centre as a refuge from the flood.'

'I'm not so sure it was a good idea, Jack,' said Nessa.

'Why?'

'Well, the place looks like a disaster hit it,' she said.

'Let's go down and have a closer look,' I said.

We bounded down the hillside. I waved to Chris as we approached.

'Hey Jack! Nessa! Come to join us, have you?' he said by way of greeting. He smiled at Nessa and nodded.

'We've come for a look round,' I said. 'For the moment, we're staying put at home. But if we can help, we'll gladly do so.'

'We'll need your help with that,' he said. 'Some of us in the village are trying to organise a few of them junior-sized wheelie turbs to be set up here, just as you suggested.'

'First check the generator,' said Nessa. 'You may not need the mini-turbs.'

'Who are all these people?' I asked, gesturing to his companions.

'Oh, I keep forgetting you've been away so long. These are people from our village,' he replied. 'Let me introduce you.'

He introduced us to several people whose names went in one ear and out the other.

'And more people are on the way,' said Chris. 'We're going to make a stand here. No bit of water is going to force us from our homes, and not the council either.'

'Let's go inside and see what's what,' he added.

We went in with them. Sure enough, the shopping centre was a wreck. The *Da Shi* was a Big World true to its name, but, we saw, a largely empty one. The security guards must have buggered off, and the looters had had a free hand. The world of cheap plenty had disappeared as though tossed into the waters of the Great Flood – a little ahead of time, since the flood hadn't actually arrived.

Rubbish of all description was strewn across the wide hallways – bits of clothing, broken toys, a tennis racket devoid of its strings, a bashed-in tea kettle and part of a hoover. Just by the main entrance was one of the food courts. Here and there lay not only the usual plastic bottles and cups, but also half-eaten portions of whatever the looters couldn't carry with them or didn't fancy.

'Disgusting,' said Chris.

As we stood there, surveying the dismal scene, more people appeared at the door behind us, among them Jenny Towton and her two daughters and some others whose faces were familiar.

Jenny gave a cheerful greeting that soon wilted as she looked around.

'Come on, then, let's get to it,' she said. 'First, we'll find the cleaners' closets and get some brooms and mops.'

'All right,' said Chris. 'Volunteers to help remove rubbish, please!'

I admired the way the villagers set themselves to the task of making the shopping centre liveable, but I now regretted suggesting the use of the shopping centre – the task of making it liveable was harder than I'd expected. But they did it.

'Come on, Nessa,' I said. 'Let's find the computer shop.'

We found it soon enough and saw at once that the computers had been nicked by looters. But that didn't matter to us. We weren't interested in computers. We were interested in someone who could help us de-cipher the turb smartchip. Not surprisingly, there was no one there. No one turned up for work at an abandoned shopping centre.

But there were books – lots of books on programming languages. There were several books on Emerald – the programming language used in the turb smartchips.

'Jack, it's no use,' said Nessa. 'Even if we had the background knowledge to understand these books, it would take us weeks to get through them. And we haven't got weeks.'

'You're right,' I said. 'But let's take them anyway. They might come in handy.'

We walked back out of the centre the way we had come in. Everywhere we saw the people of Upper St John hard at work, cleaning and putting things right.

'Jack,' said Nessa. 'We ought to help.'

'We will,' I said.

We joined shoulders with the villagers for several hours, clearing rubbish, trying to seal windows and gathering anything useful. Chris Porter and PC Bartle had got the generator to work, so there was no need to rig up any turbs at the centre. Finally I told Nessa we had to go.

'I want to get to the *Hope and Glory* project before dark,' I said. 'We've done out bit here, for today. We'll come back.'

We entered the hills again. The hills in Oxfordshire aren't very high. No question of anything snow-capped like the Pennines, even in that wet winter. Still, it was what counted for wilderness in Oxfordshire. It felt different from the woods on our property. English wilderness. Not so wild as I imagined, say, Alaska, to be, but wild enough.

I had under-estimated the time it would take us to hike to the project, and the winter sun began to set.

'Nessa, we're going to have to camp,' I said. 'I've got the gear.'

We picked a spot just below the crest of a small hill, less exposed to the wind, but with no tree cover.

'I've got a lean-to shelter,' I said. 'I prefer them to tents. Less weight to carry. And tents don't really keep you warmer. If the weather gets rough I can hang flaps on the sides. I'll just set the shelter side to the wind.'

'That's fine. I'm used to basic shelter,' she said. 'Just make a fire and I'll cook us something to eat.'

I gathered some damp dead wood and twigs and made a fire using starter blocks. The damp wood smouldered but eventually broke into flames.

'What've you brought?' I asked.

'Meat in tins that I found in your house, and potatoes and onions,' she said. 'Salt and pepper and some spices.'

She set to work with a knife and a pan and soon flavours rose from the fire.

Despite the thick cloud cover, the night was cold. We huddled together for warmth under the lean-to. Dawn came, dull, cold and damp. I was the first to wake. I struggled out of my bedroll, and pulling on my boots, reached out to the fire. Just as I grabbed a log, a white spear thudded into the ground inches from my hand. It was a turb blade.

It was gone as soon as it appeared, but the thudding sound woke Nessa.

'Look!' she cried.

High above us stood a turb. Its blades spun so fast they appeared almost a blur. Its red mast light blinked through the mist. From its head, a green slime dripped down the length of its long pole.

'Run toward it,' I shouted.

'What?' cried Nessa. 'Why?'

There was another thud. The blade hit the earth by Nessa's feet. She screamed.

'Run for your life!' I cried. 'Toward the turb!'

She waited no longer, and sprinted toward the turb.

By staying within the radius formed by the turb's own height, we could be safe from the blades. The trick was to keep moving as the turb moved, always staying as close as possible to the base wheels. I say that as though I'd done it a thousand times but at that moment, I hadn't. This technique was what they taught wind engineers in turb training, in case you got a turb that might fall over. I hadn't used it in practice till that morning.

Thankfully it worked. We huddled near the turb's wheels. This was a two-wheeled model, which meant it was highly agile. Fortunately, it seemed to be alone.

The wheels turned in a jerky motion, this way and that.

'It's, uh, it's *looking* for us,' said Nessa, gulping.

'It can't spear us so long as we stay near the base,' I said.

Suddenly the turb seemed break into a sprint. Its two giant

wheels began rolling quickly up the hill.

'Try to keep up!' I shouted.

We managed, barely, thanks to a small gulley on the hillside that caused the turb to slow. Until you've seen a turb moving at top speed, tower bent forward like a charging beast, you can't imagine that such a large object can move so fast. Of course, that endangers their stability and for that reason they usually move more slowly, which, I think, is why most people describe their motion as a kind of lumbering.

We weren't out of danger. We'd only got a reprieve. The thing played cat and mouse with us for most of the morning. It moved this way and that. It seemed to entertain itself by skewering birds. Its blades spun, then stopped, then spun.

The more tired we became, the more dangerous it was for us.

Then I had an idea, an idea so simple I kicked myself for not having had it sooner. So simple, so elegant. But it required me to go back to our camp site and that meant going beyond the turb's blade radius.

'Nessa, I'm going to walk up this hill as far as I can without going further than one hundred and fifty metres exactly,' I said.

'Are you mad?'

'Anything but,' I said. 'I know this turb model. It's a Korean-made Air Slice 40, height exactly one hundred and fifty metres.'

I began to put distance between myself and the base of the turb.

'Look, it's following you!' cried Nessa.

'Not exactly a pleasant thought,' I commented, crouching as I moved up the hill. The turb lumbered along behind me. Still moving away from the turb, I made an arc towards our camp.

'Now Nessa, you move away from the base – but stay within the radius of the blades. And start shouting – make some noise,' I called when we reached the crest of the hill.

'You can't be serious,' she hollered.

'I think they're attracted by sounds,' I explained.

Nessa began to speak in a loud voice, in Chinese.

The turb began to bob in her direction, as though trying to

touch its own wheels, which of course it couldn't do.

'Jack, this turb is hot for me,' she said. 'I don't like it.'

As soon as I saw that, I made a dash for the camp, found what I wanted and scurried back inside the radius of the blades.

'Now we'll see if this works,' I said to Nessa. 'You take the hunting knives and I'll use the hatchet. We're going to puncture this turb's tyres.'

It was easier said than done. The tyres were of a thickness found in articulated lorries, three or four inches thick. We slashed and slashed at the rubber until great strips came off. Huge holes now appeared in the tyres and the great tower began to wobble.

'Nessa!' I cried. 'Get over here – now!'

At that moment the turb tower leaned backward at a sharp angle. I dropped the hatchet and yanked Nessa further away from the tyres.

The turb tried to move forward, and that was its undoing, for the tyres no longer turned and the tower tipped further backwards.

Suddenly, it seemed, the beast appeared to understand its situation, for with a jerk the tyres moved in the opposite direction, as if to right itself. But it was too late. The tower hovered above us for a moment longer and then crashed to the ground. It fell, slowly, as if silently. It seemed to float downwards. But when the blade struck home there was a boom like an explosion. The ground shook beneath our feet. A spray of snow and earth flew into the air from where the blade struck, and in the immediate silence following impact we heard the flapping of wings as flocks of birds took flight.

The sound of the crash reverberated across the hills. I remembered studying as part of my training a turb collapse in Northern Ireland decades ago – the sound was said to have been heard seven miles away. I was sure this also could be heard very far away.

For a moment we stared at the fallen turb, unable to believe our eyes.

'Unbelievable,' said Nessa, gazing at the fallen turb.

'Look at the tendons,' I said.

Modern turbs models were designed with tubes – called 'tendons' – running along the length of the blades. The purpose was drainage, to allow water to run off the blades. If the blades were in a horizontal position, and therefore water run off was not possible, small pumps installed in the turbs' heads enabled the turb to pump water off.

I stepped closer to the blade, now plunged into the earth, and examined the tendon.

'It's filthy,' I said. 'But not any more filthy than any other turb I've seen.'

Turbs, I should explain, only appear white and clean and shiny when seen from the ground. The reality is that the wind splatters them with all manner of filth, both natural like leaves, bird droppings, soil and sand, and man-made pollution.

'It looks like rust, doesn't it?' said Nessa. 'But it can't be – this turb's blades are made of plastic.'

Small, round red flecks ran up and down the tendon.

Just then came a crash that sounded like a tree falling.

'More turbs are coming,' said Nessa. 'We'd better get out of here.'

8

BOOM

We returned home cold and wet and exhausted. And utterly terrified. We sat in the lounge, for a few moments in total silence.

Without thinking I poured two whiskies and handed one to Nessa, not thinking that she wouldn't drink it.

'That was more like a wild animal than a wind turbine,' she said at last.

This made me think of my rambling discussions with Frank about the turbs being a 'new species.'

'"Does it matter what *we* call it"?' I recalled saying to him.

'Where did that turb come from?' Nessa asked.

'Almost certainly from our very own wind farm,' I said.

'I think so, too,' she said. 'Jack, we talked about livestock kills – way back in the past, before the computerisation of turb herds. Could this be something like that?'

'It's not a million miles away,' I said. 'But it's different, though, isn't it? This wasn't an accident. The turb wasn't just leaning too far over, spinning its blades. It deliberately attacked us.'

'I've never heard of such a thing,' said Nessa. 'We have just over two hundred million turbs in China, and I've never heard of a single deliberate attack on people or animals. The turbs just aren't programmed to do that.'

I thought of something else I'd said to Frank.

'Suppose the smartchips in the turbs override the control computers,' I said.

'What do you mean?' she asked.

'I mean, the independent movement of turbs, on a large scale, disregarding what the control computers tell them to do,' I said.

'Jack, that's the deviation factor. We're looking into that, in fact, we've only just begun. But, given time, we'll get to the bottom of it. That has nothing to do with turbs attacking people.'

'Hasn't it?' I asked. 'I'm not so sure.'

'Why?' she said suddenly. 'Why would a turb attack a human?'

'Sometimes, technology has strange, unintended effects. Side-effects, if you will,' I said. 'The short answer to your question is: I don't know. *Yet.*'

'But it did. It did attack us,' she said. 'Here, you can drink this whisky. I'll make us something to eat.'

It was almost dusk. Nessa cooked up a storm of stir-fried beef with onions and new potatoes. I made a fire in the lounge and after dinner we sat before it, still talking about what had happened in the forest. There came a pause in the conversation, and I thought about asking her to marry me then. But every way I thought of to raise the subject didn't seem right. Words played around in my head, but my lips didn't open. For a while neither of us spoke.

Then Nessa said: 'Jack, has it occurred to you that the farmer and his wife – '

'Yes,' I said.

' – were killed by a turb?'

'Yes,' I said again. 'The police think it was refugees or looters. But now, in light of the turb attack on us, we have another theory.'

'Let's talk it through,' said Nessa. 'Exactly how might it have happened?'

'Well, it must have been like the attack on us,' I said. 'Only the Fergusons didn't know much about turbs. They didn't know they'd be safe if they stayed within the radius of the blades. Seems they were killed separately. June must have been terrified, to confront a turb alone. Thom, our theory goes, died second. So he must have seen what happened to his wife. He must have been sick with grief and terror.'

'He seized on the idea of the combine because it was the only tool that might work. Because it was made of metal, like his attacker. Because it had blades, like his attacker.' I said. 'Because his attacker was a turb.'

'And as far as his wife is concerned, we can toss out the supposition of a tall man with an axe – her wounds are better explained by the slice of a turb blade,' said Nessa.

'That's right,' I said.

'Do you think they recognised the turb that attacked them?' Nessa asked.

'What a strange question,' I said. 'And yet, an intriguing one. No, I don't think so. Thom paid no attention to the turbs installed on his land. And June certainly didn't.'

'Why do you say *one* turb attacked them,' Nessa continued. 'Why not turbs – maybe there were more than one.'

'True, it's possible,' I said. 'But I don't think so. We'd have seen more evidence of that in the drive, in the fields – the marks made by turb tyres – they're enormously heavy, as you know, and they leave an imprint.'

'I think we need to go back to the forest, to that dead turb,' I went on. 'We need to get the smartchip from that turb and study it as well. To see if it's any different from the first chip we took.'

'I agree,' Nessa answered. 'When?'

'Soon as we can. But we're going to need some tools, and some weapons, in case of another turb attack,' I said. 'It was near impossible to cut that turb's tyres, even with those sharp hunting knives.'

'We need a chain saw,' she said. 'Or something like it.'

'The big shopping centre, that's the place,' I said. 'There's a garden centre that might have some useful things.'

*

The Big World's garden centre lay beyond the west car park. It consisted of a forecourt filled with young saplings, all dead apart from the firs and pines, and various models of lawn mowing tractors. It struck me, as we entered the next morning, that the tractors would be useful for getting around the hills.

Inside the centre was a single large showroom, also full of mostly dead plants and an array of gardening tools. The centre had been left untouched by looters – what good were plants? The thieves hadn't thought about gardening equipment and tools.

Among the plants, pots and tools stood, or sat as best they could, a hundred or so old people. It seemed they had gravitated to the garden centre to form a community. They had divided themselves into a men's section and women's section, and had set up a line of clay pots between them.

The mood was subdued. Many of the old folks sat staring into space. Some were reading. Some were huddled around a screen from the centre's CCTV security system, which had been adapted for use as a television.

'This is GCHQ TV broadcasting from Cheltenham,' I heard a presenter's voice say, 'giving you the information you need to survive the flood, twenty-four hours a day.' Then I saw Toby Lang in the screen. He was talking about the internet.

'People may have noticed that since the flooding began, the internet isn't always there,' he said. 'Smartphones are pretty useless without it, I know, and I know everyone needs information at a time like this. Unfortunately, one of the effects of the flooding has been to damage underground fibre optic cables that are part of the physical infrastructure of the internet. We're working…'.

I didn't need to be told that the internet was on again, off again, but Lang at least made me feel that the government were doing something. The garden centre residents watching the TV screen hardly stirred.

'This is what the English call "cheap and cheerful",' I said.

'Cheap, yes,' Nessa observed. 'But it's not my idea of cheerful.'

We found the chainsaws without too much trouble. There were six models to choose from and we each took one.

'If you are trying to steal those, I'll tell someone from the council. But if you've got a bottle of gin for me, I won't,' said an old man, approaching us

'That sounds like a fair bargain,' I said. 'What's your name?'

'Reggie,' he said. 'What's yours?'

'Jack,' I said. 'This is Nessa.'

'Pleased to meet you both,' he said. 'You're not from the council, are you? They're all such prats and you seem like such a nice young couple.'

'It's very kind of you to say that, Reggie,' I said. 'I don't happen to have a bottle of gin with me, but you'll get one, maybe two, when we come back. That's a promise. Say, we're on the prowl for some axes as well, for fire wood. Have any idea where they are?'

He eyed us. He was a tall, thin man with wispy grey hair. I wondered what kind of work he had done in his prior life.

'It's wetter than usual this winter, isn't it? Makes for a damp cold that goes right into the bones,' he replied. 'You'll need firewood. I saw some axes over there at the far end. Say, could you – ?'

'What, Reggie?'

'I don't like to ask, but could you possibly arrange some tonic to go with the gin?' he asked. 'We don't have anything to drink here.'

'We'll see about a bit of fresh lemon, too,' said Nessa.

We left Reggie and found the axes, taking one large one each.

'Jack, all this is heavy. How are we going to carry these things back to the house?' Nessa asked.

'Let's see if there's any biofuel in that big lawn tractor over there,' I said. There was, a bit, at least enough to start the engine. Luckily, I found a full jerry can of fuel nearby and emptied it into the tank.

'Looks like petropha,' I said, referring to a kind of plant-petrol fuel blend.

'Other than for carrying things, I'm not sure these tractors are going to be very useful,' I added.

'You never know,' said Nessa. 'But they're fun.'

'Let's get all this gear home – we can stop at the petrol station and fill up the jerry can on the way home,' I said.

Now, I thought with satisfaction, we had a store of weapons, a very special store of weapons for disabling and killing turbs.

*

Even after many sought refuge in the shopping centre, the F Café remained the focal point of Upper St John. It buzzed with new faces and old, people swapping rumours and possible facts. They came ostensibly to buy fuel – the nearest other station was miles away on the A40 – but they came also for information.

Of course, the hot topic remained the Great Flood. Every scrap of information was discussed and analysed. Would the flood really reach Oxfordshire in a few days' time? No one quite believed that, but then no one knew for sure. Would the Americans come to save us? There was no sign of that – they were having their own troubles with flooding. What about Canada and Australia and the Commonwealth? No one had any hard information. What about technology? – 'they' could do anything these days.

The deaths of the Fergusons had also made an impression, making people uneasy about their security.

'I tell you I saw what they did to Thom and June,' said one man in the F Café. I overheard him as Nessa and I stopped in to buy biofuel.

'What who did?' another man asked.

'Them refugees,' said the first man. 'Probably foreigners.'

'What?' asked the waitress. I recognised her. Her name was Sally. She'd worked at the café forever.

'I tell you, June Ferguson had her head cut off!' said the first man.

'That's 'orrible,' said Sally.

'Now, such a thing might have been an accident,' another man put in. 'I hear Thom was killed in his combine, maybe *by* his combine. Suppose there was something in the mechanism that made it dangerous.'

By the sound of him he was an educated man and his voice was pleasant. A few heads turned to listen to him.

'All the things that our civilisation depends on have got so complicated that we don't understand them anymore,' the man went on. 'This isn't anything new. It's been that way for several generations now. Ask the average Englishman how the Voice Control Drive on his car works. He wouldn't be able to tell you.'

'There've been some terrible accidents with the Voice Control,' the man went on, fingering his unlit pipe. 'Remember that pile up on the M6? A lorry driver said "south" when he meant to say "north" and the lorry went the wrong way up the motorway. I don't remember how many people died – lots.'

'Sometimes I wonder if all our technology has a mind of its own,' said a woman in a tweed coat.

'Exactly,' said the pleasant-sounding man, gesturing with his pipe. 'Now take the turbs. Let me ask you all this: how many turbs are there in England today?'

No one knew.

'More than twenty five million, according to government figures, including the offshore ones,' the man said. 'With seventy million English people, that's one of them for every three or four of us, give or take.'

'What are you getting at, professor?' asked the second man.

The first man smiled. 'I'm not a professor,' he said, and then: 'Only this: if they started to slice us up, they'd make quick work of us. Look how a single turb can chop up a flock of birds in no time.'

'I read that those attacks weren't by a single turb,' said the tweed lady. 'There were packs of them.'

'Precisely my point,' said the professor. 'They seem to be operating together. Like a species.'

Several people appeared lost by the 'professor's' argument.

An odd little man who hadn't said a word now piped up.

'Sorry, does that mean that, like wolves or dogs, they fight amongst themselves over which one gets to eat the kill?' he asked.

The professor appeared nonplussed.

'I hadn't thought about that,' he said, stroking his chin. 'Well, yes, I suppose they might bicker about that.'

'A bit like people in Waitburys supermarket on a busy Saturday,' said a large, florid woman.

All at once Sally screamed.

'Look!'

A white, gleaming turb blade hovered just outside the window, between the café and the fuel pumps.

All eyes in the café turned to stare at the massive, razor-sharp hunk of metal. It made slight movements, this way and that.

Those closest to the window pressed their faces against the glass to see the height of the monster. Outside, none of the customers at the fuel pumps seem to have noticed it.

'What's it doing?' asked one man.

'It's, uh, *sniffing*,' cried Sally.

It looked as though it might have been, but I knew that was impossible. Nessa and I were at the till in the back of the café, well away from the window.

'Everyone, get away from the window,' I called out. 'Fast!'

'But why, Jack?' asked Sally.

'Just do it!' I cried.

People began to move toward the back of the café. But not all of them. Some stared fixedly at the turb spear.

At the pumps a lorry driver with his back to the café was putting the nozzle of a hose into his fuel tank.

Sally began pounding on the window. Others joined her.

'Get away,' she cried.

A sudden swish of the turb blade sliced right through the hose. The cut off end of the hose jerked upwards, spewing fuel across the ground.

The lorry driver looked puzzled by the slack in the hose and turned around. By then it was too late. The giant blade stabbed him the groin and lifted him off the ground, slamming him into the side of his lorry. The blade went through the man and pierced the lorry like a hot knife through butter. Then it twisted, ever so slightly, and pulled out of the man's lifeless body, leaving it to drop to the ground.

There was a gasp from those watching inside the café.

The blade now returned to its earlier position, quivering, as it were, before the café window.

'Don't anyone go outside,' I shouted. This time they all listened to me.

'I can assure you that I have no intention of getting any closer to that monster,' said the professor.

'What's that dripping from the tip of the thing?' said someone.

All eyes focused on the blade.

'It's blood,' said the woman in the tweed coat.

'Oh, my God!' screamed a voice. 'Everyone, look!'

The petrol-biofuel mix streamed toward two men on the pavement, not ten metres away from the café. They were engaged in conversation and hadn't noticed a thing. One of them was making a point, gesturing with an unlit cigarette in his hand.

'He's going to light it!' screamed Sally.

The people inside the café pounded on the window, waving their arms and pointing at the river of fuel, but the two men were looking the other way. One fumbled in his pocket and produced a lighter. The one with the fag leaned forward. The last thing I remembered before the explosion was the river of fuel set alight and the flames racing back to the storage tank. The force of the blast shattered the café window, leaving those inside cut by shards of glass.

Luckily we were at the back of the café. I was knocked down by the blast but otherwise unhurt. Nessa had banged her head against a cabinet and was bleeding from the forehead. Dazed, we stood up and looked around us. I had never seen such a scene. People were screaming and blood was everywhere.

'Nessa, let's get some water and start dressing wounds,' I said. 'Tea towels – we can use the tea towels.'

Others who were only lightly hurt joined us. By the time the emergency services arrived we'd managed to address the worst cases and get the less seriously injured to start dressing their own wounds. The main wounds were, of course, cuts from the shattered window. Outside, the fuel tanks continued to burn but at least the fire wasn't spreading.

I spied Withers among the emergency workers, but I avoided him. My mind was too unsettled by what had happened. Above all, I didn't want to share with him – not yet, anyway – any of our thinking about the turbs.

'That's the second instance we've seen of a turb attacking people – first the one in the forest that attacked us, and now this,' I said to Nessa as we headed home.

'I couldn't believe it before and I can't believe it now. I've never seen anything like it,' she said. 'But why did it attack and then go away?'

'It shied away as soon as the biofuel tank exploded,' I replied. 'I didn't expect that. I thought the turb would remain aggressive, like the one in the forest. Must have been the fire that drove it away. What do you think?'

'I think you've hit on something. Perhaps we've discovered a new weapon: fire,' she said.

'I would put it differently,' I said. 'We've re-discovered one of the oldest weapons known to man.'

How we would use it was, at that point, unclear.

*

The next morning bright and early Nessa and I made for the dead turb in the forest. We wanted to get our hands on the turb's smart-chip. It took us some hours to find the thing. Fresh snow during the night had covered the hills and, under other circumstances, we would have enjoyed the view. As it was, every moment we looked about for turbs.

The force of the fall had driven two of the turb's blades deep into the earth. This didn't surprise me, as turbs of this model had a total weight of many tens of thousands of kilograms. They were almost as heavy, in fact, as the jumbo jets of the past.

As a result, the turb's head was only about twenty metres off the ground. There was no point to crawl through the entire length of the turb on the inside if we could reach the head directly from the outside. The blades were too sharp to risk shimmying up them, even if we had protective clothing, which we didn't.

But the turb was equipped with metal rungs on the outside which, fortunately, were on the upper side of the beast. So up the rungs we went.

'Turb wrench, please,' I said as we reached the hatch on the tower, just below the turb's head.

We climbed inside the turb's shaft.

Before us was the turb's yaw drive and the motor that controls the yaw.

'Up here,' I said, leading the way up a set of rungs, and I opened a second hatch leading into the turb's head.

A foul stench greeted us when I pulled open the hatch.

'Ugh,' I cried. 'This is what I expect inside a turb head – plenty of foul-smelling plants. The one we climbed a few days ago was relatively clean. I'll never get used to that foul smell.'

'Plant gloves, please!' I said, pointing to my rucksack.

'I got used to it a long time ago,' said Nessa, handing me the special gloves used by wind engineers inside turb heads. 'I had to get used to it in order to study the plants.'

'You told me you're an expert on turb plants, but we've never talked about it,' I said. 'I guess now's the time.'

'Jack, turbs have been full of plants for as long as you and I have been wind engineers, or longer,' she began. 'It started with the use of plant oils as lubricants for turb gears and rotor blades. They have certain advantages over petroleum-based oils. First and foremost, they're less polluting.'

'I know,' I said. 'The green lobby doesn't mind if plant oil leaks into the ocean from offshore turbs, but they would feel differently if something akin to motor oil dripped from countless offshore towers. Same for onshore turbs.'

'That's right,' she said. 'Using plant oil instead of petrole-um based oil makes environmental sense. Besides that, plant oils are cheaper.'

'What wasn't foreseen was that the use of plant oil would give rise to plant life inside the turbs. Plant oil was introduced into millions of turbs before anybody noticed the plants,' said Nessa.

'At first people attributed the growth of plant life inside turbs to seeds carried by the wind into the turb heads. The warm, moist interior is a good environment for plants, especially during high summer temperatures,' she went on. 'Eventually it was realised that the plant oils played a role in creating the perfect environment for plants to grow.'

'In any case, the appearance of plant life inside turbs was welcomed. For if the turbs generated their own plants, and hence their own plant oil, there would be less need for externally introduced lubrication,' she continued. 'So turb manufacturers developed ways of capturing free flowing plant oil within a turb's head and introducing it into the lubrication system.'

'And I decided that learning about the plants would help my career as a wind engineer,' she added.

'I would say most people in the wind community haven't given much thought as to what type of plants they are,' I said. 'In any case, wind engineers aren't botanists – most of us don't have the background to understand what we're looking at. You're unusual in that regard. Besides, it's not easy to de-plant a turb head, and it's expensive – so the wind industry decided just to ignore the plants.'

'Not entirely,' said Nessa. 'The appearance of plant life inside the turbs has sparked some curiosity. I'm only one example. *Wind Tech Times* recently published an article on the plants in offshore turbs. Did you see it?'

'Yeah,' I said. 'Something about plants in the turbs being hundreds of millions of years old.'

'That's right. The author claimed that they resemble some of the oldest plants on the planet. Though as always with plants, there's no fossil record to support the theory,' she said.

'He also claimed that the plants in both on and offshore turbs are carnivorous – something that those in the wind community I've talked to find a little amusing and, at the same time, disgusting,' she continued.

'Yeah, that I've heard,' I said. 'I can believe it. Look at the bulbs on these plants. Do you see that small indentation in the centre? It looks like a mouth, doesn't it?' I said.

'It is a mouth, Jack,' she said. 'And it's true. They're meat eaters.'

'Once, on a maintenance detail, one of them bit me,' I said. 'There was an ugly scab on my finger that took weeks to heal. The memory of it has kept me from further curiosity about the plants. Since then I've been very careful to wear my turb plant gloves.'

'As you should,' said Nessa. 'Keep your fingers clear of them, especially the bulbs. And try not to step on them.'

'That won't be easy,' I said, eyeing the floor of the turb head. It was slick with plant oil. Here and there were the ugly bulbs I'd seen before.

I said that a turb head is tall enough for a man to stand upright, but that we couldn't do under the circumstances, as the turb was driven into the earth at an angle. We had to lean backwards and keep hold of something to maintain our balance.

For a moment we looked around us.

'Well, it's a newer model than the other one,' I said. 'It's got a single shaft generator.'

But in other respects, I could see, this model was old. Single shaft, or direct-drive, turbs had been around for a long time. There were other characteristics of the turb that told me it was an older model. Chiefly, the enormous size of the *neodymium* permanent magnet generator testified to the beast's age. Technology had made the generators much more compact.

'Over there,' Nessa pointed to the rear of the head. 'That's the generator. The smartchip is behind that.'

'I know,' I said. 'I know this model like the back of my hand.'

The generator was a cylindrical hunk of metal of a greyish hue, perhaps a metre in diameter, fitted into the back of the turb's head.

It was covered with the hideous bulbs. Most were about four to six inches around, but some were considerably larger. They were dark brownish in colour. Their surface had a moist, shiny appearance. Right in the centre of each bulb was what resembled a pair of lips, presumably an aperture for taking in food. No doubt about it, they were revolting-looking creatures.

'Look at the casing around the generator, it's cracked,' said Nessa.

'So it is,' I said. 'What does that tell you?'

'It tells me the plants have come into contact with the *neodymium* inside the generator,' he said.

'Hm,' I said. 'What's the significance of that?'

'I'm not sure,' she said.

'One of us has to get behind the generator somehow,' I said. 'I'll do it, but I'm not sure how.'

The turb being at a steep angle, with the rear of the head down, and the generator located at the rear, this wasn't going to be easy. We'd brought a rope, which I wound round my waist. Nessa slowly lowered me deeper into the turb head.

For support I clutched the shaft with both hands, inching down towards to the generator. But my gloves quickly became wet from the plant oil covering the shaft and I began to slide out of control. Nessa tried to grab my arm but it was too late. I landed on my bum with the soles of my feet against the generator, like a leg press in the fitness centre.

'Nessa, stay back,' I said. 'There's no sense both of sliding around in this slime.'

'All right,' she said. 'Let me know if you need help.'

'I – ouch! One of these damned bulbs nearly bit me.'

I slapped it with the back of my hand and it went flying.

'Right, up!' I said, grabbing metal ridges on the generator casing as Nessa held the rope taut, trying to avoid at all costs the bulbs covering the thing.

There was just enough room to pass between the generator and the outer wall of the turb head, to get where I wanted to go. Gingerly I squeezed myself behind the generator. Here it was easier to see, because a thin shaft of light penetrated via the opening to the wind vane outside, at the back of the turb head. Still, I needed my small torch. Clutching it between my teeth, I could see what I was looking for. There it was.

I pulled a screwdriver from my pocket and went to work. The screws turned but not easily. After some unrewarded effort, I fitted the head of the screwdriver into the gaps between the screws and the casing and try to pry the screws off, at the risk of stripping the screw threads. That didn't work either, so I went back to using the tool as normal and, gradually, the screws began to turn.

Two screws loosened, then a third and a fourth. I could twist them with my fingers now and the plate on the turb's controller came off.

I peered inside, and felt around inside the controller with my fingers.

'Got it!' I shouted. 'I got it!'

Before me was the task of climbing back up the slimy, slanting head of the fallen turb.

'Nessa, have you got hold the rope?' I called.

'Yes, got it,' came the reply.

'Get a good grip on something and pull me up,' I said.

She pulled, and I struggled to keep upright on the oily floor of the turb head, reaching for support wherever I could. Grabbing a pipe, I felt a tickling under my wrist and jerked my hand away. I'd touched another bulb, but felt nothing – it hadn't bitten.

'Keep pulling,' I said. 'Another one of these bloody plants – they're everywhere!'

Close enough now, Nessa reached out and, grasping my right hand, drew me to her and gave me a big hug.

'You made it!' she said.

'Let's get out of this turb!'

'Sure, but I want to take a plant sample,' said Nessa. 'Do you have a plastic bag or something like it?'

I fished around in my rucksack and found a ziplock plastic bag.

'Thanks,' she said.

She carefully cupped her hand around a couple of bulbs and lifted them off the floor of the turb, taking care to retain as much of the liquid that seeped from them as she could. Then she tossed the mess into the bag and zipped it shut.

'I'd like to have a closer look at it,' she said. 'As you said, let's get out of this turb.'

Outside, the cold winter air felt refreshing after the dank, fetid air inside of the turb.

We made our way back through the forest, across England's clouded hills. A few slanted rays of winter sun lit the way, turning the heavens a bright pink as only an English sky can be. As we neared the old Roman road by Buckley, I spied smoke rising from the trees ahead of us. This was unexpected – I didn't think anyone lived in the marshland there. As we reached the Roman road I switched off the tractor engine and we stopped to listen.

9

FOUNDLING

We soon heard the clip-clop sound of horse's hooves from somewhere beyond a dip in the road.

'Down quick,' I said to Nessa. We couldn't very well crouch in the open so we moved back from the road.

Slowly two shapes rose from the dip in the road, first a pair of heads, then their shoulders and their arms. The two figures wore black hunt caps. One held a shotgun, the other what appeared to be a machine gun.

'I don't believe it,' I said.

'Jack, who are they?' Nessa asked.

'They look like hunters,' I said. 'But we haven't had hunters in England for a long time. And hunters didn't carry guns.'

'So, who are they?'

'I don't know,' I replied.

Suddenly another horseman galloped up from behind. On his mount he held a young boy.

'I found this lad in the last village, hiding in a cellar,' he called out.

The first two riders turned round and one of them said something we couldn't make out.

'No he's not,' cried the galloping cavalier. 'He'll work like the rest. You'll see to it.'

He sidled up to the others and pushed the boy onto the rider nearest to him. The boy almost fell, his arms outstretched, but he caught himself. The horsemen laughed as he screamed.

The cavalier now took a position ahead of the other two riders. He was obviously the leader. I studied him through my field glasses. He looked to be about my age. He sat tall in the saddle, and his hat made him look even taller. He wasn't wearing a hunt cap like the others. He wore a hat made of dark cloth with gold braid, festooned with feathers. His unlined face was smooth and glistening. I caught sight of his hands – they were smooth like his face. He might have been a City banker wearing the fancy dress of an English Civil War cavalier. The effect would have been ridiculous but for his cruelty towards the boy.

We watched as they rode toward the smoke rising in the far trees.

'That must be their – camp, or whatever it is,' I said. 'Come on, let's follow on foot. Maybe we can help the boy.'

'Jack, don't risk it,' said Nessa. 'This isn't our business.'

'Hell, Nessa, aren't you curious? I've never seen anything like them in Oxfordshire.'

We walked in the direction of the smoke, through the scrub and marshland land along the Roman road. Soon, in a clump of trees, we saw a farm. Smoke puffed from the chimney of a the farmhouse, the only place around with any signs of life. Evidently they saw no reason to conceal their presence.

Near the farmhouse was a large barn, a silo and some smaller outbuildings. In front of the house was a well, and behind it, a penned field with horses. Next to the field stood three small turbs, by the look of them, the same model as at my house.

'Let's circle round through the woods behind the barn,' I said.

From there we could see the barn clearly, and the house through the gap between the barn and the silo.

'Put the boy in the barn with the others,' said the cavalier to one of the horsemen. As the horseman opened the door, we could see light from within, but we couldn't see inside.

'I can make it to the barn and see what's inside,' I said. This meant covering about a hundred metres of open ground. The sun was by then behind the barn so the ground was in shadow.

The barn was a rough piece of work, with gaps between the planks wide enough to see inside. I peered through one gap, then another and then a third. I saw a group of people huddled in one corner. But I didn't see the boy. Then, through another gap, I saw him. His back was towards me, and he was bent over a table.

'Boy,' I whispered as loudly as I could. 'Come here!'

He turned and looked in the direction of my voice.

I punched the wall softly with my palm.

'Over here, don't worry,' I said. 'I'm a friend. We've come to get you out of here.'

He cocked his head and stared at the spot in the wall where my voice came from. He took a step in my direction and then turned his head toward the barn door.

'What's your name?' I called out.

'David,' he said.

'How old are you David?' I asked. He was approaching me now.

'Thirteen.'

'Look here, the gap here' – we made eye contact – 'I and my friend, we saw them take you. We saw how that man on the horse tossed you around,' I said.

'You did?'

'Where are they all now?'

'They're in the house or they've gone out to work,' he said.

'What work, what are they doing?' I asked.

'Stealing things from people's houses,' he said.

'When will they come back?

'When the sun goes down,' he said. 'Then they said they'll give us something to eat.'

'Now, David, who are these horsemen? Where do they come from?'

'Gloucestershire,' he said. 'They're hunters. That's what they said.'

'Good, David, good. Can you keep a secret?'

'Oh, yes!' he said, his eyes full of interest.

'Good. The secret is – I'm going to get you out of here, understood?'

'Are you a policeman?' he asked.

'No – a friend,' I said. 'Walk with me, and I'll tap the wall when I want you to stop.'

I moved along the side of the barn till I found what I was looking for, a plank that was sufficiently eaten away to allow a young boy to slide under it. I tapped on the wall and then curled my fingers around the gap.

'OK, David, slide under,' I said. He wriggled through and I grabbed him by the arms, pulling him up. We sprinted back across the field to Nessa.

'Nessa, this is David,' I said. 'He's thirteen. New member of the team.'

'Hello, David,' said Nessa. 'Where are you from?'

'From Buckley,' he said.

'Where's that?' she asked. 'Is it far?'

'No,' he replied. 'It's just to the north of here, on the Roman road that leads to Biscott.'

'And where are your parents?' she asked.

David looked away without replying.

A gust of wind distracted us, and I looked up at the sky.

'Let's save getting to know each other for later,' I said. 'Better to get away from here.'

'Why – say, a storm's coming,' said Nessa.

The wind picked up and began to howl.

'That's not a storm,' I said. 'Look!'

Out of the grey sky emerged the red lights of turbs, lots of them. For a moment we watched them.

'They're coming this way,' said Nessa.

The sky had cleared and moonlight shone over the farmhouse. I quickly estimated the height of the turbs and their distance from us. It might get very nasty, I thought. We could see the Gloucestershire men around the house. One man was on the roof, and two mounted men stood guard by the horse enclosure. They all had guns.

They'd made a great bonfire in front of the house. Perhaps that would keep the turbs away – I wondered if they knew that – but I didn't want to wait around to find out what might happen.

'David, do you want to come with us?' I said. 'You don't have to, but you're welcome to.'

'I want to,' he replied.

'Off we go then,' I said.

We walked back to the tractor and, squeezing the boy between us, headed for home. Nessa took him upstairs straightaway and put him to bed.

'Let him sleep as long as he needs to,' she said.

I settled into my chair in in the lounge to try to make sense of the source code in the two smartchips we'd got – one from the *Hope and Glory* turb and one from the dead turb in the forest. Hopefully the exercise of comparing them might tell us something. But I made little progress.

I didn't notice David till he was standing at my elbow.

'That programme you're looking at, it's written in Emerald,' he said.

'Oh, David, you're up?' I said, adding, 'I know that.' There was some irritation in my voice, not at him but at myself, because of my lack of understanding.

'You can read programming languages?' I asked, after a pause.

'Yes,' he said, 'I've learned some languages pretty well. That one, for example – Emerald.'

'Can you write them as well?' I asked. 'Can you write changes to the source code?'

'Sure,' he said.

'Well, come sit by me and let's try to read this together,' I said, pulling up a chair for him.

I pushed the screen and keyboard towards him and sat back to watch. He scrolled up and down, eyes intent on the screen.

'I need to play with it,' he said. 'And maybe do some research.'

'Well, the internet connection is spotty here so that may take some time,' I said. 'But I've got some books here on Emerald. They might be useful.'

'Then, uh, then, I'll just have to experiment,' he said. 'What kind of changes do you want to make to the source code?'

'I want to see if we can change this source code to accept direction from another computer, that is, not override its own control computer,' I said.

'Is that what it's doing?' asked David.

'Yes,' I said, adding: 'These chips came from turbs.'

'I hate them,' he replied, recoiling from the screen. 'They killed my parents. I hate them.'

'How David? What happened?'

'In the village,' he said. 'My father was – '

He whimpered and then began to cry.

'Tell me about it,' I said. But he remained silent, crying.

'OK, we'll talk about it another time, when you are ready,' I said.

Suddenly he stopped crying and looked again at the screen.

'Why would these chips override their control computers?' he asked, his eyes glued to the screen.

'Good question,' I said, looking at the boy with new eyes.

'I mean, normally, the instructions in the software which the chip gives to whatever it's connected to – a machine, a car or even a turb – won't change, especially if there's a control from another computer, as you say,' he said. 'The software in the chip will be written to accept direction. There must be some outside influence, malware, for example.'

'Hacking, you mean?'

'Yes,' he said.

'You mean someone might have hacked the turbs' smartchips?' I asked.

'If they not doing as they've been instructed to do, it's the most likely explanation,' he said.

'David,' I said, 'I know turbs much better than you do. I'm a wind engineer. But I need to get to know them better still. I know they've been behaving – well, we can't explain their behaviour, yet. Maybe you can help.'

'Will you stay with us for a while?' I asked.

'I haven't anywhere else to go,' he said sadly.

Nessa came just then into the lounge. She saw at once that the boy was sad and went to him with open arms.

'You've slept, have you?' she said, embracing him. 'I've made something to eat for you. Beef with noodles. Are you hungry?'

'Yes, very,' he said.

'All right, come and eat,' she said, taking him by the arm.

I followed them into the kitchen. She sat him down and put a plate of food before him.

'Jack, you too,' she said, putting a plate on the table for me. I sat down and dug in.

'Nessa, what's that smell? I asked. 'It's coming from over there.'

I gestured toward an over-sized wash basin in the corner of the kitchen.

'It's the plant samples,' Nessa replied.

'What, from the turbs? You've got them in the kitchen?' I exclaimed. 'They stink!'

'I needed to look at them,' she explained.

'Look at them?' I asked.

'I cut one of the bulbs open,' she said. 'I wanted to see what it was eating.'

'What did you find?' I asked, still unhappy about the smell.

'Jack, I don't know, and I won't know till we get the plants to a proper lab for analysis,' she said.

'Come on, you must have found something,' I said.

'Yes, I found something,' she said. 'I found the bulb's stomach. As least I think I did.'

'How do you know?' I asked.

'Trust me, the turb plants are my passion,' she said.

'All right,' I said. 'What was in the, uh, "stomach"?'

'It looks to me like the remains of an animal – there were bits of cartilage and some small bones,' she said.

114

'What are you talking about?' asked David.

'Nothing, David,' I said. 'Eat your food.'

'My father used to say that,' he said. A sad look crossed his face and he put down his fork.

I didn't know what to do. I wasn't a father and I had little experience with kids. Nessa came to the rescue. She got up and embraced the boy, whispering something in his ear. A smile came to his face and he looked up at her. She whispered again, and the smile got larger. He picked up his fork and began eating again.

Later, after she'd put him to bed, we sat before the fire in the lounge. I wrapped my arm around her and we kissed. Watching the fire, I thought again – for the thousandth time – about how I would propose to her. But I wasn't ready. I told myself the time wasn't right.

'Jack,' she said, 'this is a little ridiculous, isn't it? We're trying to solve the deviation factor by ourselves. I mean, here I am cutting open plant bulbs in a wash basin and you're trying to crack the turb smartchips with the help of a thirteen year old boy. We've got to get help from your boss, Phil Burnley. Access to a plant laboratory, and real computer geeks.'

'You're right,' I admitted. 'But for the moment, we should do what we can ourselves. Phil will be in touch – soon as I get a signal in my smartphone. Tomorrow morning, I'll climb one of the hills – or one of the turbs – to get a signal. Or maybe we'll go to the shopping centre – there's bound to be a signal there.'

'That man Patel's bound to turn up again very soon,' I added.

*

The next morning I rose early to climb the nearest hill in the hope of getting a signal in my phone. But something caught my eye.

There was a caravan parked by the road near our house. To be more exact, a small flat-bed lorry the size of a van, with a caravan on its bed. I didn't like it. Strangers. Maybe men like those who'd taken David. Maybe worse.

I dropped my gear to reconnoitre, slowly descending the hill toward the strange vehicle, trying not to make myself obvious. At a distance of perhaps fifty metres I could see that there was no one inside.

I decided to take a closer look.

I came down the hill to within twenty metres of it – still no sign of life – and jumped to the road.

'It's a shitty old caravan,' I said to myself.

I climbed onto the van and peered into the windows. Three was nothing out of the ordinary: dishes, washcloths, books.

Then I turned round to see a man pointing a shotgun at me.

'I've got two shots,' he said. 'Both for you. You'll have a great, big hole in the middle of where your stomach used to be, and blood and guts everywhere. I'll have to give my caravan a good wash.'

His voice told me he wasn't going to shoot. It was playful, a bit of the Irish.

'Friend, I wasn't looking to steal your stuff,' I said. 'It's just that I live up this hill and I saw a strange vehicle and I wanted to know what was what.'

'Strange? You call my vehicle strange?' he laughed. 'It's more than strange, it's bloody bizarre. Did you notice the oaks beams I built into the ceiling? It's the only caravan in England with oak beams.'

At that point I was quite certain he wouldn't shoot me. I moved my eyes off the shotgun and onto the man before me. He was a large man with a large belly, and his face told of evenings with a bottle.

'I stopped to do a bit of hunting,' he said. 'I fancied a rabbit. Actually, I fancied anything. I'm famished.'

'Where have you come from?' I asked.

'Keighley, near Leeds,' he replied, 'My son's got – had – a haulage business up there.'

'Where are you headed?' I asked.

'I'm not quite sure,' he replied. 'South, I guess, where it's warmer.'

'Where's your son?' I asked.

'He buggered off to Ireland with his wife, he said, 'They didn't need me hanging about, with the flood and all. Say, allow me to remind you that as the one holding the shotgun, I should be asking the questions.'

Saying that, he lowered the shotgun and then slung it over his shoulder.

'Fair enough,' I replied, but seeing him lower the gun, I had already made up my mind to invite him to the house and give him something to eat. Call it intuition or a feeling, however it is that we make judgements about other people. This man was harmless, I felt. And he might be useful. My mind was racing ahead about his shotgun. Maybe he would part with it for something in return. I was wondering how much ammunition he had.

I also decided then and there to invite him to park his caravan on our land for a time – if Nessa liked him. If she didn't, I would find a way to ask him to move on.

He said his name was Danny and he was sixty two years old. He launched into what he called the short version of his life story. Originally from Ireland, he'd spent most of his life kicking around Africa in various businesses connected to mining. He went on and on. I wanted to ease the conversation around to the subject of his weapon and ammunition, but there was no opening.

'My friend, save the life story for as payment for your meal,' I finally broke in.

'That's very kind of you,' he replied. We made our way up the hill to the house.

'Nessa!' I called out as we entered. 'We've got a guest. His name's Danny.'

'Good morning,' she said, coming to the door. 'Would you like something to eat?'

'You read my mind,' he said.

'What does that English expression mean?' Nessa whispered to me.

'It means he's hungry,' I said.

We brought him into the kitchen and Nessa warmed the beef

and noodles from the day before, adding a heaping of onions and put a plate before him.

'That's very kind of you,' he said. 'I don't know how I will repay your kindness.'

'Never mind that,' I said. 'Tell us about your journey here. What was it like?'

I was interested in what he'd seen coming down the length of England from Leeds to Oxfordshire.

'I decided to come south via the Peak District,' he related. 'I laid on five jerry cans of biofuel. I thought the elevation would be too high for flooding, and it was. I kept to the smaller roads and avoided cities and towns, as far as I could. I saw hardly any traffic.'

'Except I saw a lot of them wind turbines. Quite a few of them in the Pennines, you know, put there to catch the wind in the mountains. But they all seemed to be on the move. I'd never seen a wheelie turb – that's what the newspapers call them – move of its own accord. I mean, I'd read about turbs with wheels. There were so many moving together, they looked like great herds of African elephants!'

'We know a little about turbs,' I interjected gently, so as not to interrupt him.

'You do? Well, then you can educate me,' he went on. 'Each day I passed hundreds of them turbs moving across the mountains, all heading south like me. There was a funny ringing in my ears and I couldn't figure out why till one day it hit me: it was the turbs.'

'What do you mean?' I asked.

'They gave off a – they *vibrated*, if that's the right word, like giant musical tuning forks! It was horrible. Or it seemed that way to me, because near Birmingham, I put the last herd behind me and the ringing in my ears stopped. So I figure it was the turbs that caused it.'

'Anyway, I kept to the smaller roads because I was afraid there'd be a lot of traffic on the main motorways. I thought there might be lots of people on the move, refugees and such. The smaller roads were quiet. Not much traffic. Looked like a lot of the countryside was emptied out.'

'The problems started when I had to pass through more populated areas,' he related. 'Most of the petrol stations I saw were boarded up, and those that were working were mobbed and there were arguments – I even saw a couple of fistfights. Lots of abandoned cars and lorries on the motorways, and some of them had been broken into.'

'But Oxford was the worst. I figured it being a university town, everything would be quiet. Nothing like it. I drove into a firefight,' he said.

I offered Danny a glass of whisky and he took it gladly.

'I'd heard from another traveller that Oxford had plenty of food and fuel, so I decided to chance going into the town. I came in from the north via the A4165. The road was deathly still, not a soul to be seen.'

'In the centre of town was a pedestrian zone, but that didn't seem to matter anymore so drove I right through it. It was a mess, shop windows all broken and things strewn about.'

'On my left was a round building which a sign said was the Radcliffe Camera – funny name for a building – and beautiful it was, only it was just a burned out shell, the walls all blackened. Further on I saw more university buildings just as beautiful, made of stone with towers what they call them "dreaming spires" rising above them. Just as I pictured Oxford to be. The sad thing was that most of them were burnt shells.'

'I saw a signposting for the High Street but just as I turned into it, I heard gunfire. It was close by, I reckoned. A few shots, then a few more. My vehicle is rather conspicuous' – he laughed – 'so I decided not to make myself a target. Well fuck me, I thought. I jammed my foot back on the pedal and the first sign I saw was for the A40 and here I am.'

We talked some more – Danny regaled us with stories about Africa – and then saw him out to his caravan, which I'd let him park near the house, and left him to rest.

'I think he's charming,' said Nessa. 'His stories about travels in Africa were fascinating. And I like his old-fashioned manners.

What do you think about him?'

'He seems harmless,' I said. 'Might even be useful,' I added, still thinking about his shotgun.

'The story he told about coming down from the north – it's incredible,' I went on. 'Seems like order is breaking down all over the country.'

It was still only the middle of the afternoon.

'I'm going up one of the hills,' I said, putting on my boots. 'We've got to know what's going on.'

Once I reached the crest of the highest hill by the house, I got a signal and saw at once there were several unread messages – all had been there a couple of days.

'Blast!' I said to myself. 'While we were wandering around the woods…'.

10

THE WRATH OF GOD

Patel texted he would return to collect us – *both of us* – and bring us to an RAF base to join the turb working group. He wrote he'd come 'soon' – when was that, I wondered.

I lit a cigarette, gazing down at the house.

Phil texted he'd intervened to get Nessa approved for the mission. And he asked if we were making any progress at the *Hope and Glory* project – anything to share?

And there was a message from Frank. He said Phil had asked him to join the working group – hardly a surprise, I thought. He would be needed.

I replied to each message in turn.

'*When are you coming?*' I texted Patel.

I turned to flick the ash off my smoke and on the other side of the hill I saw the red tower light of a turb.

'*Tx,*' I wrote to Phil. '*We'll need Nessa – esp for plant analysis. We've got two turb smartchips – working on them.*'

'*See you soon, where are u now?*' I wrote to Frank.

I turned again to flick the ash. There was now a second turb in the distance. It occurred to me that soon I would run out of cigarettes and there weren't any more to be had, now that the F Café was closed.

A reply came from Patel.

'*Meet me tomoro at the Big World shopping centre on the A40. I'll put a chopper down on the roof,*' he texted.

'*What time?*' I replied.

'*Not sure exactly. Afternoon,*' he texted.

I tapped the smoke and turned. There were now four red turb lights away over the hill.

The phone beeped again. A message from Frank.

'*I'm at some kind of base in Yorkshire. Came yesterday,*' he wrote.

The thought of Frank made me smile. I took another drag, recalling him disappearing in the mist on the motorway and the bizarre journey up to London from Dover.

The fag was nearing its end. I took another puff, stood up and snuffed it out with my boot. Before going back down the hill, I turned to look again over the crest of the hill.

'What the – !' I exclaimed.

There before me were dozens and dozens of turbs. So thick was the herd that I could hardly see the sky. They'd come in the time it had taken to smoke a cigarette. They were just on the other side of the hill, and moving towards it, fast.

I turned and bounded down the hill to the house.

'Nessa!' I called. I found her in the lounge, with David, sitting in front of my computer.

'What is it, Jack?'

'Turbs – lots of them, just over the hill behind the house, and coming this way,' I said.

'What are we going to do?' asked David, obviously frightened.

'The first thing we're going to do is not be scared,' said Nessa, putting an arm around the boy. 'We've got time to think.'

'There's no reason to believe they're dangerous,' I said, not convincing anyone, least of all myself.

'Jack, they're dangerous,' said Nessa. 'We know that. If we stay inside the house – .'

'But we can't – I've had a message from Patel. We're to meet him at the shopping centre. He's bringing a helicopter to take us up north.'

'I see,' she said. 'When?'

'Tomorrow afternoon.'

'It'll be dark soon,' she said.

'Yes, and before it gets dark, I think we should go up the hill and take a closer look at our visitors,' I said.

'Agreed,' said Nessa.

I grabbed a pair of field glasses and a chainsaw. 'David, go and ask Danny to give you a jerry can filled with biofuel. I know he's got some – I saw them in his caravan.'

David returned a few minutes later with the can.

'We might have to make a fire,' I explained. 'David, you stay in the house. Warn Danny to come inside, too.'

Thus armed, Nessa and I scrambled up the hill. There, as we reached the crest, we saw the herd.

We were curious – professionally curious. We stood and watched them. They were still too far away to pose any danger.

I recognised some of the models from our *Hope and Glory* project. But there were many that weren't from our project, made in countries as diverse as Brazil, Korea, China and Nigeria. Most were HAWTs with long, sharp blades curved like scimitars but some were flat-bladed models. Some of the turbs were fitted with vortex generators to control the stall. Others had slewing drives to manage the furling effect and reduce wind drag. Some of the older models had externally mounted pitch controllers and wind vanes connected to the controller.

In terms of blade count, most were eight, ten or twelve bladers, but it was difficult to count the blades at a distance – and they were spinning, which made it even more difficult.

The sizes varied. A couple were really huge, I could see, two hundred plus metres tall, with huge blades – the higher the turb mast, the bigger the rotor blade. Those were not from our farm – we had nothing so large.

Judging from the degree of forward leaning mast angle, the herd was moving at speed.

A couple of the really big ones had brightly painted nacelles which oddly enough reminded me of war paint.

'They're our turbs, but there are others mixed in. I find that odd. Look at those really tall ones, for example,' I said. 'They seem to be the leaders of the pack.'

'I'm not convinced yet that turb herds have "leaders",' Nessa replied.

'Look at all the broken tethers they're dragging along,' I went on. 'That must slow them down.'

'Still, spinning with a blade tip speed of three or four hundred meters per second, they'll cut anything in their path to bits,' Nessa observed.

I counted the herd as best I could, though this wasn't easy given the distance and intervening hills partially blocked our view. I reckoned the size of the herd at about two or three hundred.

We watched them for a while as they drew nearer.

'You know, in a way, they're sort of graceful,' I said.

'Not in my eyes,' said Nessa. 'Look how they lurch when they move. They're ugly and they're scary.'

'You're a wind engineer,' I said. 'These turbs are your life's work. I don't think you've always felt like that.'

'You're right,' she said slowly. 'Something's changed. I mean, we're seeing things now that we didn't see before.'

I could not argue with that.

'Jack, look, they're not heading toward us,' she said. 'They're heading over that other hill, to the south.'

'Yes – why, they're heading toward the shopping centre. It's directly in their path!'

'We'd better get back,' I said. 'We've got to go to the centre. We've got to warn them.'

'We haven't got any choice,' she said. 'Let's go.'

We scrambled down the hill.

'What are we going to do with David?' asked Nessa as we reached the house. 'We can't just leave him here alone.'

'He's not alone. We've got Danny. He'll take care of the boy. We'll invite him to move into the house,' I said.

'I don't know, Jack. David has become our responsibility in a way. We offered him the chance to escape those men.'

'He'll be fine with Danny,' I said. 'Besides, I want him to keep working on those smartchips.'

'All right, we'll go,' she said. 'But first, I'll make us something to eat.'

*

It was eight or nine o'clock in the evening by the time we reached the centre. The lights were on, so someone had got the generator to work. The doors of the west entrance stood open, but we saw no one outside.

The south car park was seriously flooded. The waters had risen quite a bit since our last visit to the centre – the flood had arrived. But that didn't concern us just then.

Inside, at first, everything seemed almost normal. Someone had got the mall music system operating – a pleasant, droning sound echoed through the halls as we entered. Someone had even got the escalators to work. The sight of them gently rising and falling made it seem like there'd been no flood, no crisis.

But the moment you took off your rose-coloured glasses, things had a different hue. We walked past the bedding department – it looked like whole families had slept in the beds.

But they weren't there. No one was there.

We walked past some clothing shops. I saw a mannequin and opened my mouth to say hello and ask where everyone was. Then I stopped. It was naked – all the mannequins were naked. I figured people had taken the clothes.

'Jack, there's no one here.' said Nessa.

'I can see that,' I said.

'They're all in the cinema,' came the voice of Chris Porter.

'Chris, good to see you,' I said. 'You remember Nessa.'

'I do indeed,' he said. 'How is the lovely lady this evening?'

'Fine, thank you,' she said. 'You haven't come for a Chinese meal yet.'

'Sometime soon, I hope,' he said.

'So, what's going on?' I asked. 'I need to speak to whoever's in charge – is it the council?'

'Not any more,' he said. 'We've elected an emergency committee of people from the village. Jenny's the head. The bloke Pritchard's on it, too. That woman – the council leader – she buggered off.'

'Chris, you've got to learn to get along with the powers that be,' I said. 'I'll bet she still has authority to get Withers to lock you up.'

'They've already tried that,' he said. 'But that's another story.'

'All right,' I said. 'Why are people in the cinema – watching a film at a time like this?'

'No, it's not a film,' he said. 'There's a preacher speaking about the flood. I suppose it's a form of entertainment.'

'Chris, this isn't the time for entertainment,' I said. 'There's a big herd of turbs headed straight for this centre. Where's Jenny?'

'She's in the cinema, along with everyone else,' he said.

We made our way there. It was full to capacity. A placard on the stage announced the topic as 'The Meaning of the Great Flood' and below that, the name of the speaker, Gerald De Souza.

I caught sight of Jenny and Withers in the front row.

'Jenny!' I called out. But she hadn't heard me, for just at that moment De Souza stepped out from behind the curtain and a shout went up from the audience. People were taken by his appearance. His clothes seemed intended to draw attention to himself – a long black cape hung over his shoulders down to his ankles. He wore long, black hair that fell to his shoulders. He looked foreign, with dark skin and long dark hair, perhaps from South America or India. But when he opened his mouth to speak all suggestion of foreignness melted away, for he spoke English in the received way, without any trace of an accent.

'All right, let's listen for a bit,' I said to Nessa. We settled into seats at the back.

'My friends,' the speaker began. 'It is very kind of you to come to listen to me speak here today. I've been travelling the length and breadth of this England, this Sceptred Isle, to speak about what we now call the Great Flood. But I've been listening as much as I've been speaking. I've been listening to the people of England. Hearing what they say. Understanding what they say.'

'Do you know what they say?' He paused and looked the audience over. Here and there he made eye contact and smiled.

'They ask a question: what is the meaning of this Great Flood?' He paused again and looked down for a moment, as if deep in thought.

'Have you asked yourself that question?'

'Yes, I have,' said a man in the first row. I recognised him as one of the men who was in the F Café when it blew up.

There were approving murmurs. Looking round, I saw several other familiar faces.

'You know, my friends, since time out of memory when humans have been afflicted with misfortune – and I mean both as individuals and as societies – they ask what they have done to deserve such misfortune. Did not this question first arise in the Bible with the story of Job? Yes, it did.'

'This flood is right out of the Bible,' a man shouted. 'We're going to have to build an Ark to survive!'

A few laughed at this, but many more looked earnestly at the speaker, waiting for him to continue. But the preacher paused, and replied to the man.

'You may be right, my friend. The waters have risen round this shopping centre, where you've all taken refuge. I saw them as I arrived here,' said the preacher.

'But I would like to point something out to you, something you already know. And that is this: misfortune, my friends, must have a cause.'

'Behind every misfortune is a reason – a reason why. A reason that men and women can understand. Isn't that so? Trial and punishment don't come out of the blue without any reason. Trial and punishment come for a reason. Isn't that so?' he repeated.

There were more approving murmurs.

'Now I ask you: what could the reason be? I mean the reason

for this flood which we are now experiencing? The flood which has driven you to seek refuge in this shopping centre. Which has created refugees from all over England, especially from the coastal areas. Which has shut down our airports and our seaports. Which has shattered the Kingdom's peace and created lawlessness and disorder throughout our islands, so that thievery and pillage are now the order of the day.'

The preacher paused. There was silence in the hall.

'The reason is well known to you,' he said softly.

'They call it *climate change*,' he went on, emphasising the words. 'Let me repeat those two words: *climate change*. You've heard them before. Many times, I would have thought.'

'What do those two words mean?' he asked.

'They mean the world is getting warmer,' yelled a man far in the back of the hall.

'No, colder,' said a woman near the front, the woman in the tweed jacket from the F Café.

The preacher raised his arm for silence.

'Thank you, friends,' he said. 'Yes, warmer, colder. But change all the same. *Climate change*.'

'And what could be the reason for this – *climate change*?'

No one said a word.

'Could it be that humans just burned too much fossil fuel?' De Souza continued. 'And the holes – those great, big holes – we've all seen pictures of them haven't we? – those holes appeared in the ozone layer and the governments could not agree what to do and the climate changed and the earth got warmer and the seas rose and human civilisation was destroyed? Could it be that our civilisation has come to end for that reason? A sort of technical, "Oops, we made a mistake" end of our planet?'

He paused again.

'Does anyone here today believe that?' he asked almost in a whisper.

Negative sounds filled the hall.

'I agree with you. I don't believe it either,' said De Souza. 'But there is another explanation, of course.'

'It could be that climate change and the resulting Great Flood are just random events,' he went on. 'Some scientists have said so. Natural events like this, they say, occur periodically. The history of our planet bears this out, they say. Look at the Ice Age. Look at the extinction of the dinosaurs. Look at the evidence that our planet's climate has changed from time to time. In the Phanerozoic Eon, from five hundred and forty two million years ago, until today, until this very day, there have been many changes in our climate. That's what some scientists say.'

'But I would ask them this: how can an act of nature not be an act of God?'

Nessa's eyes began to close. She elbowed me and gestured toward the door.

'Wait,' I whispered. 'It's just getting interesting.'

De Souza went on about God for a while and then returned to the flood.

'So, my friends, we are dealing with water. What does the Bible tell us about water? What does the whole of human thought and philosophy – from the Ancient Greeks and Romans to the Moderns – tell us about water? That it is the source of life. Water is the symbol of life, synonymous with the female, with love and even – if I may – with the act of sex.'

'We may regard the Great Flood as a gift of life –.'

'Tell us more about the sex!' shouted Chris Porter, but De Souza ignored him.

'– a gift of life to wash this world clean of sin,' he continued. 'Clean of greed, clean of vanity, clean of pride, selfishness, gluttony – all the sins. And when these waters subside – yes, my friends, they will subside – what a world there will be to behold! It may be diminished in a technological sense, but in a spiritual sense, it will be very much richer.'

'You're not C of E, are you?' a woman called out. It was the woman in the tweed coat from the F café.

Again the speaker ignored the interruption. He was off in a

reverie about the cleansed world. I caught something about divine justice and the possibility that the flood was the work of a malevolent God, which he did not dismiss out of hand.

'I ask you again, my friends,' said De Souza. 'How can an act of nature not be an act of God?'

'And I will answer my own question, if I may – if I may reveal to you the word of God that I have heard. God willed this flood to cleanse the world of sin. Yes, this flood is God's will!'

At this the crowd exploded into shouts and murmurs.

I had had enough. I rose.

'Sir, I don't know who you are or why you are here,' I said as loudly as I could to make myself heard.

'I've done you the courtesy of listening, but now I've got to interrupt you,' I said. 'There's a large herd of turbs headed directly for this shopping centre' – the commotion grew louder at this – 'and the people here have to take measures for their own safety.'

'What measures, Jack?' said Jenny, rising.

Before I could answer De Souza spoke.

'Ah, yes. The wind turbines,' he said. Heads turned in his direction.

'You know about them?' someone shouted.

'Yes, my friend, I know about them. They're running amok, aren't they?' said De Souza. 'They've broken their tethers – that's what people say, all over England – and now we lack for electricity, just at this moment of crisis. They're roaming the land, like great dinosaurs. Can there be any doubt that these monsters were sent by Satan –?'

'Will you shut up?' I said, moving down the aisle toward the stage.

De Souza eyed me. He opened his mouth to say something, but then apparently thought better of it.

'My friends,' he said after a pause. 'Our ministry is so very grateful to you for being here tonight. And to show our gratitude, we will humbly accept any sum you are generously prepared to offer.'

Music began to play and two statuesque women appeared on stage holding collection plates.

'We accept notes of the European Bank of England,' he said. 'But God's work flourishes with gold - rings, jewellery or gold coins if you happen to have any.'

I reached the stage and mounted the steps. De Souza stepped back as I reached the stage.

'Don't hit me!' he cried.

'Bugger off,' I said. 'Now.'

He hesitated, looking at the women moving among the audience with the collection plates. Then he spied DCS Withers' uniform.

'Constable!' he called out.

'I'm the Deputy Chief Superintendent,' Withers called back. 'You'd better do as Jack here says or −.'

'Our ministry has concluded God's work here this evening,' said De Souza, retreating behind the curtain.

He was gone.

'Enough of that,' I said, looking round for Nessa. I soon found her and we left the cinema. Outside stood Chris.

'What did you make of that bloke?' he asked.

'I guess I'm not the spiritual sort,' I said. 'I don't think religion can be counted in gold coins.'

'Jenny will be along presently,' said Chris.

I went outside for a smoke whilst waiting.

I chose a bench facing the centre, part way into the empty car park. As I sat down I turned and looked at the field and sky beyond. The sky was clear and the field below the hill open and wide.

'England's pleasant pastures,' I thought. And then: 'Maybe this is all a bad dream,' I mumbled to myself. But it was no dream.

I lit a fag. The shopping centre stood before me. 'God, it's ugly,' I thought.

Nessa came outside to join me.

'Jack, turn around and look,' she said slowly. 'The turbs are here.'

11

THE HOWLING

The field beyond the car park was filled with advancing turbs. Then, suddenly, they stopped. Away on the left some began to gently bob. The wind picked up, cold in our faces.

'The blades should start turning in this wind, shouldn't they?' said a voice.

It was Jenny. She and some others had come out of the centre.

The wind blew harder. The bobbing turbs on the left ceased their movement. Everything was still.

'They should turn,' I said. 'At least, that's what they are programmed to do.'

'Jack, you're the expert here, you and Nessa,' said Jenny, nodding to Nessa. 'What should we do?'

I climbed onto a bench.

'Listen, everyone,' I said. 'Stay well away from the turbs – beyond the radius of the blades, which I reckon is about a hundred and fifty metres for most of them.'

'I'm not about to go near them,' said Paul Pritchard, in his sardonic way. 'They look like triffids.'

'Jenny, Paul – you're on the village committee,' I said. 'Can you organise things?'

'Sure,' said Jenny. 'Go on – what do we need?'

'Right. First of all, they seem to be afraid of fire.' I said. 'So if we could gather as much flammable material as we can – sheets and towels from the bath department, wood furniture, anything that will burn – and place them at intervals around the centre we might be able to create a barrier they'd be reluctant to cross.'

'We can do that,' said Paul. 'What else?'

'They seem to be attracted by sound. So if we could place speakers from the centre's public address system outside, well away from us, and somehow get them to work, it might draw them away.'

'That might be possible,' Jenny said. 'There's a sparks here – he might know how to do that.'

'Good,' I said. 'Let's get cracking.'

It took a couple of hours to prepare the centre's defences. In that time, the turbs remained perfectly still. But instead of making people feel less worried, the lack of movement had the opposite effect. It gave the feeling that something was coming.

'It's like they're waiting for something,' said Paul. 'But for what?'

'I've done a bit of online research into turbs, that is, when my pad gets a signal,' he said. 'The turbs aren't supposed to move beyond the limit of their tethers. That's how the electricity is derived from the wind turning the blades. Their movement is controlled by computers – isn't everything these days?'

We stood outside the west entrance of the centre, eyeing the herd.

'Yes, Paul, what you discovered is correct, but it isn't the whole story.' I said.

'What is the whole story?' he asked.

'Like any system using technology, there are quirks,' Nessa put in. 'Things go wrong, problems have to be investigated.'

'This doesn't look like a quirk to me,' he said. 'Why, there are several hundred turbs out there. All of them were moving in this direction. Their movement seemed to me to be quite deliberate. And now they've stopped. What's going on?'

'Paul, we don't know everything,' I said. 'At least, not yet.'

I didn't want to go into the deviation factor, not in front of all these people from the village. It might make them even more scared than some of them were.

'Sorry, I didn't mean to put you on the spot,' said Pritchard. 'But I just think you know more than you say. I've got a discussion going on my blog – whenever I get the internet – it seems this is happening all over England – like that preacher said – and in other places as well.'

'What are people saying?' someone asked. I turned and saw it was the 'professor' from the F Café.

'They're saying turbs are on the move, all up and down the country,' Pritchard related. 'They're saying there've been some attacks against people.'

In the internet age, information was everywhere, even if the connection was spotty.

'Paul, I wasn't trying to hide anything. It's true what I said: we don't know the whole story. But we're trying to find out. We came here to meet someone from the government who is coming tomorrow to take us up north to join a working group on just this subject.'

There was a brief silence as people considered what I'd said.

'Can't the government help us?' asked the professor.

'Yes, will you bring help?' asked a woman. It was Sally, the waitress from the café.

'I don't know yet,' I said. 'But in the meantime, you've got to be able to help yourselves.'

'We can,' said Jenny. 'You've given us the basics. We ought to be all right. After all, we don't know that these turbs are any danger to us.'

'I think there's a good chance they are,' I said. 'It's best if everyone stays inside, at least for tonight. We'd better all get some sleep.'

People began to move inside, but not all of them. Some lingered at the sight of so many turbs.

'How can we sleep with them turbs out there?' I heard a man ask. But then he, too, turned to go inside the centre, leaving the silent, motionless herd of turbs lit by a pale winter moon.

'We'll find the two of you somewhere to sleep,' Jenny said to us. 'And some bedding. It won't be five stars, but I hope you won't mind.'

'Anything you've got will be fine,' said Nessa. 'It's very kind of you.'

We ended up in the sporting department, on a billiard table. I had hoped for something a little more romantic. What the billiard table lacked in privacy, it made up for in tenderness. She was in my arms, and we let each other sleep only after an endless embrace. During that long embrace I was rehearsing the latest version of how I would propose to her.

*

Nessa nudged me.

'Wake up,' she said.

There was urgency in her voice.

'What is it?'

'That sound – do you hear it? What is it?'

'I don't hear anything,' I said.

'Let's go over to that window,' she said, getting up.

I followed her to a window and I put my hand by the frame and felt a cold draught. Then I leaned my head down. I caught a faint sound. I stood there a moment, bent over, with my head near the frame.

'I don't hear anything,' I said. 'Maybe something faint.'

'Open the window,' said Nessa.

'I don't know if I can,' I said, struggling with the latch.

The window came open and with it came the howl of the turbs. It was a piteous whine that quickly filled the corridors of the mall. People turned toward the sound, then away, bringing their hands to their ears. But that brought no relief.

We staggered away from the window, slamming it shut. But the sound kept coming, through the window frame and the frames of dozens of other windows.

It grew in intensity till it occupied every space in the mind.

'The living God!' a woman shrieked, crumpling to her knees.

'Turn it off!' another woman screamed.

But we couldn't. No one could.

A dog began whimpering hysterically.

'Shut that dog up!' a man shouted, 'I'll kill it, I swear.'

The centre's few babies began to wail, louder and louder.

The howling intensified. People made for restrooms, cleaners' closets and any inside room they could squeeze into. They struggled to shut the doors on the prying fingers of those left outside.

'Let me in, please,' pleaded a man by the door of a handicapped toilet. I saw it was the professor. He was slumped by the door, clutching his hands to his head.

Whoever was inside paid no attention to him. The door remained shut.

'I can't bear it!' he screamed. 'Someone help me, please!'

Nessa helped him to his feet and steered him toward a small closet marked with a fire symbol. She opened it and pulled out a fire extinguisher and a large bucket.

'Squeeze yourself in there,' she said gently.

He looked at her and managed a weak smile.

'Thank you,' he shouted to be heard above the howling. 'That's very kind. I didn't notice this closet.'

Nessa, her hands pressed again to her head, leaned over to me and put her lips to my ears.

'Right,' she said. 'Let's get down to the cellar – it should be better there.'

We made our way along the wide mall. Everywhere people staggered about, their hands clapped to their ears.

Things that had previously been of no interest to anyone had suddenly acquired value. People grabbed anything they could flatten to the sides of their heads – bedsheets, towels, jumpers. But still the howling penetrated. At the chemist's in the middle of the mall we saw a dozen or so people engaged in a fierce struggle.

'Give them to me!' a man shouted, and in the next instant he struck a woman across the head. 'I saw them first!'

Whatever it was that he wanted fell to the floor, for we saw him and the others lunge downwards, their arms flaying to fend off rivals. On all fours a man punched another in the head. The man who was hit struck back and the two men embraced in a fury of blows and kicks.

A newcomer joined the fray, planting his foot squarely in the spine of the man on all fours. A woman rolled over onto her back and soon a couple of knees were in her stomach. She screamed bloody murder but those astride her paid no mind, so obsessed were they with wrenching something from the hand of a very young girl whose other hand held tight to the prostrate woman. The girl's grip gave way and what she held rolled across the floor.

Cotton balls. They were fighting over cotton balls.

One man grabbed some and rose in triumph, stuffing the cotton into his ears.

'Thank God!' he cried. 'I – argh!'

The woman jabbed her fingernails into one of his ears and plucked the precious balls away, leaving a red gash in one of his earlobes. She turned to run but he was faster. He threw himself upon her and she fell with a scream. He raised his arm to strike her.

'I'll teach you – ,' he cried.

We moved to help the woman.

'Enough!' I shouted, pulling him off her.

I punched him square in the face.

'You've broken my jaw!' the man yelled.

'No, I haven't,' I said. 'But my next punch will, if you don't come to your senses.'

The man rubbed his jaw.

'I'm sorry,' he said. 'This noise – it's driving me mad.'

'You're not the only one,' said Nessa, tending to the woman.

'All right,' I said, helping the man to his feet.

'Let's move on,' I said. Nessa needed no encouragement.

There was more. We soon saw similar melees in the winter clothing department, where people bitterly fought over earmuffs, wool caps, scarves – anything they could wrap around their ears.

In the bedding department there were little hillocks on every bed, where whole families cowered together under duvets and blankets for relief from the howling. In the bath department fights had broken out over towels.

The hideous howling of the turbs didn't let up. The pitch changed, it seemed to now rise and now fall, but the intensity, the piercing urgency, of the wail penetrated every corner of the brain, drowning out every thought except escape.

We ducked into a stairwell and headed down to the cellar. Bounding down the stairs we saw the Big World's fitness centre, half a level below ground. I pushed open the door and stuck my head inside. It was full. People had sought refuge from the howling in the many closed spaces that offered a measure of relief – changing rooms, toilets and the sauna. They crowded into every available closed space.

We took a few steps inside, toward the sauna. Perhaps as an overthought, it had been left on. A dozen or more people had squeezed into it, and the temperature had risen wildly with all the bodies. We saw a woman who had fainted being pushed out by those inside, while hands outside eagerly pulled her out to make more room.

'Let's get out of here and find the cellar,' I said to Nessa.

'Jack, that woman, can we help her?' she asked.

But there was no need. Another woman emerged from the sauna and emptied a bucket of water over the fainted woman's head.

'Come on, back to the stairs,' I urged.

We shoved open a door marked 'Maintenance' and continued downwards. Another flight and we came to another door that led into a dimly lit room full of pipes mounted to the ceiling.

In the poor light, Jenny stepped forward.

'It's better down here, isn't it?' she said. 'You can still hear it, but it's a little more bearable.' She was wearing a pair of earmuffs.

We squinted and looked round. Behind her were many people, some of whom moved closer to listen.

'It is,' I said. 'But still, it's not something we can live with. The sound penetrates even down here.'

'It does, damn it,' she said. 'We've got a lot of the villagers down here. It's been chaos. We're trying to sort ourselves by point of origin,' she went on. 'This is the Upper St John neighbourhood. Further down that way are the Clacton and other estuary refugees. And back the other way, that's where the Isle of Sheppey people are. The water pipes down here make it a bit warmer.'

Our eyes adjusted better and we could see that the labyrinthine passages and rooms were full of men and women. They struck me as wretched-looking, clutching duvets, mattresses and what-not that they'd dragged down from the centre's showrooms.

'There are still quite a few people upstairs,' I said.

'Some people are just too disorientated to listen to us,' said Jenny.

'What is that sound, Jack? What's causing it?'

It was Withers, the policeman. Behind him stood Paul, Chris and several others from the village.

'The blades of the turbs have stalled,' I replied.

'You'll have to explain that,' he said. 'That sounds like what a car does, or an aeroplane that's going to crash.'

'It's something similar,' I said. 'The more wind, the more the angle of the blades' attack increases until the flat sides of the blades are perpendicular to the wind direction. That's called a stall. The effect is to dramatically increase the noise level produced by the wind striking the blades. That's what causes the howling.'

'The opposite effect is called furling,' Nessa put in. 'That's where the edge of the blade faces directly into the wind. Modern turbs have what is called a slewing drive that regulates the blades' pitch or angle of attack. Those turbs out there are certainly equipped with slewing drives, using a hydraulic system or an electric servo-motor, to manage the torque load on the blades.'

'The latest models have curved blades to reduce these effects, but you still need to control the pitch,' I said. 'The computers do that.'

'It's a bit like an aeroplane, as you said, Deputy Chief Superintendent,' I continued. 'But the turbs don't fall over – crash, like an aeroplane – because the wind pressure on the total blade area, even when fully flat against the wind, is insufficient to create enough pressure on the tower to fall over.'

'Instead, you get the howling,' I said.

Withers looked at us with a blank face.

'So, what can we do about it?' he asked.

'It's nothing new,' said Paul. 'Sorry to break in. I read in the internet that the sound made by turb blades flat into the wind was recognised as a health hazard decades ago. A "howl" they called it. It creates mental stress – in other words, it drives people mad. For example, I saw an article from twenty years ago in a tabloid and the headline was: *Howling turbs drive Welsh farmers bonkers.* It was about a family in Wales driven mad by a turb farm built near their home.'

'Of course, the pro-turbers denied that turbs made any noise at all, or at least that "howl" wasn't the right word for the noise they make,' he went on. 'But according to what I've read, those who've had heard turbs howling in the wind swore it brought an end to normal life for anybody living nearby.'

'It's true what you say,' said a voice. 'I've also read that. Makes people mad.'

I turned and saw the woman in the tweed coat from the F Café. Several people behind her nodded in agreement.

'But aren't you used to it, both of you? You're wind engineers,' said Jenny. 'You're working with these things every day.'

'Yes, we're working with turbs as part of our jobs,' said Nessa. 'But the howling – that doesn't normally happen. The control computers prevent the blades from turning flat into the wind.'

'I don't understand,' said Paul. 'If their computers tell them not to turn their blades flat into the wind, what's making them do it?'

'We don't know,' I said. 'I told you – we're going up north to try to find out.'

'Jack, can't you tell us anything?' he asked.

I paused, trying to make up my mind whether to say anything more. There was no longer any point not to tell the villagers what I knew.

'It's a long, complicated story,' I said. 'The short version is that the turbs have become independent of their control computers. Each one has a smartchip, of course, but they seem to be taking direction from some other source. It may be because they've been hacked. It may be for another reason. I personally think this howling is related to this factor – we call it the "deviation factor".'

'The "deviation factor",' Paul mulled. 'Good name. But how is that related to this infernal noise?'

'Maybe all those blades aren't turned flat into the wind by chance,' I said. 'Maybe it's deliberate.'

'It's funny you say that,' said Jenny. 'My first thought when I heard the howl was that it seemed, uh, like a chorus. So many of them howling at the same time. Like a pack of hyenas.'

'It's not accidental and not just a natural effect of the wind passing over the blades,' I said. 'At least, I don't think so.'

'What's the purpose?' said a voice from among the villagers.

'To weaken our resistance, I suppose, and to drive us so mad we'll run outside and then they'll kill us,' I said.

A gasp arose.

'It can't be,' said Jenny.

'Jack's not making it up,' said Paul. 'I read about that in the internet.'

'It's unbelievable,' said Jenny. 'Why, Jack, what do they want?'

'That's what we're going to find out,' I said.

'Well, all right, then,' said Withers. 'The first thing we are going to do is stay inside. It'll be light soon, then we'll see.'

Jenny showed us to a corner where a mattress was laid out. We managed to get a few hours' sleep.

*

Morning came without any let up in the howling. It had slithered down into the cellar, via the stairways, pipes and air ducts. It woke me around six o'clock. Others were already awake.

'It's still there. I can't stand it,' said Paul. 'We should go upstairs and have a look round.'

'Maybe there's a way out without going upstairs,' said Chris. 'Maybe these tunnels lead out of here – under the car park to the garden centre, for example.'

No one knew.

'Quite possibly there's a plan for all these tunnels in the management office on the first floor,' Jenny put in.

'That's a good idea,' said Paul. 'Let's go up and have a look.'

'There are people still up there, in the fitness centre and the closets,' I said. 'We might be able to persuade them to come down here.'

'Why?' asked Paul. 'It's not much better down here. It's getting worse, in fact. We've got to find a way out.'

'I wouldn't be in too much of a hurry,' said Withers. 'If half of what Jack and Nessa say is correct, it's still too dangerous.'

'Well I'm going to take that chance,' Paul declared. 'I can't stand this howling anymore. Who's coming with me?'

'I'll come,' said a short man I recognised as the village chemist. Perkins was his name.

'I'll come, too,' said another man.

'All right,' I said. 'Nessa and I will come up with you.'

'You know the turbs best,' said Jenny. 'If something happens –.'

'Nothing will happen if we stay inside,' I said.

We made our way up the stairs. At the top I turned.

'Prepare yourselves,' I said.

I pushed open the fire door and the howl burst on our ears.

'Jenny, the management office is up those stairs. Go and see if you can find the building plans,' I said.

'I'll go with,' said Paul.

'Jack, look – that closet where we helped that man – the door's open,' said Nessa.

Just then the woman who'd fought for the cotton balls appeared. She still had them stuffed into her ears but I saw at once that something about her looked odd. She shuffled her feet and her gaze was fixed in an odd way.

'Madame,' I said. 'The man who was in that closet – have you seen him?'

'He went out,' she said in a kind of drawl. 'They all went out.'

'Where? How many went out?' I asked, grabbing her by the shoulders.

'Out there,' she said, pointing to the field. 'Lots of people went out there.'

We turned and saw the entrance door to the mall standing wide open.

'Oh My God!' said Jenny, cupping her hand over her mouth.

The turbs had moved closer to the centre. I reckoned they were now less than a hundred metres away – within blade range.

I ran to the open door.

'I don't see anyone,' I said, scanning the field, which sloped away beyond the car park.

'Where did they go?' asked Withers. 'Maybe they got away.'

'Listen, everyone!' Paul came running down the mall. He shouted to be heard over the howling.

'I've just been over on the east side of the mall – there aren't any turbs on that side. We can get out of here!'

12

GOOD VIBRATIONS

'Paul, assuming you get out of here alive, where are you going to go?' I asked.

'Why, back to Upper St John. There's shelter there. Must still be some food in some of the shops or abandoned houses. It's got to be better than staying here – we'll all go mad,' he said. 'Come on, who's with me?'

The little chemist Perkins was in, and so was another villager I knew by sight.

'He's right. If we stay here we'll go out of our minds,' said Perkins. 'Besides, I want to see if there's anything left in my shop. Maybe some medicine we might need.'

'I think you're mad already to want to go out there,' said another man from the village. 'I'll take my chances here. Let's all get back down to the cellar.'

Voices rose on either side of the issue. In the end, those who wanted to go were free to do so.

'I'll not stop anyone from trying to get out,' said Withers. 'It's your right as Englishmen to return to your homes. In fact, if I can find PC Bartle, I'll send him with you.'

'That's that, then,' said Paul. 'Off we go.'

'Just a minute, Paul,' I said. 'Nessa and I will come with you to the other side of the centre. Give it a look.'

'Sure,' he replied.

We moved. The east side of the Big World was exactly the same as the west side – with a car park the size of many football pitches laid out in a giant asphalt rectangle along the side of the building.

I pushed open the door and took a few steps outside, looking this way and that. The sun was higher in the sky and the day promised to be bright.

'I can't see any turbs,' I said. 'You should be all right. But you'll have to be careful. We set no defence measures on this side of the centre – no bonfires and no loudspeakers.'

Just then a policeman appeared.

'I'm PC John Bartle,' he said. 'The Deputy Chief Superintendent sent me to accompany those who want to leave.'

'Right,' said Paul. My name's Pritchard. This is my group. We're ready to go.'

I cast my eye over the police constable of the mid-twenty first century. He was laden with electronic gear – around his waist were a taser stinger, a laser paint gun, a GPS navigator, a National Identity Card bio-metric reader, a DNA scanner and electric-charged hand cuffs. From his protective headgear, hung a CCTV camera with microphone.

'Take care, Paul,' I said, shaking his hand.

'We'll be right as rain,' he said cheerily.

'See you soon, I hope,' said Nessa.

She gave him a peck on the cheek.

The small group of half a dozen or so walked out into the car park, and we turned to go back inside the centre.

The cellar offered less of a reprieve from the howling than before. The noise level there had risen. More people had come down from their hiding places upstairs, and they were all talking. Jenny was already there.

'The turbs are really at it,' she was saying.

'The howling ripples through the herd,' she went on. 'Starting with those far in the distance, moving up to those nearest the centre and then back again. They're baying as a pack, the way football fans use to rise and sit, in a wave. Know what I mean?'

'Yes, I do,' said Nessa. 'You saw them?'

'Yes, on our way down from the management office,' said Jenny. 'Look, we found the complete plan of this shopping centre. There *is* a tunnel leading from here to the garden centre.'

'They weren't all baying, by the way,' said Jenny. 'Some of them were sort of pecking at the ground.'

Jenny and Chris unfolded the shopping centre plans.

'Jack, come and look at this,' she said.

'Sure, Jenny, in a minute,' I said. I pulled Nessa aside, into a corner under the ceiling pipes and gave her a kiss.

'Patel should be here soon. Then we'll have to go,' I said.

'Did you hear what Jenny said about the turbs pecking at the ground?' she said.

'No, what could that mean?' I asked.

'I'm not sure,' she said. 'But I'd like to get a look at that.'

There came a piercing scream from somewhere above, clearly audible despite the howling. Carried into the cellar along pipes and ducts, it rose and intensified and then it levelled into a continuous moan that lasted God knows how long. It never seemed to end. Then finally it did, in a terrifying cry.

All conversation among us stopped. Jenny looked up from her plans. Chris turned toward me.

'What in God's name was that?' Withers whispered.

'Wasn't an animal,' said Chris. 'No animal we've got around here could've made a sound like that.'

'It sounded like a human cry −,' someone began.

Suddenly, through the pipes and ducts, from above, came another loud shriek. It was as if pain had been turned into a gas and pumped into the cellar in the form of a scream, and it mixed among us, producing pure fear. And fear produced silence. No one spoke.

The wailing went on, pitiful and heart-wrenching. I looked at Jenny. Her face was contorted, as though it were she who was being tortured. I looked at Nessa. She was a cooler customer, as I expected, but still, her eyes betrayed extreme discomfort. It was unbearable.

Then it died away.

'We've got to –,' Withers began, but stopped, as again we heard the sound of a scream from above.

'That's enough!' he shouted. 'Can't we shut that noise out somehow?'

'I don't think so,' I said. The third scream did not last as long as the first ones, yet it somehow conveyed an intense sense of pain, like a sharp object on skin, that made all of us wince.

'Cut to pieces,' muttered Chris.

'Who? How do you know that?' Withers confronted him. I could see he was angry at his own impotence.

'You know who – Paul and the others who went out there,' said Chris. 'Those weren't no animal cries. They were human. That was them.'

'What exactly happened to them?' a woman asked.

'How the bloody hell should I know?' Chris shouted. 'I'm stuck down here same as you. Do you think I've got eyes in the top of me head?'

'Settle down, Chris,' I said. 'We're all a little on edge.'

'Look, I've found a tunnel that leads under the car park to the garden centre,' said Jenny. 'What are we waiting for?'

'At least we'd avoid getting caught out in the open,' said Chris. 'Like them.'

'Yes,' Withers agreed.

'I don't know,' I said. 'In the garden centre we'll be in the same situation – maybe the howling will be worse.'

'From there we could make a sprint to the woods,' said one villager, obviously keen. 'Them turbs can't move about in the woods, can they?'

'Come on,' Jenny went on. 'Let's gather up everything we'll need.'

People began to busy themselves with grabbing anything useful. Just then a very faint scream penetrated down to the cellar and everyone froze.

'We've got to get out of here before we go mad,' said Jenny, clutching her ears.

Nessa pulled me aside.

'Jack, I want to go upstairs first – to get a look at what the turbs are doing,' she said.

'All right, I'll come with you,' I said. 'We'll catch up with the others later. Let's just see where the tunnel that Jenny found is.'

We followed the villagers till we were sure of the way, and then turned to go up the stairs. Passing the fitness centre, we saw that there were still some people inside, with towels wrapped around their ears to shut out the howling. In the mall itself, there were also pockets of people who didn't know what to do or where to go – driven to distraction by the incessant, whining howl, and terrified by the screams.

Nessa touched my elbow.

'Not that way, Jack,' she said. 'I want to have a look at the east side – where Paul went out.'

We made our way there, and immediately spotted some turbs outside.

'So, there are turbs here too, now,' she said.

We took a minute to count and catalogue them, a similar mix of models and sizes. But something was different. There were a number of the two-metre tall mini-turbs, which were moving about and bobbing. They reminded me of lion cubs, playful and competitive.

'The centre's now barricaded by turbs on two sides,' said Nessa. 'The north side has the reservoir. That leaves the south side – maybe we should have gone out that way.'

'I think it's flooded. Besides, it's just another huge car park,' I said. 'No place to hide.'

'They're pecking at the ground, Jack, just as Jenny said – those two way over there,' she said. 'Like the way a bird pecks at something with its beak, only the turbs use their blades.'

'There's certainly been no software written for turbs to instruct them to do that,' I observed.

'See how the big ones move,' she went on. 'They won't let the mini-turbs near whatever they're pecking at. I'd like to get a closer look.'

'Later, Nessa. We should catch up with the villagers,' I said. 'They may not know what to do if there are turbs at the garden centre.'

'Jack, Patel's going to be here soon and we'll leave with him,' she said. 'There's a limit to what we can do to help the people of your village.'

'I know that,' I said. 'But Patel's not here yet. Let's go.'

We soon caught up with the others in the tunnel. They were moving slowly amid the pipes and other fixtures, weighed down by their belongings. Some of them, I guessed, really thought they might be able to go home. Others were probably just looking to escape the howling. And it was fainter in the tunnel than it had been in the centre's cellar.

We eased ourselves past the column and found Jenny at its head.

'This should be it,' she said, pointing to a door just ahead. 'There should be some stairs leading up to the garden centre.'

Stairs there were and, climbing them, we soon came to another door.

'Open it, Jack,' said Jenny.

I turned the knob and pushed with my hand. But the door was heavy and I had to lean against it to get it to move. Slowly, it opened.

'What's there, Jack?' asked Chris from the bottom of the stairwell. 'What do you see?'

I blinked. The morning had brightened and the light in my eyes made it hard to see after the dimness of the tunnel.

'We're in the forecourt of the garden centre,' I said. I stepped outside, followed by Nessa and Jenny. Then came Withers and others. For a moment we all stood, looking around.

'Fresh air,' said Jenny. 'Feels good.'

'Hang on,' I said: 'Just listen for a moment.'

The only sound I could hear was the wind.

'Listen to what?' asked Jenny. 'I don't hear anything.'

'Neither do I,' said Withers.

'And me neither,' said Chris. 'What are we supposed to be listening to?'

'The silence,' I said. 'It's stopped. The howling has stopped.'

'Why – you're right!' Jenny exclaimed. 'Glorious silence!'

A door of the garden centre opened and out came Reggie. He put his hands on his hips and for a minute just stared at all of us. We must have looked a sight.

'Of course you don't hear anything,' he said. 'That infernal howling stopped a few minutes ago – when *that lot* turned up here.' He pointed toward the road.

There, just over the road, in a clearing in the woods, stood a newly arrived pack of turbs.

This new herd was smaller than the howling herd back at the main centre. They stood about a hundred metres from the garden centre. More, I could see, were partially concealed in the woods beyond. Most of them did not appear to be giants. They looked to be in the eighty to a hundred metre height range – older models dating back thirty years at least. Still, they would be fitted with smartchips.

What struck me as unusual was that a single, tall turb – much taller than the others – stood at the centre of the pack. It caught my attention not only because it was taller than the others, but also because it stood perfectly still, whilst almost all the others were bobbing up and down. Funny, but it looked to me as if they were *kow-towing* to the tallest turb in the pack.

The people living in the centre now approached the window, staring open mouthed at this new pack of turbs.

'I think we'd all better go inside,' I said.

'Agreed,' said Withers. 'Till we see what's what with these new turbs. Best for everyone to go inside the garden centre.'

'You won't need to tell me twice,' said Chris.

We shuffled into the centre, whose residents moved forward to help us, lightening loads and offering water.

Nessa and I took a drink of water gladly and then went to the window, to eye the new herd.

'Look at that tall one,' I said. 'See how it doesn't move but the smaller ones around it seem to be bowing to it.'

'I've never seen anything like that before,' she said.

'Do you agree now that turb packs seem to have natural leaders?' I asked. 'Like other animal species.'

'That one certainly looks like a leader,' Nessa allowed.

Just then the tall turb moved forward toward the garden centre.

'Are they going to attack us?' asked Withers.

'I don't think so,' I answered. 'Reggie, when they arrived, were they howling like the turbs over at the main centre?' I asked.

'No, they weren't,' he replied. 'Quiet as the grave, they've been.'

'I don't hear a thing,' I said.

'I can hear *something*,' said Jenny.

'It's like a ringing, isn't it?' said Reggie.

'No, no it isn't,' said another man. 'It's more like a humming. Like an air conditioning unit.'

'You're both wrong,' declared Chris, who came over to gaze at the new herd. 'I can hear a whooshing sound, like cars passing on a motorway.'

'I think it's more of a swishing sound,' Jenny put in. 'You hear that *ish, ish, ish.*'

'I would call it a whine – like an aeroplane's jet engine,' said someone else.

Withers turned toward me with a puzzled look.

'How can all these people describe the same noise differently?' he asked. 'I mean, if the turbs are making a noise – like the howling – it's got to be heard by everyone the same.'

'No, this is exactly the opposite of the howling.' I said. 'What we're sensing now is a vibration emitted by the turbs. No one hears it the same because each person's ear is different. It's infrasonic noise, that is to say, inaudible noise. It's at very nearly the lowest frequency that the human ear can hear. In the industry it's called "infrasound".'

'It's making me a little uncomfortable,' said Withers.

'Me, too,' said Jenny. 'I don't like it.'

'It's giving me a headache,' said Chris. 'What is it, Jack?'

151

'We think it's caused by the vibration of the turbs blades. It affects the eardrum and tiny hairs within the ear. Each person describes it differently because the impact of the vibration on the inner ear differs from person to person.'

'I've heard about this,' said Jenny. 'I saw something on television months ago. The manageress of an old folks' home in Humberside claimed all the residents had ringing in the ears after a turb forest was set up near them. Some of them got *tinnitus* – a permanent ringing in the ears.'

'What was that foreign word you used?' asked Withers.

'*Tinnitus*,' said Nessa. 'It's the Latin word for the medical condition known as ringing in the ears – but as Jack said, some people will hear a ringing, others will hear other sounds.'

'It's an ancient condition, said to have afflicted the Roman emperor Titus after he destroyed Jerusalem seventy years before the birth of Christ,' I added.

'So, it's not a real sound?' asked Chris. 'I can tell you the noise inside my head isn't my imagination! It's giving me a bleeding headache!'

'Headaches are one symptom of turb infrasound,' said Nessa. 'The infrasound also causes dizziness, anxiety, loss of balance, nausea, mood swings, palpitations, depression memory loss and a host of other harmful effects.'

'Blimey, 'said Withers. 'Do you two hear it as well? I mean, you're around these turbs all the time.'

'Our ears have been treated with special drops,' said Nessa. 'All wind engineers get them. Over time, we've built up a tolerance.'

'Built up a tolerance?' said Withers.

'Yes,' said Nessa. 'Unlike the howling of the blades, which is basically a loud noise attacking the ear, the effects of the vibration are more insidious and build up more slowly. The vibration attacks the outer hair cells of the cochlea – the part of the inner ear that enables you hear sound – sending neural signals to the brain. The more time you spend near vibrating turbs, the more damage results. So the industry has devised protective measures.'

'Why does it happen?' asked Chris.

'The vibration in a turb, like vibration in any mechanical device, can be caused by imbalances in the moving parts, such as uneven friction, meshing of the gear teeth and so forth – or, in the case of turbs, by the blades,' I answered. 'When the brakes are applied to the rotor so that the blades are unable to turn normally, they vibrate. The vibration is so slight that from ground level, you'd never be able to see them move.'

'Sorry, stupid question,' said Jenny. 'But why would the rotor brakes go on?'

'Oh, that's easy,' I replied. 'They shouldn't go on. The smartchips in the turbs should prevent that from happening.'

'But it is happening,' she said. 'And it's giving me a headache. So, if it shouldn't be happening, then why is it?'

'That's what we want to find out,' I said. I didn't think that answer would satisfy her – she was a smart woman with a keen sense of curiosity – and it didn't. She frowned and fell silent.

Among us, the effect of the vibrations began to intensify.

Reggie began moan, his hands clutched to his ears.

'Make it stop!' he cried. 'Make it stop, please!'

Chris began to hum a tune. It sounded like *God Save the King*.

'Chris, what are you doing?' I asked.

'Humming drowns out the whooshing sound in my ears,' he explained in a loud voice, though he was standing near me.

'No need to raise your voice,' I said. 'I can hear you.'

'Of course you can, sorry,' he said. 'It's this whooshing in my brain. Getting worse. Sure it's because of them turbs?'

'Quite certain,' I said.

Others began to show their discomfort. They remained silent but their faces assumed strange expressions, as though they'd tasted something that had gone off. Mouths twitched, eyes glassed with tears, and nervous tics appeared in cheeks and necks. Jaws slackened. Hands reached up to heads and fingers helplessly probed ears, too big to get inside. I could see I had to do something.

'Oh my God,' screamed Sally. 'They're coming, look!'

All eyes turned toward the new turb pack. The two-wheeled monsters were now moving swiftly toward the garden centre. Cold, sharp fear added to the disorienting inner ear torture, and people broke in panic.

'The tunnel!' I cried. 'Let's get back inside the tunnel! We'll be safe there.'

In an instant the villagers became a surging mass of humanity, with the elderly residents of the garden centre fast on their heels. It was surprising how nimble they could be, and strong, too. Withered arms showed impressive strength when their owners sensed a question of life or death. Frail legs acquired new strength. Slouching old men now stood bolt upright, casting their gaze ahead to the exit from the garden centre, intent on getting into the tunnel. The men proved stronger than the women, but with some notable exceptions. One old woman knocked a man flat out with an elbow across the side of the head.

Those at a disadvantage, those with canes or wheelie-walkers, were swept aside.

'So much for the politeness of the English,' Nessa commented.

13

UP, UP AND AWAY

'Come on, we've got to get up to the roof,' I said to Nessa as soon as we reached the main centre. ' We've got to see what's going on.'

We continued straight up from the tunnel, clambering up one flight and then two more, till we came to a locked door.

'Turb wrench, please,' I said, turning round. 'Fish it out of my rucksack, will you?'

In an instant I had the door open, and a gust of cold air greeted us.

'Bloody useful things, these turb wrenches,' I observed. 'Now, please, the field glasses – they're also in the rucksack somewhere.'

Nessa handed me the field glasses. I looked through them, and gave them back to her.

'Well, I've never –' I said without finishing the thought.

The turb herd laying siege to the Big World had doubled in size. They stood silent and motionless. The howling had definitely stopped. Whether the turbs near the garden centre were still emitting low frequency vibrations, we couldn't tell – they were too far way.

'They're are all around the shopping centre,' said Nessa. 'We're surrounded.'

'There are probably sieges like this taking place all around England,' I said.

'And in China and everywhere else in the world,' said Nessa.

'Jack, what's the solution to the problem?'

'We'll find out soon enough, when we join the others up north,' I said. 'In the meantime, the centre has to be defended. This many turbs are here for a reason and I can see only one reason – they're going to attack. I'm more convinced than ever that the howling and the vibrations were only a prelude.'

'We should get everyone into the cinema and explain to them again how to defend themselves,' I said. 'Everyone we can find.'

It took us the better part of an hour to walk through the centre, looking into the various departments, banging on doors, rooting out those still in the fitness centre and other refuges from the howling. Withers and Chris joined in, helping us to round up as many people as we could, urging them to come to the cinema straightaway.

'Settle down and listen to what Jack has to tell us,' said Withers, when they'd got there. 'Everyone, listen up!'

'I think the turbs are going to attack,' I announced, without any preliminaries. I glanced around to see the reaction. Some people looked surprised, while others were plainly sceptical. The younger ones looked ready for a fight.

I concentrated on self-defence: 'Stay inside the centre, but if you're caught out in the open, it's essential to stay within radius of the turbs' blades.'

'Try not to move or make noises,' I said. 'If the loudspeakers we set round the centre are working, stay away from them. Use fire if you can. Carry something sharp to cut the turbs' tyres if you get close to them. Be careful, because we haven't got much in the way of first aid. There's no doctor here.'

I finished and looked out over the audience. In the front row sat Jenny and her daughters Isadora and Rebecca. Near them sat a group of young men from the village, some of whose faces were familiar to me.

'Anyone have any questions?' I asked.

'Show us again how to cut the tyres,' said one of the lads.

'Can we climb inside them?' asked another. 'How could we do that?'

'Will they burn?' asked a third. 'I mean, can we use fire to set them alight?'

I answered the questions in turn, and there followed a brief silence. Finally Chris asked a last question.

'What are our chances if they all come at us?' he said.

'Well, that may depend on the circumstances,' I said.

'Come on, Jack, give us the truth.'

'All right, Chris,' I said. 'There's been no precedent of turbs attacking a building like this one. I don't know if it will happen, but I think it will. We'll be in difficulty if they drive their blades through the roof and it collapses, or if a fire starts – because we haven't the means to put one out.'

There were no other questions. People left the cinema. As far as I could tell, the mood was mixed: the younger ones were up for a fight, but the older people seemed apprehensive.

'Let's go back up to the roof,' I said to Nessa. 'Have another look round before Patel gets here.'

On the roof, I lit a cigarette as we surveyed the turbs. They were still motionless and silent, brooding, it seemed to me.

'Jack, when are you going to quit those things?' she asked.

I was about to answer – 'soon' – the same answer I always gave her on the subject of quitting smoking – when the whirr of a helicopter caused us to look up at the sky. We watched as it circled the shopping centre and then began to descend.

The chopper hovered ever closer, and then slowly put down on the roof of the centre, its rotor blades still turning. A door flung open and Patel leaned out.

'Your lift's here,' he shouted. 'Get aboard.'

We clambered into the helicopter.

'I'll explain things when we're underway,' Patel shouted through cupped hands as we climbed into the chopper. 'Belt up.'

'Patel,' I shouted back, 'I think the people here are in trouble. See all those turbs out there? They're not friendlies.'

Before he could answer, the chopper began to shake and the radio crackled with the pilot's voice.

'We're getting blown around,' he yelled.

'Bloody hell,' I said, looking out at the turbs.

The nearest turbs, which had been motionless only a moment before, had moved closer and then turned round so that we were in the wake of their blades – which began to spin faster and faster.

'Get airborne now!' I shouted.

'You heard the man,' said Patel into his mike. 'Get away.'

The chopper's rotor blades turned more quickly and the thing lifted off the roof, buffeted by the turbs' mast wake that made it shake like a baby's rattle. And then, with altitude, we were clear of the wake.

'We'll have a smoother ride now,' came the pilot's voice.

And we did. After a couple of hours flight, the helicopter came to land amid a large and strange base – a military base, it seemed – but strange, because it was full of huge, white domes that looked like giant golf balls.

I could see it was on high ground, so there was no flooding.

'Home sweet home,' smiled Patel.

'Where are we?' I shouted above the engines' roar.

'Near Harrogate, in Yorkshire. Welcome to the Texas of England!' he shouted back. 'This is RAF Fenwith Hill.'

I'd never heard of the place.

'Let's get you two sorted,' he said as we left the landing pad, 'I'll show you to your royal suite and then we'll get you something to eat.'

'We can do that later,' I said. 'If Phil Burnley is here, I'd like to see him straightaway.'

'I think he's in a meeting at the moment,' said Patel.

'We'll join the meeting then,' I said.

'All right,' said Patel.

He led us across the sprawling base, which seemed to consist broadly of two parts, one with buildings for offices and accommodation and one with those giant golf balls. In between the two parts of the base was a great field which served as the helicopter landing pad. The golf ball part of the base was even bigger than the residential part. This was where Patel was leading us.

'You'll be billeted over there,' he said as we walked.

I looked where he pointed and saw blocks of flats and small family bungalows. There were also shops, a bank and what looked like a cinema.

'Looks like you've got a small town here,' said Nessa.

'It is,' he replied. 'A small American town.'

We passed several people as we walked. From their accents I noticed they were all Americans.

'So it is,' I said. 'Lots of Yanks about.'

'Yes,' said Patel. 'They run the show here.'

As we walked I counted twenty eight golf balls, of all sizes.

'Aren't they for eavesdropping on people's phones?' I asked Patel.

He touched one of his ears.

'Yes,' he said. 'Listening in the broadest sense' – he touched an eye – 'they can read, too, e mails, text messages, tweets,' he laughed. 'Maybe they can smell as well.'

He led us into a building where a uniformed soldier behind a table took a DNA scan off my English National Identity Card and Nessa's Chinese passport.

At the end of the corridor he opened the door to a conference room full of people. I looked over the faces as we entered.

'Phil!' I cried. There sat Phil Burnley, my boss. I went over to him and we shook hands warmly. I noticed he was wearing military fatigues, which made his large frame seem larger. He looked jovial as ever.

'Hello, Jack. There's someone else you should say hello to,' he said, pushing back his chair.

'Frank!' I cried.

'In the flesh,' he said, grinning from ear to ear.

I reached out and embraced him.

'You both remember Nessa,' I said.

'Of course,' said Phil. 'Glad you didn't go home with the others in your delegation – we'll need your help.'

The man at the head of the conference table motioned for silence. He wore thick, black glasses that matched his black hair, which was touched by grey at the temples. He reminded me of a teacher I'd had at school.

'Gentlemen, please,' he said. 'Sir Philip, who's just joined us?'

'My best wind engineer, Jack Mason, and a colleague from China, Nessa Chao,' he replied.

'Welcome, glad you are here,' he said. 'For our newcomers, my name's Singh. I'm permanent secretary in the Home Office, or the National Security Department, as it's now called. Sir Philip, please continue with your description of the project.'

Phil was in the middle of a talk on the Thames Array project, its history, size and location, the number and type of turbs and so on. It was all information that I knew practically by heart.

'Thank you,' said the civil servant after Phil had finished. 'Now let's hear from Captain Wake of the Royal Navy on the current naval operations at the Thames Array.'

'Right,' said a naval officer, rising from his chair. He clicked a mouse and a map of the North Sea off the coast of Suffolk appeared on the wall.

'At the moment we're hitting the turbs with Spearfish here and here and here,' he said, using a laser pointer. 'But we're not getting the results we want.'

'Sorry,' I interrupted. 'What's a Spearfish?'

'Torpedo,' said Wake. 'The heaviest one we've got.'

'Can you just explain it a little,' said Singh. 'For our wind friends.'

'The Spearfish is launched from a submarine by a gas turbine engine and proceeds to the vicinity of its target by guide wire, then it does a "look round" as it were – it has a microprocessor that enables it to make autonomous tactical decisions – and then proceeds to the target by active sonar. The detonation is either by contact with the target or by proximity fuse. That's it in a nutshell,' the officer explained.

'So, what's not working?' asked the civil servant.

'We can sink sea turbs,' the officer replied. 'We've sunk quite a few. But as Sir Philip said, there are over twenty thousand turbs in this project alone and we haven't got twenty thousand Spearfish torpedoes. Budget cuts, you know.'

'They cost 80 million euros a piece,' another man put in. 'That's eight million pounds in old money. Sorry, I'm Jenkins, from the Treasury.'

'What about surface ships?' asked the civil servant.

'HMS Ocean's doing the bulk of the work,' replied Captain Wake. 'She's got a total of eighteen helicopters, twelve Sea Queens and six Manx. About two thirds of them are operational at any one time and they're giving it to the turbs with air-to-surface missiles. But sooner or later we'll run out of missiles.'

'Then there are the IUA's – ' he said. He paused and looked at me.

'That's "Indigenous Unmanned Aircraft",' he continued. 'They're the result of the Taranis programme launched some years ago. Drones, they used to be called. They're fired from frigates of the Type 26 Global Combat Ship class, HMS Demon, HMS Deadly and so on. But, again, we haven't got nearly enough of them.'

'Phil, what's all this about?' I whispered. 'They're shooting torpedoes and missiles at the offshore turbs?'

'The sea turbs have broken their tethers. They've been attacking our shipping, disrupting vital supplies to the few ports still functioning,' he explained.

'So that's the only answer they've found – blast the things out of the water?' I was incredulous.

'That's the military's way of dealing with things,' said Phil.

'Phil, can I say a word?' I asked.

'Be my guest. But it's not my meeting – it's his,' he said, gesturing toward the civil servant.

'Sorry, Mr Singh, may I speak?' I asked.

The civil servant gave Phil a questioning glance.

'All right,' he said. 'But please be brief. I want to wrap this up before the minister arrives.'

'It seems to me we've got to do more than blow up sea turbs.

First, we've got to identify which of them we think might be the leaders, and see what we can learn from them. Then we've got to figure out, if we can, how they exercise that leadership. We may be able to learn lessons that will help us with the land-based turbs.'

'The ultimate objective is to understand the deviation factor,' I said. 'And to do that, we will need to analyse turb smartchips and figure out why they're disobeying control.'

'I think we also have to analyse the plant life growing inside the turb heads,' Nessa put in. 'And, if we can, parts of the generator.'

'Why the generator?' asked the civil servant.

'I suspect the rare earth metal *neodymium* which is used in modern turb generators has an effect on the plants,' she said. 'I'm not yet sure how.'

The civil servant looked again at Phil.

'Sir Philip, do you support this?' he asked.

'Without reservation,' he answered.

'All right. How do you propose to go about this?' the civil servant asked me.

'I suggest we try to identify a leading sea turb, and then winch us down to it from a Royal Navy helicopter. Hopefully, it will be one fitted with a platform above the machine house at the back of its head. We'll put down on the platform and enter the turb's head via the hatch and extract its smartchip and bring it back for study.'

Singh remained silent for a moment.

'Is it technically feasible to winch your team down out of a helicopter onto a floating turb on the high seas? I mean, it's moving about, isn't it?' he asked.

'Yes, but it's feasible. It's a little dangerous of course, but it was a routine part of sea turb maintenance back before the flood,' said Phil.

'But there is one key difference in this situation,' he continued. 'During routine helicopter maintenance operations, the turb's rotor blades were always switched off. Here, we can't be sure the blades won't be turning. In fact, I'd say it's quite likely the turb will resist once it senses the helicopter.'

'I see,' said the civil servant. He seemed a little unsure what all that meant.

'Who would be in your team?' he asked me.

'We're sitting right here,' I said, gesturing to Nessa and Frank.

'Have you done this sort of thing before?' asked the civil servant.

'Dozens of times,' Nessa spoke up again. 'In the South China Sea.'

Singh seemed impressed.

'Still, it seems a little risky,' he said.

'I'd stake my life on it,' said Phil.

'It's rather their lives, isn't it?' observed the civil servant.

Then another man stood up. He wasn't wearing a uniform. He was wearing a plain, dark suit and tie, like Patel. He didn't introduce himself.

'A man from my department must oversee the operation,' he said.

Singh considered this for a moment.

'Any objection to a man from Mr Edwards-Knight's department?' he asked, looking at Phil and me.

'You're from Cobra, aren't you?' asked Phil.

'Yes,' said the man simply.

'Well, I certainly could not object to a representative from HM government going along with my engineers,' Phil replied. 'But operational control must be with my team. They know the turbs best.'

'Agreed,' said Singh. Edwards-Knight did not look pleased. He was scowling, and as he reached up to brush hair back off his forehead, I thought I saw a defiant nod which immediately disappeared into a hard smile. I looked him over. He was a few years older than me, obviously very fit, with a piercing pair of black eyes. I told myself I wouldn't want to pick a fight with him.

'Could we come back to your point about the turb leaders. How will you know which ones are the leaders?' Singh asked me.

'Sir, I know the Thames Array like the back of my hand,' I replied. 'Anything I don't know, Phil – I mean, Sir Philip – knows.

Anything he doesn't know, Frank here knows.'

'When could you move?' he asked.

'Fishburn, I'm with the Met Office,' a man wearing a bow tie broke in. 'Probably tomorrow, sir. The weather conditions should have improved by then.'

There came a knock at the door.

'Ah, that'll be the minister,' said Singh, the civil servant.

A man whose face I recognised entered the room with a couple of aides. He was grinning like a Cheshire cat. I stared at him for a moment and then it hit me: it was Toby Lang, the deputy prime minister!

'Good morning, ladies and gentlemen – got it all planned, have you?' he inquired brightly.

'Yes, minister,' replied the civil servant.

'Anything I need to know at this stage?' he asked.

'No, minister,' replied the civil servant.

'Well Singh, we've been working together long enough that you should know "yes" and "no" answers don't satisfy me. What have you approved?' said Lang.

The civil servant explained the mission.

'Who's running it?' asked Lang.

'That young man over there,' he replied, gesturing toward me. 'He's a protégé of Sir Philip Burnley.' Lang smiled and nodded at Phil, who rose from his chair.

I also stood up.

'What's your name?' Lang asked me.

'Jack Mason,' I replied. 'I run the Thames Array offshore wind project.'

He cast an eye over me and I at him. He wasn't tall – I was taller – and his youthful looks were belied by thinning dark hair. The trademark grin was fading as he regarded me.

'Think you're up for it, are you?' he asked. 'We're depending on you – you and your team.'

'My team are these wind engineers – Nessa Chao and Frank Cross,' I said, moving aside so he could see them.

Lang looked at Nessa and Frank. I could see his glance lingered slightly on Nessa.

'Ms Chao is from the Chinese Institute of Wind Science and Turbine Design,' I explained.

'Right then,' said Lang. 'Godspeed and good luck.' He turned to leave but then stopped and looked at me.

'I've got to say something to the English people about the turbs – the wind turbines, I mean,' he said. 'What would *you* suggest I say?'

'Tell people that fire drives turbs away and that noise attracts them. Tell them if they get close to a turb, to stay within the radius of the blades,' I replied. 'Tell them turbs are dangerous.'

'But why?' he asked. 'What's driving them?'

'That's what we're going to find out,' I said.

'We haven't got much time,' said Lang. 'What with the turbs breaking their tethers, we're getting less and less electricity from them, just when the flood is seriously disrupting imports of fuel. We've got to do something.'

With that, he turned and left the room.

*

The 'royal suite' promised by Patel turned out to be a small, low-ceilinged room with two single beds in a pre-fabricated building amid a host of other, identical pre-fabricated buildings. The first thing I did was push the beds together. Then I went and banged on Frank's door and told him to go and find us something to drink. He came to our room a little later.

'I got that spook Patel to get us this,' he said, smiling and holding out a bottle of whisky from the Isle of Skye. I told him if we're going to be winched onto an angry sea turb we'd need a little Dutch courage beforehand – not on the day, of course.'

'Patel seems all right,' I said. 'But that other one in the dark suit, who is he?'

'His name is Edwards-Knight – Phil calls him "EK." I got here a few days ago and Phil's been filling me in. He said EK's from GCHQ at Cheltenham, where the government are – he acts like he's running things,' said Frank. 'Phil warned me to be careful what I say around him.'

'It strikes me that Phil knows a lot about what's going on,' I said. 'Maybe more than he feels able to tell us.'

'I don't know,' said Frank. 'But I think those two don't like each other. I've been here a few days, and I've picked up on a few other things. Edwards-Knight is definitely interested in the rare earth *neodymium*.'

'Why didn't he say that at the meeting?' I asked.

'My guess – and it's just a guess – is that not everyone in that room was cleared to know that,' said Frank, adding: 'Everything around here seems to be about "clearance".'

I didn't have any answer to that.

'Frank, all these government types and military men – what do *they* say about the deviation factor, about what's making the turbs hostile?' I asked.

'That's a good question,' said Frank. 'And the answer is, I don't think they know any more than we do. At least, that's my assumption. No one has told me in so many words what the government know or think.'

'Didn't they ask you about your opinion? After all, you're a wind engineer,' I said.

'No, no one here has been interested,' he replied.

Just then Nessa came into the room from the bath, a towel piled on top of her head. She gave me a big kiss.

'We've already got two turb smartchips – we took them off turbs near Jack's house,' she said, drying her hair.

'Have you found anything?' Frank asked.

'Not yet,' I said. 'You know I'm no computer whiz. We've actually got one working on them though. Well, a young one – he's thirteen.'

'Doesn't sound very encouraging,' said Frank.

'You never know,' I replied. 'He's a very bright kid.'

We all relaxed and our party, such as it was, gained wings. Even Nessa took a sip of whisky.

In the morning, we had a brief meeting with Phil and some men working for Edwards-Knight.

'This'll be easy for a pair of blokes as experienced as you,' said Phil.

'Then why don't you try it, Phil?' said Frank.

He patted his ample mid-section.

'Love to, but I'm just not as fit as I used to be,' he laughed.

Edwards-Knight's men confirmed what Frank had surmised, that they wanted a piece of *neodymium* from the turb's generator, as well as the turb's smartchip.

'All in all, it's an easily do-able mission,' explained one of the men. He said his name was Lloyd and he would be coming along 'for the ride.'

The day had dawned grey and dull and cold. Frank, Nessa and I clambered into the chopper – it was a Manx Mk16, the principal all-round reconnaissance, transport and combat helicopter in English service.

We flew south to an RAF base in Norfolk, re-fuelled and then took off again, heading out over the North Sea. After what seemed an eternity, the pilot came on and said, 'There they are, look out the right side.'

There they were – the thousands of sea turbs in the Thames Array.

The pilot brought the chopper down to an altitude of what seemed to me to be about four or five hundred meters, still well above the turbs. There was no small talk among us. We stared at the turb pack. It had started to rain heavily, obscuring the view.

'There she is,' the pilot announced. 'On the right side, about four o'clock.'

It was a gigantic turb, really a monster by any standards – the tallest in the pack. It stood, or floated, two hundred and twenty meters above the waves. Sure enough, it was fitted with a platform above the machine house at the back of its head.

'That is turb number two-six-six-zero,' crackled the pilot's voice. 'Is that the one you want? Do you check?'

'Check,' I said. 'That's our girl.'

We dropped to about two dozen meters above the turb's head. I could see its blades were still.

The navy winch man threw open the helicopter door.

'Right, then,' he said. 'Who's first?'

Frank won a coin toss and slid forward into the winch bucket. The winch man pulled the straps tight under his arms and fastened the hook to the cable above his head. In a flash he was out of the chopper, floating downwards.

He landed on the platform, undid the hook and waved to us. Next went Nessa and then Lloyd, both landing safely.

The pilot's voice crackled.

'This turb's starting to spin.' he said. 'We're getting blown around by the wake. Get the last man off fast.'

So intent was I on the winching that I hadn't noticed that the turbs' blades had begun to turn. I felt sure this was no coincidence. The turb had sensed us.

The blades spun faster and faster with a *whooshing* sound, and the helicopter was shaking.

The winch man grabbed me by the shoulders and shoved me into the harness.

'Off you go,' he said, sliding me out the door.

For a few seconds I floated down like the others. Below I could see Frank and Nessa waving me down. Lloyd crouched on the platform.

But the wake of the rotating blades was pushing me back, away from the platform – I was over the sea. I looked up and saw that the helicopter was now far above me – the pilot was gaining altitude to get above the turb and out of its wake, and in the process he let out the cable holding me as far as it would go.

Now the chopper flew forward, out in front of the turb, pulling me over the platform. I felt a jerk as the winch cable became taut with the force of the turb's wake. Frank and Nessa were just below me now, grabbing at my ankles. They got one ankle, then the other.

'Release the cable!' Frank shouted.

I fumbled with the thing, trying to grab the lever.

'Let go of the cable!' Frank shouted again.

At that moment one of the turb's blades must have cut the cable, for I suddenly went flying backwards.

My backside hit the platform railing and I reeled over it. Were it not for Frank and Nessa holding fast to my ankles, I would have gone straight over the railing. As it was, I was left hanging upside down, with the underside of my knees wrapped over it, gazing at the churning sea far below.

'Pull me up, quick!' I yelled.

Frank grabbed the straps across my chest and began to pull. I felt Nessa take hold of my arm. Together they heaved me up, and we all fell onto the platform in a pile.

'Are you all right?' Nessa shouted.

'Fine,' I said.

'What do we do now?' Lloyd yelled, crouching nearby.

'We – what the hell – ?' I said as the platform suddenly began to tilt. The tilt grew to a sharp angle, and the three of us slid across the wet surface bang against the opposite railing. Lloyd slid into us.

'It's trying to throw us off!' Frank shouted.

The whooshing of the blades made it almost impossible to hear each other.

'We'll use the hooks to get to the hatch,' I shouted, pointing at some metal hooks in the platform, used for securing cables to lower heavy machinery.

The turb lurched again in the opposite direction and we slid with it, but I managed to grab one of the hooks and Nessa and Frank held fast to my legs. I couldn't see Lloyd, but then the turb angled again and he came crashing into us. My grip on the hook held. I extended my arm and reached for one hook and then another. In this way we moved across the rain swept platform to the hatch.

'Nessa, turb wrench!' I shouted. She crawled onto my back, undid my rucksack and handed me the tool.

'Got it,' I shouted. 'Keep hold of my legs, both of you.'

I wedged the tool into the hatch and pried it open. Once free, it was caught by the wind and flew across the platform and over the side.

'Nessa, you first!'

She turned and lowered herself into the turb's head. Then Frank followed.

'Lloyd!' I shouted. He was holding fast to one of the metal hooks. 'Get over here. You've got to get in there now.'

He gave me a hesitant look but began moving toward the hatch.

'In!' I repeated.

He turned and lowered himself into the turb's head. I clambered along after him. We were all soaking wet.

'Ugh!' was the first thing Lloyd said once inside. 'It stinks in here.'

'Watch out for those plants, Lloyd – those bulbs,' said Nessa. 'They bite.'

'My God they're ugly,' he said. 'Agh – one of them bit me!'

I went to Lloyd and looked at his wound. Blood oozed from his calf. A fragment of the plant's 'tooth' was stuck in the wound and I pulled it out. Then I tied my scarf around the wound to stem the bleeding.

'All right, Lloyd, favour that leg. You'll be stitched up back at the base,' I said. 'Right, then – the smartchip from the controller, a piece of metal from the generator and some plant samples. Frank, help me with the first two. Nessa, the plants are yours. Let's get to work.'

Suddenly the turb angled again and we were all thrown against the wall.

'Everyone all right?' I shouted.

'Listen, you bloody wind engineers, we may die here,' Lloyd yelled back. 'Because the chopper won't come back with the turb blades spinning and this thing swinging this way and that. It won't be able to pick us up.'

'Just wait, my friend,' said Frank. 'When we've removed the smartchip, the turb will be disabled – the blades will stop turning and the beast will just float on the ocean waves.'

Lloyd did not look convinced.

Frank and I moved slowly toward the rear of the turb's head, gripping anything we could with our thick turb gloves.

We eased our way back behind the generator at the rear of the turb's head. We found the smartchip soon enough because we knew exactly where to look – in the control panel above the generator. Using a control box key I removed it and shoved it into my rucksack.

But the turb went right on swaying. Its violent motion continued for another few minutes. Frank and I looked at each other in the darkness, waiting, holding fast to any pipe or hook we could grab. Then the swaying gradually slowed, and assumed a natural motion with the waves.

'She's out cold,' said Frank.

'The generator,' I said. 'We need a piece of the generator.'

A metre in diameter, it was located just below the control box. It wasn't new and the combination of plant growth and sea air had exposed many cracks in the casing.

I unsheathed a hammer and pick axe from my rucksack and began to hacking away at a large cracked piece of the casing. It soon came away. Under the casing was the rare earth *neodymium*. It shimmered in the dim light with a kind of light greenish hue. It was also full of cracks. I hacked away again and a large chunk came loose.

'Put it in your rucksack,' I said to Frank. 'And be careful with it.'

In the meantime Nessa was scurrying round the turb head with a sharp knife. She soon gathered up dozens of the plant bulbs and put them in a thick plastic bag which she shoved into her rucksack.

'OK,' said Nessa. 'I'm good to go.'

The turb was now swaying only slightly with the motion of the sea. We climbed out of the head onto the platform as Lloyd barked into his radio. Soon the chopper appeared overhead and a winch cable came down.

'First Nessa,' I said. She hooked herself to the cable and disappeared into the sky, waving as she reached the helicopter. The winch came down again.

'Now you,' I said to Lloyd, and he hooked the cable to the straps across his chest. He was standing quite close to Frank but he favoured his wounded leg with a hand on Frank's shoulder. As the cable lifted him I saw Frank being pulled toward Lloyd.

'Well fuck me − !' I heard Frank shout.

I looked up. Frank's rucksack was glued to Lloyd as they both flew upwards.

'It's the magnet' I shouted. 'The *neodymium* is a magnet! Have you got any metal on you?'

'Just my weapon,' Lloyd cried, pulling at his waist.

'No, don't pull it out!' I yelled.

But he did, with great effort, struggling against the pull of the magnet in Frank's rucksack, and when he'd got his pistol in his hand and tried to swing it free, Frank grabbed the gun, smashing his fingers between the weapon and the magnet.

There was nothing left to hold him to Lloyd except his smashed fingers, and they soon slipped out from between the magnet and the gun, and Frank fell into the sea, two hundred meters below.

I watched in horror.

'Frank's gone,' I said to myself. 'I lost my best friend.'

My first impulse was to jump after him − but I knew that would kill us both − and then the winch cable dropped in front of my eyes. I grabbed it and hooked it to my straps.

14

WAR OF THE WORLDS

I was mad with grief and shock and for a while I didn't speak. I just couldn't. I stared out the window of the chopper. Then anger took hold of me – red hot anger. I was angry at fate, Frank's fate. It shouldn't have been. For a thousand reasons, it shouldn't have been.

I focused my anger on Lloyd. It was his fault, I told myself. He let go of my friend. But why? Was it only a mistake? It was, of course it was. I found it hard to accept that, yet I couldn't see anything more in it, and there wasn't anything more in it to see. Lloyd let go. He should have held Frank but he let him go.

I stared sullenly at the back of Lloyd's head. Once he turned around and our eyes met. He looked as if he was about to say something, but didn't. His lips parted but no words came out.

I didn't have any words either. At least, for a while. Then I did. I let loose a torrent of accusations against him. At first he made no reply.

'I'm sorry,' he said after a pause in my shouting.

I wanted to say that wasn't good enough, but I stopped myself. I leaned back in my seat and went numb.

Then I cried quietly and Nessa held my head in her arms.

The chopper landed at Fenwith Hill.

I spotted Phil among those waiting for us on the tarmac. He was in a knot of men, and among them I recognised the civil servant, Singh, and Wake, the Royal Navy captain.

Phil came forward as we crouched, our heads beneath the helicopter blades.

'You two look all right,' he said by way of greeting, obviously relieved. 'Jack, I'm sorry about Frank.'

'Phil, I can't speak about it just yet,' I said. 'Give me a little time.'

'Sure,' he said.

'Glad you're back safe and sound,' said Singh. 'I'm sorry about your colleague.'

'Thank you,' I muttered.

'We've a guest who's just arrived,' he continued. 'This is Mr Chuck Wayne, one of our American cousins. He's been sent here by his government so that we can co-ordinate our efforts on wind energy problems.'

Standing next to Singh was a hugely obese man with a big, friendly smile on his face. He laughed.

'That's British understatement for you,' he chuckled. 'What my friend meant was, we're going to pool our efforts to understand why turbs are breaking their tethers and running around like scared herds of longhorn cattle!'

'I'm glad to meet you,' he beamed, pumping first my hand and then Nessa's.

'Where are you from?' he asked her.

'I'm a senior wind engineer from the Chinese Institute of Wind Science and Turbine Design,' she replied. 'Our delegation is, or rather was, visiting the English energy department, till the flood came.'

'I'm very impressed,' said the American.

An army officer standing nearby stepped forward.

'We'll take those bags,' he said, gestured to the rucksacks containing the turb plant samples and the chunk of *neodymium*.

'Actually, I'd rather keep them for the moment,' I said. 'I want to talk over with Phil here what we're going to do with them.' I glanced at Singh.

'That's all right, Major Brooke. Leave them with Sir Philip's team for the time being,' he said.

The army officer did not look pleased, and I thought I saw the shadow of a frown cross Chuck Wayne's smiling face. He turned toward Singh and I used the chance to look at him more closely. He was tall, which made his weight appear less noticeable, with a fleshy face and thick black hair that receded and greyed at the temples. He wore a kind of jogging suit with a big, round emblem over his heart that read 'National Security Agency of the United States of America.'

'I'm bushed from the flight,' he was saying to Singh. 'I'd like to rest a bit and then we can chew the cud.'

Just then a black SUV with dark windows pulled up and out sprang Edwards-Knight. He was in a rage.

'Lloyd, you dropped a man into the sea?' he shouted.

Lloyd stepped forward.

'Yes,' he said. 'I couldn't hold him. I'm sorry.'

'You'd damn well better explain exactly what happened,' he said. 'Let's go.'

He practically grabbed Lloyd by the collar and walked him back to the SUV, puling open the door. Lloyd dutifully climbed in.

'Just a minute, Edwards-Knight,' I said. 'The man who died was my friend. I didn't see exactly what happened, but I don't think – I don't think it was anything more than an accident.'

Edwards-Knight stared at me.

'He might have dropped the samples you brought,' he said, obviously livid. 'That would have been much more serious.'

That left me speechless. What kind of man was he?

'Jack, it's their de-briefing,' said Phil. 'It doesn't concern us.' He took me by the shoulder and Nessa took my arm.

'You two get some rest,' he said. 'Then I've got something to show you.'

A jeep brought us to the pre-fab building which served as our hotel. I held Nessa in my arms and we fell asleep, for I don't know how long, before Phil knocked at our door.

'Let's take a walk, the three of us,' he said, 'and have a little chat. It's safer to speak outside, but in a place like this, you never know for sure.'

'Take this' – he handed me a single sheet of paper – 'and you two read it as we walk. Some of it might be familiar to you.'

As we walked, I held the paper so that Nessa could read it along with me.

'Briefing Memo – Neodymium' was the title. It was not addressed to anyone and there was no information about who wrote it or why. Above the title the words *'COBRA LEVEL CLEARANCE'* appeared in red capital letters.

The text was as follows:

The rare earth neodymium (symbol Nd, atomic number 60) was discovered in 1885 by an Austrian scientist named von Welsbach. He called it neodymium after the Greek words for neos (new) and didymos (twins) because it was combined with another element.

Although classed as one of the rare earths, neodymium is widely dispersed in the earth's crust but in very small quantities and never freely – it is always found combined together with other elements and therefore must be separated in a costly and environmentally hazardous process.

The metal was first produced in its pure form in 1925.

Neodymium is the strongest magnet known, with only a few grams capable of attracting metal hundreds of times its own weight.

Its strength as a magnet accounts for its use in wind turbine generators. This is due to the single rotor shaft innovation in turbine design – a shaft turned by the wind at slow revolutions needs a strong magnetiser, stronger than traditional copper coils, to generate electricity more efficiently.

Historically, the largest deposits of neodymium have been found in northern China.

When direct-drive generators using neodymium were first introduced into wind turbines decades ago, the price of the metal spiked – and then slumped – and there were many concerns at the time – about Chinese domination of the market, about pollution from dirty Chinese mining practices and about whether our planet contained enough of the metal to fuel the wind energy revolution.

All these worries passed. New sources of the metal were found on other continents and mining practices were improved. The supply of neodymium became steady.

Apart from its strength as a magnet, neodymium has other uses.

In the form of glass slabs, neodymium is used to catalyse the smashing of atoms ('inertial confinement fusion') in huge tunnels specially created for that purpose, in order to unleash nuclear energy.

Neodymium also stimulates plant growth, and is well known as a concentrate in fertiliser.

Neodymium also reacts with light, both sunlight and moonlight in ways that are not yet fully understood. It's thought that this may influence plant growth.

The unintended result of the presence of neodymium in wind turbine generators has been to greatly accelerate the growth of plant life inside the turbines. It is suggested that this phenomenon is widespread in the wind turbine population.

There the memo ended.

Phil was right – some of this was familiar to me, as it would be to anyone who maintained wind turbines with permanent magnet generators containing the metal, that is to say, almost anyone in the industry. But some of it was new to me. All in all, the memo was written for a purpose that was unclear to me.

'I suppose I shouldn't ask you where you got this,' I said, as Phil shook his head. 'Nessa, what do you think?'

'It strikes me that whoever wrote this Memo doesn't have all the pieces of the puzzle,' she replied.

'What do you mean?' asked Phil.

'Well, what's missing is the relation, if any, between all this information about *neodymium* and its stimulation of plant growth, on the one hand, and the "deviation factor" on the other,' she said. 'The memo doesn't explain how it all connects.'

'Nessa, you're a smart girl,' Phil said. 'But then I reckon you'd have to be to get Jack.'

'See? He's blushing,' he laughed.

'Phil, I wasn't blushing, I just turned red briefly,' I said. 'But you're not too far off the mark. She is smart.' I pecked her on the cheek.

'So, what's going to happen with this chuck of *neodymium?*'

I asked.

He stopped and bent down to tie his shoelaces, first one, then the other.

'Try to keep your heads down when you speak,' he said. 'The cameras' – he nodded upwards at the CCTV cameras on every building we passed – 'they can read your lips.'

That was the second time Phil had referred to surveillance. I wondered what or who he was worried about eavesdropping on us – it was an RAF base after all. But I didn't say anything.

'The metal would normally go to the Atomic Weapons Establishment at Aldermaston,' he said into his shoelaces. 'But I'm not sure what will happen. Singh or his boss, Toby Lang, may order it to be analysed somewhere else in England or that American Wayne may get our government to give it to him.'

'Either way,' Phil continued, still tying a shoelace, 'we won't be involved – and I'd like it to be otherwise – I'd like to remain close to this investigation.'

'What about the plant samples we took from the sea turb?' Nessa asked.

'There used to be something called the Imperial Forestry Institute,' he said. 'It collected plants from all over the British Empire, which is to say, a large part of our planet. The institute was incorporated into Oxford University after the end of the empire.'

'Nessa, I want you to take the plant samples there, and work with one of their experts,' he said. 'Maybe you can discover something.'

'Phil,' I said, 'we've just come from Oxfordshire. The situation isn't good there. Near my village, the rivers have burst their banks. It's lawless – there are bandit gangs. And the turbs have been acting strangely, aggressively – they've laid siege to a local shopping centre where the villagers have taken refuge.'

'None of that surprises me,' said Phil, lowering the memo from his face. 'Still, Nessa should go to the Department of Plant Sciences in Oxford. She should see a man named Gordon. Professor Gordon.'

'Phil, I haven't been into Oxford town, but a traveller told us it's chaos there – university buildings burnt, gunfire,' I said. 'I don't want Nessa to go there.'

He raised the memo to his lips.

'Then you go with her. My information is different,' he said. 'Plant Sciences is in South Parks Road, Oxford, and they're still working, despite everything. I've told Gordon you'll be coming. Take the plant samples there.'

'All right,' I said. 'I trust you, Phil. If that's what you say, we'll do it.'

'What about the smartchip we took from the sea turb?' I added. 'Shall I take it with me to Oxfordshire?' I said, though I was still unsure whether young David would be able to crack the software code.

'Oh, that,' said Phil. 'You know me, I'm not so tech-savvy. For the time being, fine. Perhaps later we'll give it to Wayne so he'll feel he got something valuable from us. What do you think?'

'I think that's fine,' I said.

'That's settled then,' said Phil. 'You can take one of the training helicopters from the base. You still remember how to fly one, don't you?'

'Yeah, I remember,' I said.

'Good,' he said. 'I've arranged for a service in Frank's memory. Maybe you'd like to stay for that.'

'Of course,' I said. 'Phil, what's your explanation for the deviation factor?'

'Same as yours – I don't have one yet,' he said. 'Look, I think it's worthwhile trying to learn something from the plants, and to look at the metal. But I'll tell you my hunch: the deviation factor has nothing to do with either of them. I think the turb smartchips have been hacked.'

'What do the government think?' I asked.

Phil sighed.

'It's hard to say what HM government think,' he said. 'It's not an animal with a single brain. It's an animal with lots of brains, each with its own ideas, and lots of egos to match. Jack, give up the idea that the government are any smarter than you.'

*

We went back to our room to wait for Frank's service. As I stood
by the window smoking a cigarette, I saw tanks and artillery at the
far end of the great field. I had noticed them there the day before,
but I ascribed no importance to it because, after all, we were on a
military base.

Later Patel appeared and led us to an army jeep, which drove us
across the great field to the part of the base where most of the golf
balls were clustered.

Then he ushered us into a pre-fab building that might have
been the same one as the conference a day before. Or a different
one – they all looked the same. En route I noticed more tanks and
armoured vehicles ringed around the golf balls.

The service for Frank did not last long. The civil servant introduced Phil, who by his standards was very brief. Then he invited
me to say something and I did, with difficulty. It was all too fresh.
Toby Lang, who appeared toward the end, accompanied by Chuck
Wayne, added 'a word of heartfelt praise for our young wind engineers.'

Just as the service was ending and people began filing out, an
army officer motioned for silence.

'I should like to mention that the defensive measures here at the
base, which many of you must have noticed, have been authorised
by Mr Lang because of increased turb presence in our vicinity. A
herd are coming down out of the Yorkshire Dales from the west,
and there's another lot coming from the east, near Knaresborough.
Just carry on as normal.'

I turned and nearly bumped into Wayne.

'I'm sorry about your colleague,' he said. 'He was a friend, too,
wasn't he? That's what they tell me.'

'Yes, he was,' I replied. 'I'm going to miss him.'

'Jack – it's Jack, isn't it? – I'd like to ask you a question,' he said.

Without waiting for a reply, he went on: 'What's causing the turbs to run loose? I'd like to hear your view.'

'Well, Mr Wayne, it's a long story,' I said. 'But it's also a short one: I don't know yet.'

'Do you think the turb computer networks in England have been hacked by a foreign government or terrorists?'

'I'm not a computer expert. I'm a wind engineer,' I replied.

'Oh, I know that,' he said. 'And a damn good one, I hear, the best England's got.'

'Thank you, Mr Wayne,' I said.

'Call me Chuck,' he said, with a friendly smile.

Before I could say anything else, a boom of artillery sounded, and then another, causing the walls of the flimsy, pre-fab building to shudder.

'That would be our guns,' shouted the army officer who'd spoken before. 'There must be some turbs nearing the base. As I said, keep calm and carry on.'

'Sound attracts them,' I said. 'It would be better not fire any more guns.'

'You may be right about that,' said Wayne. 'It fits with our observations.'

There was another artillery burst.

'Our experience in the USA,' said Mr Wayne, ignoring the noise, 'also suggests that fire is an effective method for deterring the turbs.'

I looked at Wayne with interest. Almost everyone had filed out of the room and I glanced around for Nessa. I wanted to find her, but at the same time, Wayne had caught my attention.

'We've noticed the same thing,' I said.

'Looks like we've got something in common,' he said, resting an arm on my shoulder.

'But, Jack, if the turb computers have been hacked,' he went on, 'we haven't been able to figure out how – we've taken some chips, like you, and we're studying them, but we're still not there. We haven't got all the pieces of the puzzle.'

'Thanks for your time,' he added abruptly, and moved in the direction of Lang, who was just leaving the room. I followed him out. In the packed corridor, there were a number of people milling about, evidently reluctant to go outside where the guns were firing. Nessa waved to me.

'I've found something,' she called out. 'Follow me.'

I turned and saw the American talking to Lang. He beckoned to the American to follow him and they both disappeared along a corridor.

Nessa grabbed my shoulder.

'Let's go downstairs till this noise stops,' she said. 'There seems to be a maze of tunnels that connects all these buildings. We'll be safer there.'

I followed her down some stairs and turned into one corridor and then another. There were lights – the base surely had its own power supply – but they began to flicker.

'Where, Nessa, where are we going?' I asked.

'A left and then a right,' she said, as if to herself.

'There, there it is!'

She led me into a chamber and toggled the light switch. The lights came on, dimly, but enough to see that there was everything there needed to survive for some time – beds, blankets, tinned food, bottled water, kerosene lamps, matches and God knows what else.

'Nessa, how did you find this place?' I asked.

'I looked,' she replied.

'Glad you did,' I said.

We sat down on one of the beds.

'They all think the turb computer networks have been hacked,' I said. 'They think that explains the deviation factor.'

'Who thinks that?' she asked.

'Well, Phil, you heard him say so, and that American agent Wayne. He told me so just now – well, not in so many words but his meaning was clear,' I said.

'Well, they might be right,' she said.

'Possibly they are, but I don't think so,' I said. 'How long are we going to stay down here?'

'I found another way out,' said Nessa, pointing to sliding doors on one side of the chamber. She pulled them open, to reveal rungs in one wall leading up to a hatch in the ceiling.

'I think we can go out this way,' she said.

The hatch opened to reveal another set of rungs, this time leading up much higher than the height of the underground chamber, ending in another hatch. We climbed.

As we opened the second hatch I could see at once we were inside one of the golf balls. The cavernous space was in the shape of a dome, with a white covering that looked it was made of plastic panels or an enormous tarpaulin. In the centre a satellite dish with a diameter of at least twenty meters was fixed to the floor, with many cables running off it.

There came the sound of footsteps and voices. The footsteps were coming our way.

'We're pretty much sure our turbs' computer networks have been hacked, yours, too. But the thing with hacking is, the footprint is very hard to see. It could be the usual low-level cyber warfare with China or Russia – or both – or it could be non-state actors.'

'The debate is over how to respond. One approach is simply to remove the threat by destroying the turbs. For this approach to succeed, we would need a weapon that could be applied on a large scale. And we've got an idea – to use the *neodymium* inside the turbs to nuke them. In other words, to create atomic fusion internally in the turb heads, in the same way *neodymium* is used in an atom smasher. We'd simply blow them to smithereens! But we'd have to deal with the issue of radioactive fallout. We're still working on that one.'

'As we speak, we're working on a laser device that can bombard a turb head with atoms. Apart from the physics-related requirements, it has to be a weapon that an ordinary solder can use – hand-held or shoulder-mounted, like a WW2 bazooka. That kind of weapon could be at beta stage within a short time.'

As the men neared, Nessa and I recognised the speaker's voice – it was Wayne.

'But there's another approach – to set off atomic fusion in millions of individual turb heads without bombarding each one separately. That's something we're still working on at the theoretical level, and it may take a year to get there,' Wayne continued.

Whoever he was speaking with said something we couldn't make out.

'Oh, yes, of course,' said Wayne. 'That's another option – we call it the "special option" – a combination of the weaponry and the strategy.'

'But that's what we call a *po-liti-cul* question with a great, big *P*,' he drawled. 'It would deal with the turb problem, and it also would send an effective message to China and Russia to cease their cyber attacks against us.'

Again the other man said something we couldn't hear.

'Well, yes, it presents some of the same technical challenges,' said Wayne. 'But with the additional challenge that we would have to somehow blow up all them turbs in China and Russia and let them worry about the radioactive fallout, keeping it away from Merry Olde England, of course. '

He chuckled.

'I can tell you, God's honest truth, plain as I'm standing here, that the "special option" was discussed at the highest level last week. Yours truly was present,' said Wayne in reply to some other remark we couldn't hear.

'That's right,' he continued. 'The president holds his cards close to his chest, but I think – and I'm not alone – he can't wait to let the turbzilla nukes loose on the Chinese and the Russians. In fact he even calls them "turbzillas" in private.

'What's that?' said Wayne. 'Well, we'll use as a reason our evidence of their plans to do the same to us.'

'Will you be able to produce evidence?' asked the other man. All at once I recognised the voice – it was Toby Lang!

'Of course,' Wayne said. 'We'll have evidence of "turbs of mass destruction". We can supply some to you.' He chuckled again.

'Lang!' I whispered. 'Why would a bloke like him be listening to such crazy ideas?'

'Maybe he doesn't think they're crazy,' Nessa whispered back.

'Chuck, as I see it, England hasn't any alternative to following the American lead on this,' said Lang. 'I want you to convey my thinking to the president. I'm not sure the prime minister sees it as I do, but I'm not alone in the cabinet and there may be a change at the top. Sooner rather than later.'

'I thought you'd see it our way,' said Wayne. 'That's what our intelligence said.'

'What do you mean by that?' Lang asked sharply. 'Have you been spying on your friends?'

'Toby, don't be naïve,' said Wayne.

Just then I moved my leg and a piece of metal fell with a clang.

'What was that?' said Wayne. 'There's someone else here.'

'It came from over there,' said Lang.

Footsteps in the huge dome echoed in our direction.

'Back down the hatch,' I said. 'Nessa, you first.'

'No! You first!' she said, not budging.

'Nessa, down, now!' I said, and she moved, grudgingly, disappearing through the hatch. The footsteps drew nearer. It was now too late for me to go down the hatch. Hiding myself among the spider's web of struts and poles under the satellite dish, at the level of a man's head, I caught sight of the American's pudgy fingers stuffed into the trigger of a very nasty looking weapon.

'I don't see anyone,' said Wayne. 'Probably it was just something that was shaken loose during all that artillery fire.'

He peered again into the spider's web where I was hiding.

'Well, I guess we should be on our way,' he said to Lang. They turned, and their footsteps receded.

I waited a long while, perhaps half an hour. There was silence in the dome. Then I moved from my hiding place as quietly I could, careful with each step, watching my head didn't bang against any of the poles or struts.

I found the hatch and climbed down.

Nessa was waiting in the room below.

'Could you believe what that American was saying?' I exclaimed. 'It's madness!'

'Lang doesn't think so,' she replied curtly.

'Whatever he thinks, we've got work to do at the Plant Sciences department at Oxford,' I said. 'So, let's go borrow a helicopter.'

15

NO PLACE LIKE HOME

The artillery fire had, thankfully, ceased, but we saw at once that a whole herd of turbs still ringed the part of the base where we were, some quite close to the great field. They bobbed gently with the wind.

On the field stood a half dozen helicopters. Some were in no condition to fly – they'd been smashed by the turbs' wheels or sliced by the turbs' blades. But the smallest one, the one Phil had mentioned – a two-seater training helicopter – looked serviceable.

Broken glass and bits of metal littered the tarmac where the turbs had roamed.

'Are you sure you know how to fly one of these things?' asked Nessa.

'If I can fly any of them, I can fly this one,' I replied.

We climbed in and I scanned the gauges. I hated the gauges. I didn't understand what more than a few of them were for, and I hated the distraction of watching them. No wonder I'd never got a pilot's licence.

But I had enough flying hours under my belt on offshore turb maintenance details – albeit, as a passenger – to know what was important.

'Stick, collective, pedals,' I said to myself.

I pushed the start button and after a second the main rotor began turning.

'That's a good sign,' I said. 'The battery is charged, fully charged,' I added, spotting the right gauge. The trainer was a solar battery-powered model, but I had no idea how much flying time a full battery would give us.

The main rotor was turning steadily now.

'Put on your seat belt,' I said.

I pulled the collective up gently, and the bird lifted off the ground. I pulled with more effort and the bird began to rise, straight up into the sky.

'Oh, Jack, look!' Nessa screamed.

She'd seen the turb first. It was lunging directly at us, tilting at a sharp angle, its blades whizzing. Out of the corner of my eye I saw a second one, coming at us from the opposite direction. If we remained where we were, the two would slice us to bits from two sides.

'The helicopter's noise attracted them,' I shouted, my mind racing. I had an idea.

Turbs aren't very fast, I knew – I had a little time. I depressed my left foot on the left pedal, turning the chopper toward the first one. Then the right foot on the right pedal, to face the second one. Back and forth, keeping them in view. All the time gently pulling the collective to bring us higher, up to the level of the turb heads.

'I'll give these turbs ten seconds,' I said to myself. 'Nine, eight, seven…'.

Nessa sat glued to her seat.

'Jack, what are you doing? Fly away – get away from here!' she cried.

'Six, five, four, three, two,' I counted.

The whirling blades of the fast approaching turbs began to violently shake the helicopter.

With one second remaining, I yanked the collective as hard as I could and pulled the stick toward me. The chopper shot upwards at a steep angle.

Where we'd been an instant before, the two turbs smashed into each other with a tremendous crash. Blade struck blade, head hit head, and they seemed to lock horns like charging bulls. The force of the impact shook the earth below.

They turned, like a couple dancing, their enmeshed, grinding blades like the couple's arms.

'Too much stick,' I yelled. 'We're stalling!'

'Jack, we're going down,' Nessa said.

Our chopper began to fall into the battling turb blades.

'Anti-stall, anti-stall,' I thought. 'How to get out of a stall?'

I pushed the stick forward trying point the front of the chopper down, at the same time pulling the collective up to maintain altitude.

Still, the chopper was falling. I glanced down. In an instant we'd be caught in the turbs' blades.

'Nessa, hang on!' I yelled.

I shoved the stick forward as far as it would go, and the chopper responded – the nose dropped and we surged forward – we were free of the turb blades – but still losing altitude. I pulled the stick back, toward my chest, keeping the collective up.

But – no reaction. The chopper still pointed nose downwards. We were dropping fast. I pulled the stick closer and, slowly, the helicopter levelled itself. We began moving forward in steady flight, just as the two dancing turbs lost their balance and fell, sideways, to the ground with a boom that echoed off the faraway hills.

I released my hands momentarily from the controls and wiped the sweat off my palms on my trousers. My shirt was covered in perspiration, front and back. I lifted a corner of it to wipe my brow.

'You see, it's easy when you know how,' I said to Nessa.

'Sure, Jack,' she replied.

We were flying level now and straight ahead – quickly putting distance between us and the base – but to where?

I gazed at the gauges looking for the GPS, but couldn't find it.

'The nearest large city is Leeds,' I said. 'If we can find Leeds, and we can find the M1, and follow it south.' The day was clear, and visibility unlimited.

'How far is it to your house?' she asked.

'About two hundred miles.' I answered. 'But this training helicopter will be slower than the one we came up here in, which means – I guess – maybe three hours flying – if the battery holds out.'

Leeds came into view, and then a tangle of motorways to the south of the city.

'Now which one is the M1, do you think?' I said.

'You're asking me?' she replied. 'Really, Jack.'

I picked the one which, according to the chopper's compass, led due south.

We flew on and on. Two big towns – I reckoned they were Nottingham and Leicester – came and went.

I knew that at some point we would have to leave the M1 as it veered southeast toward London and we would have to veer southwest toward Oxford. But when to leave the motorway? It was a pilot's perfect landmark on a clear day, except that it wasn't ultimately going where we wanted to go, and its curve toward the southeast would not be noticeable from the air.

Then something by the motorway caught my eye – rows of Aston Martins all parked up next to a complex of buildings. Since I was a boy I'd coveted the DB7 model – made more than fifty years ago – but it was hopelessly out of reach on a wind engineer's salary. I fancied I saw one among the rows of gleaming, new DB27s. Then it struck me: this was the Aston plant, in Newport Pagnell, the right place to leave the M1 – from there it would head straight to London.

'We're exiting the motorway,' I said to Nessa. 'So to speak.'

I pushed the stick to the right and depressed the right pedal at the same time, my eyes on the compass. I decided to fly due west. There, I knew, I would see the M40, which for a stretch runs parallel to the M1. In between there would be no landmarks.

'Are you sure you know where we're going?' asked Nessa, staring down at the fields below.

'Sort of,' I answered.

After a while, the ribbon of the M40 came into view. I turned the stick to follow it south. On we flew.

Eventually I caught sight of a perfectly straight line on the ground, leading off to the left of the motorway. I stared at it, wondering what it was. Then it hit me – the Romans always build perfectly straight roads. This was the Roman road from Bicester leading southwest towards Oxford.

'I've found it!' I cried.

'Found what?' said Nessa.

'Do you see that straight line, just there? That's where you were, where the hunters had their camp, where we found David,' I said. 'We're almost home now.'

'All I have to do, when we get there, is figure out how to land this thing,' I added. 'I'm not very good at landing a helicopter. I've never done it before, actually.'

Nessa gave me one of her looks.

'Did you have to tell me that?' she asked.

I started looking for level fields, a bit like looking for a parking spot in a car park, I told myself. That one is too far, this one is too small… maybe the next one will be just right.

I picked a field.

'There,' I said. 'We'll put down there.'

I pushed the collective ever downwards, reducing the altitude, and pulled back slowly on the stick, raising the nose. I leaned forward, trying to make out the ground. It was coming up fast.

'Jack, too fast!' Nessa shouted.

There came an enormous thud as the chopper hit the ground. With nose up, the tail rotor blade must've hit the ground first, for it stopped turning and as a consequence the chopper began to spin, on the ground, on its horizontal axis. I'd forgotten to let go of the stick – and the main rotor blades kept turning. And the impact caused me to jam my feet against the pedals, which made the instability worse. The bird turned round and round on the ground, and then it tipped over on its side when one of the main rotor blades struck the earth. Then it stopped.

I looked at myself, up and down. No blood. I looked at Nessa, again, no blood.

'Are you hurt?' I asked.

'No, I don't think so,' she said. 'Just – let's get out of this thing.'

I pushed open my door and we climbed out.

'Where are we?' Nessa asked.

I looked around.

'A few miles from the house, I think – over that hill,' I said.

We walked up and over the hill, but our house wasn't there.

'Next hill,' I said. 'Must be the next hill. Home is over the next hill.'

And it was. The first thing we saw was the smoke rising from the chimney. Nothing looks more seductive on a cold day. But as we approached we saw the door was open and a couple of the windows were broken. No one greeted us. The house was still, silent.

'Danny! David!' I yelled.

No reply came. I thought of the Fergusons' farm, how deathly silent it had been when we'd found their bodies.

We pushed the open door back and stepped inside the house. The hallway appeared normal, everything in its proper place, but one thing was missing: all the weapons we'd stacked by the door in case of need – hoe, pitchfork and so on.

I stepped into the lounge. The first thing that caught my eye was the fireplace – the embers told that someone had been here that day or the night before, at any rate not long ago.

The second thing I noticed were the glasses and plates on the table – four. But Danny and David were two. So who had eaten there? And why had they not cleaned up – lack of time or because of some other reason?

There was mud and snow all over the lounge carpet, leading to the double-leaf glass door to the garden.

Nessa kept calling out David's name, but still there was no reply.

'I'll go upstairs,' she said.

'No, wait,' I said, opening the garden door, 'let's just look…'.

I stepped outside and looked around. I heard the sound of some twigs breaking in the woods. I stopped and waited, straining my ears.

There was no one there.

We set about putting things right. I sealed the broken windows as best I could. Then I got some logs from the shed and started a fire. Then I made myself a coffee. As I sipped it I thought I heard the sound of something moving beneath the stairs. Mum had had a storage space built there, and she wanted it concealed behind a panel that looked as though nothing were there. For valuables, she said. I looked at the panel, wondering for a moment whether I should fetch some sort of weapon before opening it. But curiosity got the better of me and I slid the panel open. There was David, shivering and terrified.

'David, it's me, Jack,' I said.

He stared at me without speaking. I reached into the cupboard to pull him out but he recoiled, and it was a struggle to get him out and in front of the fire, with a blanket over his shoulders.

'David!' Nessa cried on coming downstairs. He didn't turn to look at her.

'He's been through something horrible,' I said.

'Let's give him something to eat and he'll come round,' she said.

Whoever had eaten in the house had no taste for Chinese food – the larder was still full of noodles and rice. I found one unbroken bottle of wine in the cellar – most of the bottles had been emptied and smashed.

It was the most miserable homecoming we could have imagined.

With time David revived. We fed him and gave him some wine. I spoke to him continuously, looking into his eyes. Over an hour passed, and then he uttered our names and touched my arm. After a few minutes more, he looked into my eyes and then Nessa's. She held him. Soon he was talking, telling us what had happened.

'Danny said he saw them while he was out hunting for rabbits,' he related. 'They were on horseback. I knew it was the same men who'd taken me before, you remember the leader with the feathered cap, the one you called the Laughing Cavalier.'

'Danny had discovered the cupboard under the stairs, and he put me in there with my tablet and some food and told me not to move or make a sound.'

'Then it was quiet. Later there were sounds like a party. Lots of voices, but only men's voices – and the sound of things being broken. Then nothing.'

'Do you believe me?' he asked.

'Yes, David, we do,' said Nessa.

'David, it's best you rest now for a while,' I said.

We put him to bed under a blanket before the fire.

I walked outside to look around. First off I saw Danny's caravan was gone. There were signs of a struggle – lots of footprints in the mud and snow, some broken tree branches and deep ruts where his caravan had stood. But they might also be signs that Danny took off in a hurry. In any event, there was no sign of him.

I came back into the house.

'What did you find?' she asked.

'Not much,' I replied. 'Looks like Danny left in a hurry. There might have been a fight of some kind but I can't be sure.'

'Why didn't he stay to protect the boy?'

'Seems he decided he couldn't. Hiding David and getting away was best for both of them,' I said.

'Jack, I'm not comfortable here,' said Nessa. 'Whoever was here might come back.'

'I don't think so,' I said. 'This house doesn't have anything to offer to thieves.'

'All right, Jack, I've put all the plant samples in bags. I'm ready to go to Oxford,' she said. 'Did you contact the professor there?'

'No – as usual, no signal here,' I said. 'We'll set off in the morning.'

After a while David woke.

'Jack,' he said. 'I've cracked the software code in the chips you gave me. I've been wanting to tell you.'

16

SAVING THE PLANET

'Show me what you've done David,' I said. 'Bring your tablet here.'

He came over to me and we set his tablet and my laptop on the table.

'You see,' he said, 'it was simple once I'd figured out which pro-gramming languages were used in the source code – it was Emerald and one other.'

'It's funny when you think that thousands of human languages have become extinct but the number of computer languages grows all the time,' he added.

I looked at the boy in admiration. He was much smarter than I'd been at his age.

'Talk to me,' I said.

'Well, first of all, I wouldn't call it a smartchip. It's really a pro-cessing unit,' he said.

'So, I wanted to re-programme the processor – to insert my code in place of what was there,' he went on. 'It's running executa-ble files, and the source code is being compiled in the processor into machine code. So once I understood which languages were there, and how to work with them, I changed some of the declarations using typed language. I mean, I defined the types of data to which the unit will respond – so the computer won't respond to other data inputs.'

'Explain that to me in plain English, please,' I said. 'I'm only a wind engineer.'

'Well, it means – it should mean – the computer won't respond to a given input because it won't see that input,' he said.

'What do you mean by "should"?' I asked.

'I only meant I haven't tried it out yet, so I don't know for sure,' he replied.

'One step back, David, let me ask you this: do you think these chips have been hacked? What I mean is, have they been taking instruction from some software or malware introduced from outside?'

'It's possible I but don't think so,' he said. 'What I found in the chip was Emerald, just as set out in the books you gave me. I don't know about the other language. It's called FinianX.'

'So, why are the turbs disobeying their control computers?' I asked.

'That's what I've been trying to tell you,' he said. 'There's another input – the chips are responding to it.'

'And it wasn't introduced from outside?'

'No, I don't think so,' he said.

'OK, go on,' I said. 'What about getting the turb chips to take instructions from another computer, say a computer that we programme?'

'That should work,' he said. 'Once you've made the changes to the source code, if you put the chip back inside a turb, you could control the turb.'

'Put the chip back into the turb?' I exclaimed. 'David, we can't go around pulling chips one by one out of individual turbs, then re-programming them and then putting them back – there are tens of millions of turbs out there. We've got to find a more workable solution.'

'Tell me again about the second programming language,' I said. 'What did you say it's called?'

'FinianX,' he said.

'And you said you're not familiar with it? What role do you think it plays?' I asked, wondering if I was being a bit too hard on the boy. After all, he was only thirteen. But his voice told me he liked the give and take.

'It's not uncommon to use multiple languages in programming,' he said. 'It's not that one language has one function and another language has another function. The programmer could use a couple of languages just because he found it convenient, or because one was easier for him to write one section of code than another.'

He looked up at me.

'Do you follow me?' he asked.

'Yes, I think so,' I answered. 'But I'm still not clear on whether this second language – whether it's relevant to what we are trying to do.'

'I think I need to go a little deeper into the programming instructions,' he said. 'I mean, exactly what the chip is trying to tell the turb to do.'

I leaned back.

'My friend, I can see you're not sure,' I said. 'You've made it part of the way – perhaps a big part of the way – but you're not there yet.'

I got up and walked over the cabinet, pulled out a bottle and poured myself a glass of Islay whisky.

'All right, David, I said. 'Now, the steps you took, can you walk me through them?'

'Sure,' he said.

I grabbed a notebook lying on the bookshelf and handed it to him.

'Save every step you've taken on your tablet,' I said. 'But let's also write all the steps down in the old fashioned way – in this notebook. A little insurance. OK, let's go through them.'

We sat side by side well into the evening, as he showed me what he'd done, step by step.

'I'm tired,' I said as the symbols on the screen began to dance. 'Just flew a chopper down from Yorkshire. I've got to sleep now.'

'About tomorrow, David. Nessa and I have to go into Oxford tomorrow, a day trip. You're going to have to be here on your own

– just for the day,' I said. 'I promise we'll be back by nightfall, and then we'll go through it again.'

*

We set out for Oxford at dawn, with two extra jerry cans full of bio-fuel strapped to the sides of the tractor. I avoided the motorway and kept to the valleys. Still, it was hard to manoeuvre the tractor in forested terrain. We had to stop often to pull logs or branches out of our path, and to make detours around flooded patches. It was nearly noon before we got to Oxford. I could see that the tractor, while useful, had its limits.

The town centre appeared to be Danny had described – burned out buildings sprinkled with bullet holes – but we saw only a bit of the High Street, and what we saw looked deserted. I chose to avoid the centre by cutting across Magdalen Grove, heading straight for the Plant Sciences building. The Cherwell has burst its banks and the grove was in parts knee-deep in water.

Our smartphones beeped.

'At least we've got a signal here.' I said.

The building was intact, as Phil had said. We swung open the doors and there, in the reception, stood a young woman.

'Good morning,' she said. 'My name's Chloe Hanson. I'm Professor Gordon's research assistant. We've been expecting you.'

We introduced ourselves. She led us down a corridor and up some stairs.

'Mind if I ask you,' I said, as we walked. 'What you're doing in this research building in the midst of all this chaos?

'Partly to carry on with our work, and partly to protect the building,' she said. 'The plant samples in this building are irreplaceable.'

She stopped and rapped on a door.

'Come in,' said a voice.

Gordon looked up at us from a white table full of glassware and jars.

'They're the two Sir Philip Burnley said would come?'

'Yes,' said the young woman.

'That's right,' I replied. 'I'm Jack Mason and this is Nessa Chao – she's a botanist. I'm only a wind engineer.'

'I know. He told me. You've come about the plants, haven't you? The plants growing in the heads of wind turbs.'

'Yes,' said Nessa, laying her bag on Gordon's table. 'We've brought these samples for study.'

'Let's get on with it,' said Gordon.

He wore thick spectacles that made his eyes seem huge. The woman also wore glasses, but hers were plastic, of the laboratory kind. Both of them wore white body suits of the kind you see in films about contagious epidemics. Around their necks hung breathing masks.

Gordon tossed a pair of lab gloves to Nessa, who donned them and carefully removed the samples from her bag and laid them out on a tray on the table. Then, she carefully sliced open one and, using a tweezer-like tool, put a sample under the microscope.

'Never seen that before,' she said.

'What?' asked Gordon.

'Here, take a look,' she said. 'The contours of the mouth, I mean. They're not associated with this species.'

'You know this species?' Gordon asked.

'Yes, of course,' she replied. 'They're carnivorous.'

'Do you know which turb heads these plants came from?' asked Gordon. 'That might be important.'

'We know where they came from,' I put in. 'Those on the left from a turb the *Hope and Glory* project here in Oxfordshire and those on the right from a sea turb in the North Sea. The third sample, in the middle, was taken from a turb that fell over near here.'

'All right, let's start,' said Gordon. 'We're going to compare the DNA from these samples with the DNA from our own samples from the same species of plant, taken from a natural environment, not from the inside of a turb,' he said. 'That will take a little time. Ms Chao, we'd welcome your help. Mr Mason, you can have a seat and watch, or come back in a bit.'

I sat down and fidgeted. Then I went outside to check on the tractor. I looked up and down the street. It was quiet. I saw no sign of life. In the distance, smoke was rising from some other part of the town. I puffed on a fag. Eventually I went inside and made my way back to Gordon's lab.

He looked up as I entered. Nessa stood beside him, staring into a microscope.

'The DNA is different,' he said to me. 'The samples you've brought have been genetically changed – modified.'

'He's right, Jack,' said Nessa. 'There is a difference. They're not the same plants, or rather, they're the same, but not the same.'

'How do you mean?' I asked.

'Come,' said Gordon. 'Look into the microscope.'

I did as I was told, but comparing the left and right sides of what lay before me, I saw no difference.

'Sorry, but I just don't see anything,' I said.

'Look again, Jack,' said Nessa. Then I saw it. There were differences between the two cell shapes.

'How can you tell they're genetically modified?' I asked.

'The differences in the shapes of the cells mean they will have different traits,' Gordon explained.

'Which traits, for example?' I asked.

'Well, it could be longevity, or resistance to pesticide or disease,' he said. 'Or it could be some other trait. We won't know till we've done more work.'

'All right, they're genetically modified,' I said. 'What's the significance of that?'

'It may have no significance at all,' said Gordon. 'But I've a hunch it has.'

'Allow me,' said Nessa, again taking the microscope.

'Hang on, there's something else here – some colour spots,' she said. 'Professor Gordon, please take another look at the grey areas, the greenish-grey.'

Gordon bent over and looked.

'Yes, I see them,' he said. 'What do you think they are?'

'I think they're traces of metal,' she said. 'Take another look.'

He did, and then so did Hanson. They talked for a few minutes in a botanical language that was beyond me.

'We think you may be right,' said Gordon.

'I think the metal may be related to the genetic modification of the cells,' said Nessa.

Gordon pushed his glasses up over his forehead.

'The presence of metal might have an impact,' he allowed.

'Well, first we'll need to analyse the metal content,' said Nessa. 'Have you got facilities here for performing an assay?'

'No, but they have at the Materials Department. It's just round the corner in Parks Road.'

'Do you think anyone's there?' she asked.

'I don't know,' said Gordon. 'Chloe, please see if you can ring them. In any case, I'll take you round there.'

Nessa turned to me.

'Jack, you know, an assay can be very time-consuming, especially a fire assay,' she said. 'We'll have to stay here overnight.'

We talked it over and decided Nessa would stay for the assay results. Besides, that would give the three botanists more time to spend with the plant samples, and to discuss their ideas. I would go back to the house – after all, we'd promised David we'd be back before dark.

'Do you have a freezer or fridge for the samples?' Nessa asked Chloe.

'Yes, we'll put them in the deep cool overnight,' she replied.

'We'll find you some accommodation here for tonight,' she added. 'We can't let you wander round the town.'

'Thanks,' said Nessa.

The last thing I did before heading for home was to use the signal to send a text to Phil to tell him we'd delivered the plants to the lab and had already made some progress in analysing the samples.

'Things are heating up fast – get to the bottom of it quick as you can,' he texted back.

*

I got back to the house after dark, wet and cold. My fingers were stiff from clutching the tractor handles. I found David in the lounge, sitting in front of his screen.

'Jack, you're home!' he jumped up.

'Of course I'm home – told you I'd come back, didn't I?'

'You said you'd be back before dark,' he replied.

'I did, and I was wrong,' I answered. No sense in arguing with a kid, I thought – you'll always lose. 'Have you eaten?' I asked.

He shook his head.

'All right, let's get our bellies full and make a fire,' I said. I pulled off my coat and went into the kitchen, where Nessa had left some noodles and tinned beef in the pan. It wasn't much but we ate hungrily.

'Right then,' I said. 'I'll wash up and you make a fire.'

When the fire was going I beckoned David to his tablet.

'What've you been up to?' I asked.

'I looked more closely at the instructions in the source code. They're about instructing the physical parts of the turbs to move – speed, direction of the wheels, blade angle and so on. You know that, don't you?'

'I do, David,' I said. 'And you're right. And?'

'Well, the question you asked was whether the source code in the turb smartchips can be re-written, re-programmed I mean, without the need to remove and re-programme each chip,' he said.

'That's right,' I said.

'And you asked me whether these chips have been hacked,' he went on. 'But the answer is still "no." I didn't see any malware or spyware in the code.'

'What are you getting at?' I asked.

'Well, it occurred to me that these turb smartchips haven't been hacked. But they could be,' he said.

I looked at him blankly.

'I mean, *we* could hack them – introduce new code to change their behaviour. That's basically what hacking means.'

'Why, David, that sounds brilliant,' I exclaimed. 'We just turn the thing on its head, as it were. Instead of searching for hacking that we can't find, we do the hacking.'

'But how exactly?' I wanted to know.

'What about using a wireless signal?' he ventured.

That sounded good to my untechnical ears.

'We could introduce new source code to all the turb smartchips,' he said.

'Would that work? I asked.

'I don't see why not,' David replied.

'So, all the steps we wrote down in your notebook – we can use them to change the turbs' behaviour?'

'Absolutely,' he replied. 'But there's just one thing. You remember I told you about the second programming language? I haven't been very successful to re-writing it.'

'What does that mean?' I asked. 'Does that mean what you've done won't work?'

'Oh, I think it will work,' he said. 'I'm just not one hundred percent sure.'

I gave him a great, big hug.

'I feel we're more than halfway now,' I said. 'Just keep working on that second language.'

17

RORKE'S DRIFT

'David, wake up,' I shook him.

'I have to go away again,' I said. 'Again, just for the day.'

'Where are you going?' he asked.

'I've got to go the shopping centre, to see if they need help. We left there two days ago and I don't know what's going on. And I've got to get some biofuel for the tractor there,' I said. 'Then I'm going back to Oxford to collect Nessa. We'll be back by dark.'

'Jack, I don't like being on my own here,' he said.

'I can understand that,' I replied. 'But I can't take you with me – it's safer if you stay here.'

To my surprise and relief, as soon as I crested the last hill, I saw that there had been no turb attack on the Big World. The centre was intact. But the herd was still there, if anything larger than before.

I left the tractor in the forest and swung round on foot to the north side of the centre, where the reservoir prevented the turbs from coming closer. I passed along the edge of the pond to the building and then made my way to the entrance on the east side, where there were fewer turbs.

'Jack!' cried Chris Porter. 'You're a sight for sore eyes. Glad you're here.'

'Chris, how are you?' I said. 'It doesn't look so bad here. By the look of it, they haven't attacked.'

'They haven't indeed,' he replied. 'But morale is slipping. People don't like the waiting. Let me take you to Jenny.'

'Thanks,' I said.' Chris, by the way, I'm in need of a jerry can or two of biofuel.'

'I'll see what I can do,' he replied.

He led me to the information kiosk on the ground level where the main corridors came together, a sort of command post for the centre's defenders.

'Mason, good to see you,' said Withers.

'Hello, Jack,' said Jenny. 'As you see, the turbs haven't moved. They howled a bit more, and they vibrated like hummingbirds – drove us mad – but they've kept their distance.'

'Have you been lighting bonfires round the centre?' I asked.

'Sure have,' said Jenny. 'It's been a tricky business that, because it's meant moving across the open ground of the car park. We've found its best to make the bonfire forays under cover of darkness. My daughter Isadora's done a bang up job at leading the forays. My other daughter Rebecca's not bad at it, either, I must say.'

'Has it worked?' I asked.

'Yes, definitely,' she replied. 'They've shied away whenever we get the fires going.'

'What about the loudspeakers?' I asked.

'That's also worked,' Withers put in. 'We turn them on every few hours and the turbs move toward them. Then we turn them off, wait a few hours, and then on again. Keeps them guessing, we figure.'

'You're developing your own tactics, that's good,' I said. 'I can learn something from you.'

'Isadora here's developed something really useful,' said Withers. I turned and there was Jenny's younger daughter, wearing her Territorial Army uniform.

'Tell Jack what you've thought of,' Withers prompted.

Isadora gave a shy smile and brushed back her long blond hair.

'Go on,' said Jenny.

'Torches,' she said. 'We take long poles or any piece of wood or metal we can find here, and we stick something flammable on the end, like a loo roll. Instant anti-turb weapon.'

'Keeps the young ones safe when they go out on forays,' said Chris.

'Still, it's dangerous to go out there,' said Jenny. 'We've had one casualty, Ed Fraser, a young lad from the village. And we found Paul's body, by the way, out beyond the east car park. Seems a turb crushed him beneath its wheels. The rest of his group might've got away, but we don't know.'

'Sorry to hear that,' I said. 'Look, I can't stay long. I just wanted to know how you are all getting on, whether I can do anything to help.'

'You already have helped, Jack,' said Withers. 'You gave us the know-how. Your coming here today has boosted morale. Look.'

I turned round.

Dozens of people had gathered to listen to us – I saw faces from the village, as well as new faces, presumably refugees from Clacton, the Isle of Sheppey and other areas by the sea.

'Listen to me,' I said. 'Remember this: if the siege gets long, it might turn out that supplies, rather than cunning or courage, will decide the issue. Draw up a list of things to conserve and ration them with discipline.'

'I'll come back,' I promised. 'But I don't know when.'

I looked at Jenny and then at Withers, to see if they'd taken what I'd said on board. Jenny nodded forcefully, but Withers' head was bent as someone whispered in his ear. He then turned and said something to Jenny, who approached me.

'Jack, some of the lads have gone out the west entrance. They're fed up and looking for a fight,' she said. 'Can you stop them?'

'I'll try,' I said, bolting to the west entrance, where I found a crowd of young men and women – Isadora and Rebecca among them – fuming with impotent rage.

The mini-turbs outside were rolling on their bi-wheels right across the car park and up to the door, and then rolling back again. Backwards and forwards they rolled, and as they rolled they bobbed up and down. The effect on the younger defenders at the door was explosive.

'They're mocking us!' cried one of the lads.

'Damn cheek,' said another.

'Don't be foolish!' I shouted. 'Turbs have no emotions. Better learn that now.'

Despite my words, a band of defenders angrily sallied forth, armed with whatever they had to hand. This, surprisingly, was a lot – axes, hatchets, garden hoes and even an old hunting rifle.

'No!' I cried, and ran out after them. I got ahead of them and turned.

'Go back!' I shouted. 'We can't be wasting our strength on the little ones. Wait for the big ones. That's when we'll need every hand.'

'Isadora!' came a cry.

She'd got out ahead of all the others.

Armed with a bow and arrows from the centre's sporting goods department, she stood, her legs apart, raised her bow and put an arrow directly into the head of one of the turbs. It must have penetrated the small gap between the nose of the nacelle and the rear part of the turb head, lodging in the gears, for the blades stopped spinning and the turb keeled over.

Everyone stood there, amazed by what she'd done.

'All right,' I shouted. 'Enough. Get back inside!'

I grabbed Isadora by the arm and pulled her with me. Seeing her with me, the others followed.

It was a victory of sorts for both sides. The turbs remained in possession of the field as the defenders retreated to the safety of the centre. But the defenders had taken heart.

They gathered spontaneously in the cinema to celebrate.

'Isadora!' called out several of the young lads. 'Get up on the stage!'

It became a chant: 'On the stage! On the stage!'

Isadora was reluctant.

'Go on,' said Jenny. 'Get up there.'

She did, blushing. Her red face set off her long blond hair.

'I'm not a hero,' she began.

The chant changed immediately.

'Hero! Hero!'

'I reckon I'm just good at outwitting turbs,' she continued. 'Out-smarting them, fooling them, running rings around them, disabling them, and then killing them!'

A great cheer arose. Jenny and Rebecca sat in the front row, beaming.

'I want to say why I'm fighting the turbs,' she went on, still blushing. 'I'm fighting to stay alive, of course, we all are.'

'But not for that reason alone. I'm fighting to keep my family alive. But not only that. I'm fighting to keep my fellow villagers alive. And more. I'm fighting for those from other parts of this Kingdom who've taken refuge with us. And more. I'm fighting for England!'

At this there was pandemonium. People jumped up and down, waving anything to hand. Cries of *Victoria Cross!* arose on all sides. Another chant arose: 'VC! VC! VC!'

'This shopping centre's going to go down in English history as another Rorke's Drift,' the professor shouted.

Isadora left the stage amid loud applause. Morale had soared.

Chris touched my elbow.

'Got two cans of biofuel for you,' he said. 'I rigged some straps so you can carry them on your back. They're outside.'

'Thanks, Chris,' I said. 'I'll come back soon as I can.'

'Better not take too long,' he replied. 'Some of them big turbs have got nearer, sort of poking at the roof, like giant woodpeckers.'

'They're checking us out, by the sound of it,' he added.

*

It wasn't fun carrying forty litres of biofuel on my back up the snowy hillside. On the way out of the centre, I slipped on the embankment and almost fell into the reservoir. One of the straps snapped as I slid, and I ended up having to carry one of the cans. But I found the tractor, emptied one of the cans into the tank and strapped the other tightly on the rear. My fingers were freezing. I flexed them, opening and closing my fist to get the blood flowing.

I set off for Oxford. It was nearly dark, and the going was hard. The tractor had a small headlamp, but logs and branches kept appearing out of nowhere. I had to dismount constantly to clear the way.

I already knew I would not keep my promise to David to return before dark, but there was nothing I could do about it. I had to go on.

My heart leapt when I finally saw the Plant Sciences building in Oxford. I jumped off the tractor and mounted the steps, giving a quick bang at the door. Then I banged again, out of exhaustion. A light went on inside, and Chloe Hanson nudged open the door.

'It's you,' she said. 'I thought it might be. Nessa's inside. We're bedded down in here tonight. I'll make a bed for you.'

'Thank you,' I said, forgetting entirely about stashing the tractor away somewhere.

Chloe led me to a room where Nessa, rising from a cot, threw her arms around me.

'You're safe,' she said. 'I was so worried.'

'Yes, safe,' I said. 'I was worried about you.'

I laid myself down on the cot and my head hit the pillow.

I don't remember anything more. The next thing I knew Nessa was waking me.

'Jack, we have the results of the assay of the metal traces in the turb plants,' said Nessa. 'Come on, Gordon's waiting for us. He wants to tell you about them.'

'Coffee,' I said, rolling over in the cot.

'Here,' she said, handing me a hot Styrofoam cup. I sat up.

'It's awful,' I said.

'Drink it and let's go,' said Nessa. 'Put your trousers on.'

I did as I was told and we trundled down a corridor and up some stairs.

'Ah, Mr Mason, good morning,' said Gordon as we entered his

lab. 'You can hear this first hand.'

'Hear what?' I asked.

'The assay results,' he replied. 'Ms Chao already knows. Hasn't she told you?'

'I've just got up,' I said. 'She hasn't had time to tell me anything.'

'It's *neodymium*,' said Gordon. 'The traces of metal inside the plant cells are *neodymium*.'

I woke up at once.

'Traces of *neodymium* in the turb plants?' I said. 'They could only have come from the turbs with permanent magnet generators.'

'That's right. And there's more,' said Nessa. 'Do you remember the first turb we went inside of, just after we'd come to Oxfordshire, the one near your house that had hardly any plants in it? The assay for those samples was negative – no metal traces.'

'That was the one with the ancient, twin-shaft generator,' I said. 'That generator uses copper coils, not *neodymium*.'

'Exactly,' said Nessa. 'But the other samples we took, from the turb in the forest and from the sea turb, have significant traces of *neodymium* in the plant cells.'

'I see,' I said, thinking about the implications of this discovery.

'We found something else as well,' said Gordon. 'The plant cells from the turb with the copper generator show very little genetic modification from other, similar species. But the cells taken from the turbs with *neodymium* generators show very striking modifications.'

'How does genetic modification occur?' I asked.

'In modern commercial agriculture, something called a "gene gun" is used to shoot high energy particles or radiation into plant cells, which then penetrate the cell walls into the membrane,' explained Gordon. 'It was controversial in the past, but now it's generally accepted practice.'

'And how might it have happened that the *neodymium* got into the plant cells?' I asked.

'There are many ways that could have happened,' said Nessa.

'The metal casing of the generator corrodes over time and frag-ments come loose. There's lots of moisture in the turb head, high temperatures, wind. The fact is that it has happened.'

'There's another point I ought to explain. It's very important,' Gordon broke in. 'The precise nature of the genetic modification in the cells affected by the *neodymium* has been to make the plants carnivorous.'

'That's right. The cells where no *neodymium* was found are not the cells of a carnivorous plant,' Nessa added.

'And another thing I think is worth bearing in mind,' said Gor-don. 'The process of genetic modification sparked by the *neodymium* is still continuing. We should not regard the plants we've looked at now as being a final product.'

'They're still morphing,' I said. 'But into what?'

'I don't know,' Gordon replied. 'They could become even more dangerous.'

'Explain to me please a little bit about carnivorous plants,' I said, picking up a Petri dish and staring into it.

'Don't stick your fingers in there, Jack,' said Nessa. 'That one's a flesh-eater.'

'I think I'll let Chloe tell you about carnivores,' said Gordon. 'She's writing her thesis on them.'

'There are just shy of six hundred species of carnivorous plants,' she began. 'Most thrive in environments with a lot of light and wa-ter, but little soil nutrient. The inside of a turb head would be per-fect. They succeed in environments where other plants fail, and of course, there would be little competition inside a turb head.'

'Almost all carnivorous plants rely on a trapping mechanism to ensnare their prey,' she went on. 'That's where the samples you brought us are most interesting. Their trapping mechanism resem-bles teeth. See here, at the mouth of the bulb? These growths per-form the same function as teeth.'

'These are probably descended from *Cephalotaceae*, maybe the *Cephalotus follicularis*, better known as the Australian pitcher plant. It prefers warmer temperatures. That may be why, as you explained, so many of the turbs are moving south,' she concluded.

'How do we kill them?' I asked.

'That's easy,' she replied. 'With mould.'

'Mould?' I asked.

'Yes,' she replied. 'Most species of carnivorous plants will die if they come into contact with ordinary mould. Like the kind in your kitchen or bath.'

18

THE LEADER OF
THE PACK

'Incredible,' I said.

'And yet simple,' said Nessa.

'Hang on,' I said. 'We're not ready to go about using mould to kill the plants in millions of turbs, even if we had a way of doing so. No, there's still something unexplained.'

'Have you told Phil – I mean, Sir Philip?' I asked, turning to Professor Gordon.

'Yes, we sent a report,' he said. 'He'd asked to receive one as soon as we had any results.'

'Good. I've got to talk to him,' I said. 'Better to do it here – it's hard to get a signal at my house.'

'My office is private,' Gordon offered. He led us through a door off the lab. I spoke Phil's name into my smartphone.

'Have you seen the report on the plants?' I asked as soon as he picked up.

'Yeah, just did. I was in a meeting here in Cheltenham with government people,' he said. 'Unbelievable. Why didn't we look more closely at these plants before?'

'Because none of us in the wind industry paid any attention to the plants growing inside the turbs,' I said. 'They were just plants.'

'That's water under the bridge,' I continued. 'What we've got to focus on now is that this discovery still explains only part of the story. It tells us there's a link between the *neodymium* generators and the plant life – but it doesn't explain the deviation factor. It doesn't explain why turbs are breaking their tethers and disobeying instructions.'

'That's true,' he said.

'Listen to me, Phil,' I went on. 'The unexplained part – I think we're on to something. With the turb smartchips, I mean. I think David has cracked the source code. Don't worry – we wrote everything down in a notebook.'

'Who's David?' came Phil's reply.

'Sorry – a boy we're looking after,' I said.

'What boy?'

'We found him near my house. He's thirteen and he's been orphaned as far as we know,' I said. 'He's been fantastic with the smartchips. We couldn't have done what he's done.'

There was a pause before Phil spoke again.

'Do you mean to say,' he said slowly, 'that between us and the Yanks, and all the brain and computing power we've got, a thirteen year old boy cracked the source code?'

'That's exactly what I'm saying,' I replied.

There was silence. I looked at my smartphone. The connection was gone.

'Professor, have you got a landline here? I need to call Sir Philip Burnley in Cheltenham,' I said.

'No, Jack, we haven't had those for donkeys' years,' he answered.

My smartphone beeped.

'What have you got? Or what do you think you've got?' came Phil's voice. He sounded angry, or at least incredulous. 'Everyone here still thinks the turb smartchips have been hacked, and that's the explanation for the deviation factor.'

'We don't think they've been hacked. To be honest, we're not entirely there yet,' I said. 'But if we get there, we'll be able to take back control of the turbs. The end of the deviation factor.'

'And what do you propose to do now?' Phil asked.

'To come to Cheltenham with David and put him together with the government's computer geeks,' I said. 'We haven't got any transport by the way. Can you send a chopper?'

'Yeah, stay put in your house I'll ask Singh to send someone to get you.'

'When will the cavalry come?' I asked.

'I don't know. I'll let you know. Your boy may have saved the planet, but I'll believe it when I see it,' said Phil. He was irritated. The familiar joviality wasn't there. Then the connection was gone.

'All right, let's move. Let's get home.' I said to Nessa. 'I just remembered that I promised David we'd be home before dark and that was yesterday.'

'Thank you both,' I said to Gordon and Chloe. 'We've got to go.'

'Have something to eat first,' said Chloe. 'We've got some ham and cheese sandwiches. I know it's not much but you ought to eat something.'

'That's very kind of you,' said Nessa. We gobbled up a few sandwiches.

Outside the Plant Sciences building the tractor was nowhere to be seen.

'Damn!' I said. 'I was so tired last night I forgot to hide it. And now it's gone. That's what England is coming to!'

'What are we going to do?' asked Nessa.

'We're going to walk,' I said. 'It's only about six miles. It'll be easier if we walk along the road. I know one of the smaller roads that will take us within a mile of home. From there, we'll go over the hills.'

It was cold and it got colder but at least it wasn't snowing. After an hour or so of walking, Nessa nudged my arm.

'Look, Jack, over that hill,' she said. 'Turbs.'

'That's the shopping centre over that hill,' I said. 'I was there yesterday to see how they were getting on.'

'How are the villagers doing?' she asked.

'They're holding their own, but for long I don't know,' I said. 'Nessa, I promised them I'd come back.'

'Well then, I guess we'd better look in on them,' she said. 'David will be worried, but we're already a day late.'

As we approached the crest of the last hill, we glimpsed the roof of the shopping centre. It looked funny, crenelated like a castle wall.

At the top of the hill we could see the whole of the centre. We could see now why the roof looked crenelated – whole chunks of it had been hacked away by the turbs.

The turbs were still there, hundreds of them. But there was no sign of life inside the centre. Doors and windows hung open.

Coming down the hill, we caught a whiff of smoke and then saw the burn marks on the walls of the centre. But we saw no fires burning.

We circled round and approached the building along the reservoir embankment. At the edge of the west car park, Nessa grabbed my arm.

'Jack, there!' she said.

Before us lay a corpse. We neared it.

'It's a young man. But look at the condition of the body,' I said. 'I've never seen anything like that before.'

The young man's body seemed like it had begun to decompose or had been hacked. The flesh hung in strips loosely around the limbs.

'Yes, you have, Jack,' said Nessa. 'At the farm, that old couple. The bodies looked just like this one. It's horrible!'

'You're right,' I exclaimed. 'It's the same.' I felt nauseous.

'There's another one!' Nessa screamed.

'Let's get inside,' I said, pulling Nessa by the elbow.

We entered through the west door and followed the main mall corridor, wading in several inches of water. The flood waters had risen.

It was deathly quiet. Our own voices created an echo that made the mall seem full of people the way it used to be on a busy Saturday afternoon.

Outside one of the pubs, an empty beer barrel floated in the water. I kicked it just to watch it move.

'There's no one here,' said Nessa. 'Jack, let's get out of this place.'

'We're over here!' came a voice. It was Jenny Towton.

We hurried on to where the voice came from – by the information kiosk. There we found dozen people crouching.

Jenny stood up.

'There are more of us down in the cellar,' she said. She turned and hollered: 'Jack Mason's here!'

'The turbs attacked last night,' said Withers.

'They started pecking at the roof,' Chris Porter put in. 'Walls started to crash. Small fires broke out. People got scared. Some of the lads went out to fight.'

'We lost some,' said Withers.

'I know,' I said. 'We saw them.'

'We haven't had time yet to go out and gather them up,' he continued. 'We'll do it, though.'

For a moment I was too upset to speak. The horrible sight of those young men's bodies and the cowed sense of defeat I got from the villagers overwhelmed me. I had to do something.

'Chris, I want you to go to the garden centre – use the tunnel – and bring me back a chainsaw. And any other weapons you can find. And some biofuel for them. Quickly, please.'

'Be back in a snap, Jack,' he said.

'Jenny, where are your daughters?' I asked.

'In the cellar,' she replied.

'Well, find them please and tell them to get some bedsheets and bring them here,' I said.

'What's the plan, Jack?' asked Withers.

'I'm going to take on the leader of the pack,' I said. 'If I win, the herd might retreat.'

'You're not going out there alone,' said Nessa.

'No, I'm not,' I said, kissing her. 'You're going with me – you're the distraction.'

'Great,' she said. 'I'll be eye candy for a turb.'

Everything fell into place by the west door – chainsaw, make-shift torches made with bedsheets, an eMusic player for making noise, Molotov cocktails made with jam jars and an assortment of axes and hatchets.

'All right, let's go,' I said. 'I don't want to wait till dark.'

I strode out into the car park, Nessa at my side. The turbs had turned round to face away from the building and their blades were spinning steadily, creating a strong wind from their wake in the direction of the centre.

'Why are they doing that?' asked Isadora, running after us.

'It could be they are making wind to fan any fire that might start in the centre,' I said.

'Are they that smart?' she asked.

'I'm learning something new about them every day,' I said. 'Now you get back inside.'

'No, I'm coming with you,' she declared.

'The hell you are!' It was Jenny, who grabbed her daughter by the shoulders and held her back.

Nessa and I advanced across the car park.

I spotted the leader easily enough. It was the tallest one, at well over two hundred meters. But it wasn't only height that gave it away. It also seemed to me that the turbs around it were bobbing slightly in its direction. We'd seen that phenomenon before.

'That one!' I said to Nessa. 'Now move over that way, and make some noise!'

Nessa switched on the music – an electric guitar version of *Jerusalem* came blasting out – and the turbs perked up. First the leader, then others, began moving in her direction.

That gave me my chance. I sprinted toward the leader and got within the radius of its blades before it could react.

All of a sudden it stopped cold. Blast, I thought, it *had* sensed me. Why else had it stopped moving toward the noise? But I was safe inside the blade radius – for the moment.

I heaved off my rucksack and pulled out the chainsaw. I shook it to check that Chris had filled its tank. Then I yanked the chain and the saw roared to life. It was a vicious weapon, and I couldn't wait to use it on the turb.

Nearing the thing, I raised the saw over my head and swung it down on one of the tyres. The whirring blade flinched as it hit the thick rubber tyre but I held it fast and pushed. It slowly bit into the rubber and gained traction. I pushed harder. The saw's blade was now slicing smoothly through the rubber.

Halfway through, I pulled the blade free and made to strike from another angle. I swung the saw down – and missed. The turb had moved!

The giant wheels rolled and I ran behind, trying to get close enough to strike.

Then suddenly it stopped, and I ran smack into the tyre. I lost my grip on the chainsaw and it flew past me, missing my head by inches.

'Damn!' I yelled, and ran for the saw.

But before I could grab it off the ground the turb reversed and came at me, trapping the fallen saw under a tyre.

I looked up at the thing.

Did it know? I wondered. Did it know that stopping just there it would pin the saw, and deprive me of my best weapon? It couldn't be, I thought. I pulled a hatchet from my belt. But I didn't have time to strike. The turb moved again.

I flung the hatchet at one of the tyres, but missed. Then I un-shouldered an axe and, holding it with two hands, neared the turb.

It was turning in circles round me. I watched it and soon felt dizzy. Was *that* deliberate, I wondered? Was it trying to confuse me?

I looked down at the ground to steady myself and then at Nessa, dropping the axe. I wanted the chain saw.

The other turbs hadn't stopped – they were still moving toward her.

'Nessa!' I called, 'Drop the music player! Leave it! Get back inside!'

She was out of earshot and cupped a hand to her ear.

'Get back inside!' I shouted again, hurling a Molotov cocktail at the turbs' wheels. It exploded in flames but the turbs kept right on going for her.

This time she seemed to have heard, for she began to run. But, no, she wasn't running back inside the centre – she was running toward me!

'No!' I cried. It was too late. She nearly knocked me over with an embrace. She kissed me, and I kissed her back.

'Nessa, you're mad! You've got to get back inside the centre. Now!'

'You, too, Jack,' she said.

'All right, you go first, run – now!'

She ran. I looked up again at the leader. It had stopped turning circles. It stood motionless. I saw the chainsaw lying on the ground and reached for it. I glanced at the tyre I'd sliced open. There was a yawning gap in the rubber but, I saw, it was not enough to disable the turb. I would have to have another go at the tyres.

The turb moved.

'Bloody hell,' I muttered. The turb was chasing Nessa.

'I'll get you, you bastard,' I said under my breath, and sprang after the turb. I ran like hell, holding the chainsaw out in front of me.

I got close enough and leapt, thrusting the saw into a tyre. Then I pulled it out and jabbed it in again, and again.

Springing to the other tyre, I sliced again. I cut well into the rubber, but it wasn't enough. I shoved the saw into the gap and dragged it down with all my strength. The tyre tore open and the saw jerked free. I let go of it and looked at what I'd done.

Both tyres should now be unable to turn. The turb might soon crash and I looked round to see where Nessa had got to. She was at the door of the shopping centre, I saw with relief.

But she hadn't gone inside – she was waiting for me, waving.

'Stay there!' I called out.

The wheels of the turb groaned. It was trying to move. I knew that would be its end.

I tried to hasten it. I jabbed the chainsaw again into a tyre and sliced up and down, with the saw at my hip.

The turb's tyres jerked first backwards and then forwards, with great force, then backwards again – and continued moving backwards. I was amazed the thing could move with such cuts in the tyres.

It moved swiftly backwards – and I knew at once I would soon be caught beyond the radius of its blades. Then it would have its chance. Like a wounded beast, it still had fight in it. It was trying to kill me.

Dropping the chainsaw, I bolted to the shopping centre, as fast as my legs would carry me.

I got there in the nick of time. Just as I reached Nessa's waiting arms, the thing fell. I looked up.

'It's coming straight at us!' I cried.

One of the blades struck earth with a great boom, not a metre away from where we stood, shaking the ground beneath our feet. We were sprayed with bits of asphalt, mud and snow. The force of the fall drove the blade deep into the earth.

I held Nessa as close to me as I could.

'We're all right,' I said. 'It's over. The thing is dead.'

From inside the centre, the villagers began to emerge. They stared at the fallen turb.

'Jack, you killed it,' said Chris.

'You did,' said Withers.

'All in a day's work,' I muttered. We were covered with mud and snow. I'd somehow torn my clothes with the saw. We must have looked a sight.

'Get you a cup of tea,' said Jenny.

'Nothing stronger?' I asked with a smile. I was beginning to relax. The turb was definitely dead.

'Look,' said Chris. 'They're moving away.'

All heads turned toward the turbs. It was true – the herd was on the move. First a few, then more lurched backwards. Then more lumbered after them. Soon it became a stampede – if I can use that word for creatures that move slowly. The herd was heading south.

'I think we're safe now,' I said.

'Let's get inside,' said Jenny. 'It's cold out here. I'll get you that tea.'

'Just a minute,' said Nessa, approaching the blade. 'Look at the tendons – the water outflow pipes. They've got those flecks that the turb in the forest had.'

I stepped closer to the blade. Nessa was right.

'Jack, now that we know the plants inside the turbs are carnivorous, can there be any more doubt what these red flecks are?' she said.

'No doubt,' I said. 'It's blood.'

19

UNEXPECTED COMPANY

The people of Upper St John were in a buoyant mood. Some were merely relieved the turb threat had, for the moment at least, receded. Others wanted to celebrate, and they wanted Nessa and me to join them. Bottles of spirits emerged and toasts were offered around.

'Hang on a minute,' I said. 'It's a bit too early to celebrate and we've lost some of our own. The turbs might come back. And Nessa and I can't celebrate – not yet, anyway – we've got someone at home waiting for us and we've still a lot to do.'

We said our goodbyes. Glasses were raised as we walked out of the centre – straight out the west door where few dared to tread only a short time before.

When we got home we found David in a state of agitation that switched back and forth between anger and hurt that he'd been left alone for so long, and excitement about a new step in cracking the turb smartchips. It took some apologies and hugs and, later, some food – a big plate of spicy stir-fried beef and noodles – to put the anger and hurt right.

Nessa and I changed clothes and washed ourselves. The hot water wasn't as hot as it should have been and we shivered together in the shower. I lit a fire as soon as we came downstairs. Then, after the meal, I turned my attention to the other source of David's agitation.

'All right, David, what have you got? You've got something – I can see it by the look in your eye. Put your tablet on the table and show me.'

'I concentrated on the instructions in the source code,' he said. 'You told me they were about movement of the physical parts of the turbs – speed, blade angle and so forth – and they are.'

'But there's more,' he continued. 'There's also source code dealing with temperature, humidity and plant oil lubrication. That got my attention.'

'Why?' I asked.

'Because, in the smartchips you gave me, there's a lot more code dealing with those subjects than with physical movement of the turbs.'

'So?' I said.

'Well, I know Nessa's been looking at the plants inside the turbs, and I had the idea that maybe that's important. Because things like temperature, humidity and plant oils are relevant to the plants.'

'David, you're losing me,' I said. 'Yes, there are sensors within the turbs' heads that monitor all those things and all that information is collected in the smartchips.'

'Well, I thought the plants themselves might be sending information to the smartchips,' he said. 'And the smartchips are responding to these inputs.'

'What are you saying?' I asked.

'I'm saying what I already told you: these chips haven't been hacked,' he said. 'There's no direction coming from outside telling the turbs what to do. It's the plants that are telling the turbs what to do.'

'The plants?'

'Yes, when they need water or food or a warmer temperature, they give this information to the smartchips,' he said. 'I guess, via the sensors you mentioned.'

A light went on in my head.

'Food, you said?'

'Yes, Nessa said these plants eat meat,' he replied.

Just then Nessa walked in from the kitchen.

'I heard, Jack,' she said, sitting down beside us.

'I have a question,' she said. 'David, are you sure the inputs from the plants can instruct the turbs to feed the plants when they're hungry?'

'Quite certain,' he said, trying, I thought, to sound grown-up. 'It's the only explanation that fits all the observations.'

'And what about us hacking the smartchips to override inputs from the plants? That still goes?' I asked.

'For sure,' he said, smiling. He was a kid again.

'What about that second programming language in the source code that you were having so much trouble with?' I asked.

'Oh, that,' he said. 'I was wrong about that. It isn't important.'

I went over to the bookshelf and poured myself a dram of Jura.

'Your notebook – have you written all this down in your notebook?' I asked.

'Yes, I did,' he said. 'I figured I might have to explain it again to someone.'

'Good,' I said. 'I think you will.'

I drained the whisky and my head hit the back of the armchair and in an instant I was out. I slept for I don't know how long, till I felt David shaking me.

'Someone's here!' he cried. 'There's a big black car at the foot of the drive.'

I searched for the field glasses and ran to the window.

There, below us, I saw Edwards-Knight getting out of the car, a black SUV with darkened windows. Two other men got out with him. It had been raining for hours and the road was partially under water. The three men were quickly soaked and they flapped the sides of their raincoats to shake the rain off. That's when I saw their weapons.

Why would they bring weapons? I thought to myself. Well, why not, given the chaos.

I watched as Edwards-Knight raised his arm and pointed at either side of the property. He had that hard smile on his face. The men unholstered their guns, cocked them and set off in the directions he'd pointed to, one to one side of the house, one to the other.

Why would they cock them? I wondered. Something wasn't right.

'Come on, David, we're getting out of the house and going up the hill, now!' I shouted. 'Get your coat!'

I grabbed my coat and Nessa's and found her coming down the stairs.

'Put this on,' I said. 'We're going up the hillside straightaway.'

'Why Jack?' she asked, but she knew me well enough by then to put the coat on first and head for the door.

'Edwards-Knight, that bloke from the base up in Yorkshire. And two others. Guns. Not friendlies,' I said as we scrambled up the snowy hill.

'Keep going!' I urged, holding David's hand. 'I want some distance so we can see.'

I picked a spot and then decided to head for another a bit further up the hill, to be on the safe side.

'OK.' I said. 'Down.'

We crouched and I watched with the field glasses. The two men had circled the property and joined Edwards-Knight at the door of the house. They knocked at the door and waited, not for very long, before forcing it open. A few minutes later they emerged from the rear into the garden.

Edwards-Knight pointed and one of the men raised a hand held device that looked like a cross between an old-fashioned camera and a missile launcher. He pointed it at the hill above the house and began moving it left and right, slowly raising it. Then, the thing pointed at us, he stopped. He said something to Edwards-Knight and the three men began to come our way.

'They've seen us or found us somehow with that thing,' I said. 'Quick, let's get over the crest of the hill.'

As we neared the crest I spotted some turbs in the next valley, not far away. Its head was visible from the top of the hill, but the men pursuing us could not have seen it.

'Let's make for the nearest turb,' I said.

'Jack, why?' asked Nessa. 'It's too dangerous.'

'No, not if we're quiet in the approach,' I said. 'Let's get inside the radius of the blades.'

'I can't,' said David. 'I won't. I hate them.'

'David,' I said with urgency. 'Your life depends on it. Follow me.'

We moved down the far side of the hill at a run, my hand in Nessa's and hers in David's. Wet tree branches brushed our faces, and now and then the undergrowth caught our ankles.

'Keep moving,' I said.

We'd reached edge of the woods at the valley floor and I looked back up the hill. The three agents were there at the top, the man with the strange device searching the woods where we were.

The turb was about fifty metres from us.

'Good,' I said. 'The turb hasn't noticed us. Now, make for it, walk quickly, but make it seem like you have all the time in the world.'

We moved toward the turb. As we walked I looked backwards over my shoulder to the men on the hilltop. The man with the device, I saw with relief, was looking away from us.

We reached the base of the turb.

'Get behind it,' I said to Nessa and David. 'Get to the far side, where they can't see us.'

I fumbled in my pocket for a turb wrench and flipped open the hatch at the base of the turb.

'In we go,' I said. 'Nessa, you first, then David, the rungs will be wet, so be careful, but climb!'

Inside the turb, I made a quick calculation of its height. About one hundred and fifty metres, I reckoned.

A few of the familiar foul plants stuck to the walls up and down the tower, but most, I knew, would be concentrated in the turb's head. Of course, they stank.

'Ignore the smell, David,' I shouted. 'Keep going up.'

The safety cable flapped around the rungs, but we didn't have any safety belts.

Nessa and David were already well above me, and I struggled to catch up with them.

'I think they can't find us here inside the turb,' I called out. 'I'm guessing their device can't penetrate the turb's skin.'

But I was wrong. Almost at the top, I heard someone enter the turb far below at the base.

'They're coming,' I said. 'Hurry up, into the head, we've still got time.'

By the time I reached the head, Nessa and David were already inside.

'How did they figure out where we are?' Nessa asked.

'Doesn't matter,' I said. 'We've got the upper hand. They don't know how many we are, or whether we are armed. And they don't know turbs like we do.'

'The first thing we do is move about here inside the head, especially near the generator,' I went on. 'I want this turb to sense us. But wait, wait till I give the signal.'

'Jack!' We heard a voice from the tower. It was Edwards-Knight. 'Why are you running away? We've come to get you to safety.'

I looked down through the hatch. He was coming up, followed by the other two.

Edwards-Knight was about half-way up the turb. I reckoned the other two were maybe a third of the way.

'We're very grateful to you,' I shouted.

They kept climbing, coming closer. I could see a pistol in one of the men's hands.

'Now,' I said to Nessa and David. 'Move around, make some noise!'

Within a few minutes the turb began rocking gently on its wheels.

'Is it doing that because of us?' David asked.

'Yes,' said Nessa. 'Take hold of something. It'll get worse.'

The speed of the swaying increased.

I could see the man with the pistol was struggling to hold it and keep a grip on the rungs.

'Damn this thing!' Edwards-Knight shouted.

The turb was moving violently now, jerking this way and that.

'I can't – ' called one of his men as his foot slipped off a wet rung and he fell, and as he fell he knocked the man below him and they both tumbled down the turb tower, banging against the rungs and cables as they flew downwards and landed with a thud at the base.

Edwards-Knight stared below in disbelief. Then he looked up at me, his face contorted with anger.

'Looks like you're alone,' I shouted.

'I'll – ' he didn't finish his unpleasant thought, but re-doubled his efforts to climb. Despite the motion of the turb, I saw that he was likely to make it.

'Quick, Nessa, take David and hide in the back, behind the generator,' I said. 'I'll get him up on the platform.'

'What then Jack?' said Nessa.

'Not quite sure,' I said, scurrying up the rungs leading to the platform.

I'd got outside and shut the platform hatch just as Edwards-Knight climbed into the turb head. He'd seen me but was momentarily struck by the stench of the plants.

'Agh,' he yelled. 'Something bit my leg!'

Undeterred, he climbed the rungs toward the platform hatch. I positioned myself behind the hatch cover and waited for it to open. But I had nothing to hit him with.

He emerged and stood up, and then stumbled with the swaying of the turb, grabbing hold of the platform railing. We stood facing each other.

'You've nothing to be frightened about. You see, I have no weapon,' he said, advancing across the platform towards me.

'I only want to persuade you – and Nessa and the boy, yes, we know about him – to do the right thing,' he went on, nearly falling over as the turb moved backwards. I watched his body rather than listened to his words, none of which I believed.

He reached out his hand to me.

'Here, let's go back down with the others,' he said.

His hand came ever closer to mine but I stepped backwards, to the platform railing.

He looked into my eyes.

'Come,' he said, with that hard smile and eyes that he tried to make warm.

At that moment the turb changed direction, lurching forward at a steep angle and stopping suddenly, flinging Edwards-Knight straight at me. He tried to grab me. I felt his fingers brush my arm but he couldn't get a grip and his body hit the railing and curled over it. With a cry, he was gone, over the side.

I steadied myself. The turb was leaning at a crazy angle. I laid down flat out on the platform and, using the hooks to pull myself, crawled toward the hatch. Once I'd got hold of it, I turned my body to get my legs through the opening.

Nessa poked her head up through the hatch, between my legs.

'Jack, I'm coming out on the platform,' she said.

'What happened?' I cried. 'You removed the smartchip, didn't you?'

'Of course,' she said. 'I figured that the turb would jerk to a stop and would throw him off balance.'

'But how did you know that it would throw him and not me?'

'I didn't,' said Nessa, climbing out of the hatch. 'We were lucky.'

She stood upright on the leaning platform and I did the same. We breathed easy and gazed out over what remained of the *Hope and Glory* turb herd. The day had brightened and despite the terrible encounter with Edwards-Knight and his men, I felt almost light-hearted.

'I've got to call Phil,' I said. 'I can get a signal up here.'

He picked up.

'Phil –' I said.

'Jack, I tried to call you,' he broke in. 'There are men coming to kill that boy, and you and Nessa. They want the boy's notebook.'

'Why Phil? I mean, I know,' I said. 'We've dealt with them. Phil, about the plants −'

'What do you mean, you've dealt with them?' he asked.

'I mean Edwards-Knight is dead, but I didn't kill him. Listen, Phil, about the plants −'

'Don't say anything − people are listening. Just get here to Cheltenham. With the boy,' he said. The call ended.

20

DUNKIN DOUGHNUT

'What did Phil say?' asked Nessa.

'He said we should come to Cheltenham straightaway – with David,' I said. 'He also said Edwards-Knight was coming to kill all of us.'

Nessa frowned. She was clearly upset by what had happened. I knew that look in her face.

'Jack, while you were on the phone, I was looking at those turbs down there,' she said. 'It's what Jenny described to us at the shopping centre – the pecking – do you remember? She saw it and I thought at once it had to do with feeding. Just look at them!'

I raised the field glasses and looked. The sight was odd. The turbs were leaning over at an extreme angle, each with a single blade pecking the ground. The blades rose and fell.

'Nessa, the field is full of dead sheep. The turb blades seem to be pecking at the dead sheep,' I said. 'What does it mean?'

'Look again,' she said. 'Look closely at the tips of the blades.'

I twisted the focus and looked again.

Then I saw it. The decomposing flesh of the dead sheep was being drawn into the turbs' tendons – via the water run-off pipes – and sucked up into the turbs' heads.

'That's how the plants inside are feeding,' I said. 'It's incredible.'

What I was looking at explained what happened to the Fergusons and to the lads at the shopping centre. The strangely emaciated bodies.

I understood only at that moment what the deviation factor was all about: *The plants had taken control of the turbs.*

'David!' I shouted. 'Come up here on the platform.'

'No, I won't,' he said. 'I'm afraid.'

'Nothing to be afraid of,' I said. 'Come up here!'

His head popped up, and he emerged hesitantly. I grabbed him by the arm.

'Look out over the field, David,' I said, placing the field glasses in his hands.

He raised them to his eyes.

'I was right,' he said after a moment. 'It's what I thought. The plants are in control.'

'It's unbelievable,' said Nessa.

'All right,' I said. 'We have to get away from here, now! When that Edwards-Knight lot doesn't report back, more of them are likely to come. We'll take their car.'

'Let's go,' I said.

We climbed carefully down the rungs, and at the bottom stepped to avoid the two fallen men. I checked their pulses. Nothing.

'Jack,' said Nessa. 'Let's take their guns.'

'Can't hurt,' I replied. 'And their car keys.'

We hurried back over the hill to the house, stopping only to grab a few things.

'David,' I said. 'Get your notebook with all the smartchip re-programming notes. Bring it with.'

We set off westwards on the A40. I switched off the GPS and de-activated all the location software, hoping to blind whoever might want to track us.

'Where are we going to go when this is all over?' Nessa asked. Her voice told me she was tired and stressed – and so was I. But now we had the secret, and we had to use it.

'How about the Isle of Wight?' I said. 'It has no turbs. And it probably isn't flooded because the higher bits are two hundred meters above sea level.'

'Nessa,' I went on. 'Do you regret staying here in England with me?'

'Oh, no!' she laughed, embracing and kissing me. I turned my head and kissed her back, keeping one eye on the road.

Just then a pack of mini-turbs appeared in the rear mirror, gaining on us fast. I shook off her embrace.

'Accelerate,' I told the car, and after an interval the mini-turbs grew smaller in the mirror.

We entered the Cotswolds, hilly country and free of flooding.

'We'll be there soon,' I said. 'Now when we get to Cheltenham, I am going to stop. Nessa, I want you to take David's notebook and hide it somewhere. We'll meet up with you later. In any case, you'll be safe. David and I will continue on to where Phil is, in the government centre.'

'Hide it where, Jack?'

'I'm thinking,' I said.

Something occurred to me.

'Do you like horses?' I asked.

'Sure,' she answered.

'Cheltenham has a big racecourse, the most famous in England,' I said. 'Do you think you can find it?'

'If it's so well known, then of course,' she said.

'Come on, there won't be passers-by to ask the way,' I said. 'You'll have to find it on your own. I've been there. It's north of the town, maybe two miles, just below a big hill called Cleve Hill. It's the largest hill around. You can't miss it.'

'I'll find it,' she said.

'Good,' I said. 'Once you've found the racecourse, you'll see the stands. Right in the centre of the largest stand is the Royal Enclosure. I want you to hide the notebook under the King's seat. Got it?'

She nodded.

'Then stay at the racecourse. Hide yourself somewhere. We'll make contact after you've stashed the notebook,' I said.

'How?' asked Nessa.

'Not quite sure yet,' I said. 'But Nessa, we've got to do it this way. I want you safe and I want that notebook safe. It's our only insurance.'

'Take the GPS,' I added, ripping it off the dashboard. 'You've got your smartphone? The notebook? And the gun?'

'Yes, Jack,' she answered.

'Here, take an extra cartridge,' I said, sliding it over.

We came down out of the hills. On the outskirts of Cheltenham we saw signs of massive flooding. I reckoned the River Chelt had burst its banks.

'Here's your stop,' I said, as we entered the town.

'Jack, I love you,' she said.

'And I love you, too.'

I drove into Cheltenham. I headed for the centre of town, the Promenade, where water covered half the tyres and I wondered whether we would get through.

Here and there we saw heavily armed soldiers, but not a single ordinary person. The soldiers were my guides. I followed them. The more soldiers, I figured, the closer we would come to our destination – GCHQ – the English government's secret listening post.

'Where are we going?' asked David, who'd been silent in the rear seat.

'To the government's listening post,' I said.

'Is that a centre for spies?' he asked.

'Something like that,' I replied.

'It's nicknamed the "Doughnut" because of its circular shape,' I went on. 'But it isn't something you would want to eat or, if you did, would be able to digest.'

'When will we get there?' asked David.

'We're already there,' I said. 'There it is in front of us.'

Surrounded by ordinary housing estates, the Doughnut was marked out only by a tall metal fence, capped with coils of barbed wire. Tall poles fitted with downward-pointing cameras stood at intervals just inside the fence.

The road we'd come on led straight to a gate with guard posts on either side. In front of the gate a chunk of metal rose out of the asphalt, blocking the drive.

Somewhere in this building, I thought, were the prime minister and the rest of the cabinet, including Toby Lang. Perhaps even the King was there – the government media gave no information on the Royal Family's whereabouts.

I told the car to stop.

An armed soldier appeared from one of the posts and neared us, while others hovered behind him, their weapons raised above their hips. Above, I saw a tower with more soldiers looking down at us.

'National Identity Cards,' said the soldier.

He took our documents and went away. When he returned, he uttered a single word.

'Cleared,' he said.

The metal barrier disappeared into the asphalt.

I told the car to move, slowly, and once we were inside the gate another vehicle pulled in front of us and a hand emerged from its window gesturing us to follow. We followed it through an arch leading into the middle of the doughnut and down a ramp to a cavernous car park. The escort car stopped and a soldier approached.

'Get out and follow me,' he said.

We came to a checkpoint for a DNA scan. We were given coloured plastic bracelets that held both our DNA and a tracking device. Another man brought us to a brightly lit room with a table and some chairs and there we waited until Patel appeared. He was not as friendly as he had been before.

'Mind telling me why you turned up here in a vehicle belonging to one of our agencies?' he said, without any greeting.

'The men who drove it to my house wouldn't be requiring it further,' I replied.

'Mind explaining that?' he said.

'They came to kill us,' I said. 'Mind explaining that?'

He took that in for a moment.

'Tell me what happened,' he said. 'The short version.'

He listened and when I had finished he said simply: 'We're going to see Singh.'

'Without the boy,' he added. 'I'll take him.'

'No,' I said. 'He doesn't leave my sight.'

Patel hesitated.

'All right,' he said. 'Let Singh decide.'

'He can bloody well decide whatever he wants,' I exploded. 'I've come to see Phil Burnley. He's the man I want to see, not your Mr Singh.'

Patel shrugged.

'Singh will have to deal with you first,' he said. 'Come on, then.'

He led us down the corridor to a lift. We went up two floors, and then passed through another corridor till we came to a door that looked like all the other doors we'd passed. Like them, it was marked with a number.

'Wait here,' he said, and disappeared behind the door. After a few minutes the door opened, and Patel beckoned us to enter.

Singh was seated behind a desk.

'Get some water for them,' he said to Patel.

'Come in,' he said. 'I remember you from RAF Fenwith Hill. You're one of the brave wind engineers who risked your life. I've got to go into an important meeting in a few minutes, so I can't give you much time. Why have you come here?'

'We've come to see Phil Burnley,' I said.

'All right, I'll get Patel to find him for you,' he said. 'Anything else?'

'Yes, one thing,' I said. 'Did your ministry send three agents to my house earlier today?'

'No one from the National Security Department was sent to your house,' he replied. 'If someone had been sent, I would have known about it.'

For some reason I believed him.

'Thanks,' I said.

Singh was true to his word and Phil soon entered the room where Patel had brought David and I to wait.

'Hello, Jack,' he said warmly. 'Thank God you're all right.'

'Phil, what's going on?' I said by way of greeting. 'Why were those men trying to kill us?'

'I honestly don't know,' he answered. 'I got wind something bad was going to happen, so I tried to warn you.'

'You don't know?' I stammered. 'It seems to me you know everything that goes on around here.'

'I know they were from Cobra,' he said.

'What's Cobra?' I asked.

'A top secret unit. It does the government's dirty work,' he replied, adding, 'Has the boy really cracked the source code in the turb smartchips?'

'Ask him yourself,' I said, moving aside to reveal David, who was standing behind me.

'Well, hello,' said Phil, putting on his rather effective jovial manner. 'So you're David. Jack's told me what a smart young chap you are.'

'Thank you,' was all David said.

'He's a little shy sometimes,' I said.

'Listen, the turb chips haven't been hacked by a foreign country or by terrorists,' I went on. 'It's the plants, Phil. We've learned more about the plants than what was in Gordon's report.'

I told him what we'd seen from the top of the turb in the *Hope and Glory* project.

'Unbelievable,' he said.

'The plants have taken control of the turbs,' I concluded.

'We've got to get you in front of Toby Lang,' he said.

The mention of Lang's name made me wince – I couldn't forget overhearing his conversation with Wayne, the American agent. But I said nothing.

'Come on, I'll take you to him,' said Phil.

'David comes with,' I said.

'Sure,' Phil replied. 'We'll need him.'

We made our way through several corridors and went up in a lift to the top floor of the Doughnut. Phil proceeded to the door of a conference room, where a uniformed guard waved us to stop.

'Do you know who I am?' Phil demanded.

The guard started to speak but just then the door opened and Patel's head popped out.

'It's all right,' he said to the guard. Patel motioned us toward some chairs in the back.

So this was it, I thought to myself as I looked over the faces of the men and women gathered around the long table: politicians, civil servants, military officers, and, presumably, spies. This is where decisions are made. At the head of the table sat Toby Lang.

A tall army officer was speaking. His name tag said 'Napier' and I could see that he was a colonel.

'The overall strength of the turbs on land we reckon at about twelve to fourteen million,' he was saying. 'That figure indicates those turbs which have broken free of their electricity tethers and are now moving freely across the length and breadth of these islands. I exclude, of course, the Republic of Scotland, though we are in close contact with the authorities up there.'

'I'm afraid,' Colonel Napier continued, 'that the turbs have got the advantage. With tanks and artillery, we can hit them easily enough – and we've hit plenty, I can say with satisfaction – but the problem is we haven't enough tanks and artillery. Lack of ammunition in sufficient quantity is also a factor, again, the budget cuts. It's a bit like the First World War – not enough shells.'

'Major Brooke, the map please,' said Napier.

An officer clicked on his computer and a map of England appeared on the wall, marked with many colours.

'The red areas,' Napier continued, 'show where the turbs are concentrated. As you'll note, they're mostly in rural areas but they seem to be converging on the south – that, of course, is where most of our population is, in the Home Counties. Look here, at this red line. The turbs have nearly formed a continuous front, from Ipswich in the east, westward along to Milton Keynes and further westward to just north of us here in Cheltenham.'

'The black areas show our army concentrations,' he went on. 'As you will note, we haven't a continuous line. We have concentrations in strength, or lack of strength, varying according to the position.'

I studied the map. The black areas were dots, large and small, facing a continuous red line to the north.

Before the colonel could go on, a boom of artillery sounded, and then an another, causing the walls of the conference room to shudder.

'That would be our artillery,' he explained. 'There's a large herd of turbs approaching Cheltenham in the Cleeve Hill area, near the racecourse.'

'Sound attracts them,' I said in a loud voice. 'By firing at them, you're only drawing them closer.'

The colonel stared at me.

'You have something to add?' he asked.

'Yes,' I said. 'It would be better to silence the guns and ring the town with fire – like pyres on Guy Fawkes Night.'

'Guy Fawkes Night!' the colonel snorted.

'The young man may be right,' said Lang. 'I'd like to hear what he has to say.'

'You look familiar,' he added. 'You were up at Fenwith Hill, weren't you? One of the wind engineers who risked his life in the North Sea?'

'My name is Jack Mason,' I replied. 'And yes, sir, you saw me before the mission.'

'There's quite a bit more,' said Colonel Napier.

'It can wait, can't it?' said Lang, with just a trace of impatience in his voice.

'Mr Lang, I agree with you. I think it would be useful to hear what Jack Mason has to say about the turbs,' said Phil, rising from his chair. 'He's learned some things.'

'Go ahead, Jack,' said Lang. 'I'm listening to you.'

I took a deep breath and started talking about turbs.

'The problem, as you know, is that the turbs aren't following the instructions from their control computers,' I began. 'This is what we call the deviation factor.'

'The reason this is happening is that the smartchips in the turbs' heads are responding to the needs of the plants growing inside the turbs, and not to the control computers. The plants are carnivorous. They've been genetically modified through contact with the rare earth metal *neodymium*, which is used in turb generators. And the process of genetic modification is still continuing – we may see further mutations in the plant cells.'

'The turbs satisfy the plants' need for food by killing their prey with their blades and then they use the pump mechanism and the small pipes along the length of the blades, originally designed for water run-off. The pipes permit the turbs to assimilate food in the form of decomposing flesh.'

'That's why the turbs are killing people – in order to eat. That's why they break their tethers and as a result we lack for power. That's why, I think, they're moving south – led by pack leaders – because the plants like the warmer temperatures. And that's where the biggest source of food can be found – our population is mostly concentrated in the south.'

'The turbs,' I concluded, 'have become a competitor to the human species. Now that humankind is on the back foot, given climate change and flooding, the turbs are competing. Forget about any good the wind turbs have brought us – now, they've got the advantage. Unlike us, they don't have to grow, make or process anything to survive. They only have to kill their prey, which is us.'

The room was silent when I'd finished. Lang spoke up.

'It's incredible what you say. I find it all hard to believe,' he said.

'Toby, you're not going to listen to this nonsense, are you?' said a man sitting next to him. 'The turbs present issues that are both energy-related and national security-related. All this talk about a "competing species" is rot.'

'Well, Alastair, I'm not going to dismiss it out of hand,' said Lang.

'Sir Philip, what's your view – do you vouchsafe Jack's theory?' he asked.

'I do,' Phil replied. 'I think it's more than a theory. I think it's spot on. And I've seen the report on the plants by Professor Gordon at Oxford, which supports the conclusions as far as the role of *neodymium* in the genetic modification of the plants goes.'

'But what about hacking as the cause of the deviation factor?' Lang asked. 'My best people tell me the turb networks have been hacked by China or Russia or terrorists – by *someone*.'

'They haven't been hacked,' came David's voice. 'But they could be – by us.'

'Who's this?' asked Lang.

'This is David, my software genius,' I said. 'What he's saying is that we ourselves can re-write the turb source code to re-gain control over the turbs. In fact, David has already figured out how to do it.'

'How?' asked Lang.

'It's a bit technical,' said David.

'Well, let's find out if you're right,' said Lang. 'Get some computer blokes from the Special Anti-Turb Unit to spend some time with these visitors, especially this boy,' he said.

'If half of this is true,' said Lang, without finishing his sentence. He rose to leave.

David and I spent the rest of the day closeted with the Doughnut's computer geeks. We gave them all the turb smartchips we had. It turned out they had several of their own. The head geek was a man named Jarvis. I sat and listened to what he and David talked about, but grasped little. From time to time Phil poked his head in to see how we were getting on. Lang came down once.

'Rooms like this are where war is waged these days,' he said. 'Battlefields are a thing of the past.'

I insisted on being present because I didn't want to let David out of my sight. Still, I began to feel uncomfortable, cooped up in a windowless room, out of touch with what was happening. My smartphone had no signal. I wondered where Nessa was, whether she was safe and when I could get out of there to find her. The claustrophobic feeling was made worse by the constant presence of minders, even when we were taken up some stairs for something to eat.

Finally, Jarvis said we could go, but that didn't mean we were free to leave. We were led to a room and told to wait. That's when I really began to climb the walls. Just when I was ready to kill someone, the door opened.

'The minister wants to see you,' said Alastair, the advisor who'd been sitting next to Lang at the earlier meeting. He led us back to the conference room which, this time, was empty, save for Toby Lang.

The room was on the Doughnut's highest level, affording a view to the north. In the distance we could see the masts of countless turbs. They appeared tiny from so far away. Puffs of smoke rose where our artillery fired at them, now and then punctured by explosions and flames when a shell struck home. The scene reminded me of war game software for kids, but I knew it was real.

The advisor whispered in Lang's ear, and he turned toward us.

'Sit down,' he said, making it sound like a gesture of lukewarm hospitality, at odds with the grin fixed on his face.

'You're a clever boy,' he said to David.

'Very clever, I'd say, except that it's not working,' he went on. 'Explain, please, Alastair.'

'A special team has been testing the changes in the software by sending instructions to the turbs via radio,' said the advisor. 'But it's had no effect. We've not been able to bring the turbs under control.'

'We'd like it to work, wouldn't we?' said Lang. 'What've we missed?'

'When I was working with your team, I couldn't remember all of the steps I'd taken to re-write the source code,' said David.

'So what did you do?' Lang asked.

'I guessed,' said David.

Lang cast a sharp glance at his advisor, who in turn scowled in my direction.

'But I'll bet you saved the steps in your tablet or wrote them down somewhere, didn't you? Like a clever boy,' said Lang.

'Yes I did, in my notebook,' said David.

A look of satisfaction crossed Lang's face.

'And where's your notebook?' he asked. 'Is it in the computer room downstairs or have you left it somewhere else?'

'Somewhere else,' said David.

'Well, then, we'd better find it, hadn't we?' said Lang.

'Stop berating the boy,' I said.

Lang threw me a look that said he wasn't used to being given orders.

'Look, David warned me that he couldn't remember the exact sequence of steps he'd taken to crack the turb source code. So, the fact that all your experts' efforts to duplicate his work failed to produce results isn't a surprise to me,' I said.

'Do you know about this notebook?' Lang asked. 'Do you know where it is?'

I ignored his question.

'Three Cobra agents came to my house today,' I said. 'I think they came to kill David – and me and Nessa, my fiancé.'

'My fiancé?' I thought to myself as soon as the words were out of my mouth. Why had I said that?

'I think they came for that notebook,' I went on. 'They died, but we didn't kill them – they died when a turb – '

'I know about that,' said Lang.

'You do?' I asked, surprised.

'Of course,' he replied.

'Who sent those men to my house?' I asked.

'I've no idea,' he said.

I thought he was lying, but I couldn't put a finger on why. I had to think quickly now, because I saw my chance – perhaps my only chance – of making a deal.

'I want to speak with you alone,' I said to Lang. 'But David, you stay.'

'Very well,' he said. 'Give us a minute, will you, Alastair?'

The advisor left the room, scowling.

'All right, what is it?' Lang asked.

'I want to stop the turbs,' I said. 'But I also want a guarantee there'll be no more attempts on our lives. So I'll make you a deal: you let me out of there, and I'll bring you the notebook. We'll take one of your vehicles – stripped of tracking devices.'

'You must think I'm really naïve,' he replied. 'How do I know you won't sell it to the Chinese or the Russians, if you got the chance?'

I was shocked. So this was the kind of thinking at the highest level of our government.

'All right, I'll take with me the one man we both trust: Phil Burnley,' I said.

'Deal,' said Lang.

'Now that's done, I want to make a call,' I said. 'May I use your smartphone please?'

'My smartphone? You can't use my smartphone!' Lang retorted. 'It's for top level government communication. It's got encryption up the wazoo.'

'That's exactly why I want to use it,' I said.

Lang pulled it from his pocket and slid it across the table. I pressed Nessa's number.

'Hi, it's me,' I said when she answered. 'Are you where we talked about?' I listened. 'Good. Stay put and out of sight. I'm coming to get you.' I said.

It took some time to find Phil and ready a vehicle, a black SUV, and then I strapped David into the rear and took the wheel with Phil at my side. We drove out of the Doughnut, heading for the racecourse.

21

A DAY AT THE RACES

The racecourse, in Prestbury Park just to the north of Cheltenham, lay in the escarpment of Cleeve Hill, near the army's front line against the advancing turbs. As we approached we could clearly see the tops of the turbs on the far side of the hill, not more than two miles away. On the crest of the hill we spotted formations of tanks and artillery, blasting away at the turbs. The sound of the guns rattled David.

'Hey David,' I called over my shoulder. 'Nothing to be afraid of. Show me how brave you are.'

'That's right, David,' Phil added. 'Nothing to be afraid of.'

I turned the SUV into the main entrance to the racecourse.

Home to the Cheltenham Festival and its Gold Cup – one of the top trophies in English horse racing – the place was world famous. Starting with the King, the cream of English society came – as well as foreign royalty, Arab sheikhs, Russian oligarchs and Chinese billionaires – set down at the course's own helicopter pad or at its own steam railway station. The really rich came to race their own horses. And along with them came their accessories – expensive cars, beautiful women and paparazzi. But many ordinary punters also came, to enjoy the day and maybe have a flutter.

All of that was gone.

The racecourse had become a lake, from which the grandstand and various other buildings protruded like Lego toys. Water covered the both the old and new courses, and much of the lower grandstand. The broken windows and open-hanging gates suggested looting. There wasn't a soul to be seen, and the only sound, apart from the English artillery on the hill, was that of gates banging in the wind.

I parked on the higher ground of the north car park, by the Centaur amphitheatre.

'The Royal Enclosure,' I said, and we mounted the steps upwards, to the upper grandstand. Phil, out of shape, lumbered after us.

'Now, where did I tell Nessa to put your notebook?' I said at we reached there.

'Under the King's seat,' David replied.

'Right you are, but which one is that? They all look the same,' I said. In an age of democracy, the sovereign had no special seat at the races.

'There,' said David. 'In the middle, I think.'

'Right again,' I said, feeling with my fingers beneath the seat. I pulled up a plastic bag and removed the notebook.

'Here it is, Phil,' I said.

'Excellent, Jack,' he said. 'Done and dusted.'

He was standing on the landing where the stairs from below gave out onto the seats of the upper stand. He held a gun in his hand.

'What's the gun for, Phil?' I asked. 'I'm a little surprised.'

'The way the world is going, nothing should surprise you any more,' he observed. 'Give me the notebook, if you please.'

'I promised Lang I would bring it to him,' I said.

'He's not going to need it,' Phil replied, stepping down the aisle towards us.

'How do you mean?'

'I mean Lang is on the fence. He leans this way and that, trying to figure out which policy position might get him into the prime minister's chair,' he said. 'Oh, to be sure, there are other voices in the cabinet. I don't think it really matters what Lang or the other ministers think. The "special relationship" is history. The Yanks are determined to finish it, with us or without us.'

'Finish what?' I asked.

'The competition with China for world domination, for control of the world's resources – oil, gas, uranium, coal and everything else – the traditional sources of energy still matter a great deal,' he remarked, as if he were giving the day's weather outlook.

'You see,' he continued, 'the Yanks are going to adapt the *neodymium* in the turbs to make nukes out of them. They're going to nuke China and maybe Russia, too, if they have the chance.'

'How?' I asked. 'How are they going to do that?'

I knew about those crazy ideas, of course. We'd heard Wayne, the American agent, telling Lang.

'Oh, Jack, don't play with me, you know about the *neodymium* metal in the turb generators – and its capacity to facilitate nuclear fusion. The turbs could be turned into mobile nuclear weapons, millions of them.'

'You see, cracking the software code can be used to control the turbs, to stop them killing humans,' he went on. 'Or it can be used to turn them into weapons – with a little tinkering. And the Yanks are good at tinkering.'

'I don't think there's much doubt which side will win, and I want to be on the winning side. Besides, the winning side pays better,' he said, coming further down the aisle.

'Phil, let me ask you about those agents who came to my house,' I said. 'Who sent them?'

'Why, the Americans of course,' he replied.

'But they were English,' I said. 'And Lang and Singh said they knew nothing about it.'

'Now, Jack, don't be naïve,' said Phil. 'Certain elements on our side can see which way the wind is blowing. Lang, well, he – '

'But why did you try to warn me they were coming?' I asked.

'I don't know, a bit of sentiment because you were my protégé – you and Frank,' he said, reaching the first row of the upper stand where David and I stood. 'And a bit of self-interest. I wanted to claim the prize myself. I just needed you to lead me to it.'

'What will happen if I don't give the notebook to you?' I asked.

A burst of artillery sounded not far away, followed by an explosion. The earth shook. All the while David stayed close by me next to the King's seat, hugging my leg.

'Come on, Jack, let's get it over with. Give it to me,' said Phil, raising his pistol.

'I can't give it to you, Phil, it belongs to England,' I said.

'Jack, I've loved you like a son, you and Frank, both of you, like sons. Don't make me,' he said, now pointing his pistol at my chest.

'Phil, even a bloke as smart and experienced as you can make a mistake – and you're making one now,' I said.

'Jack, I haven't got much time,' he said. 'Give me the notebook now.'

He raised the pistol and I pushed David away.

At that moment a deafening shot rang out, then another and then a third. But I felt nothing. I knew I hadn't been hit. Had Phil fired wide to frighten me?

Then I saw. Phil leaned forward on his thick legs, his stomach hit the railing and he crumpled over it and fell from the upper stand, splashing into the flooded lower stand below.

Nessa stood, above, on the landing, holding a smoking gun in two hands.

'You shot him!' I said.

'Jack, he was going to shoot you,' she called out, bounding down the aisle.

'Yes, yes, you're right – I can't believe it,' I said.

I looked down at Phil's body, floating in the flooded lower grandstand, and shook my head. I found it hard to accept that Phil would have shot me but, obviously, I was wrong about that.

A blast sounded on Cleeve Hill, then another. The battle with the turbs was drawing closer to the racecourse.

'Jack, we have to get out of here,' said Nessa.

'Yes,' I said. 'David, come on!'

He came out from under the King's seat. I grabbed his hand

and we made for the exit and bounded down the steps.

'Wait,' I said, on reaching the ground. 'Look over there!'

At the racecourse's heli-pad stood a helicopter, its pylons sub-merged in water. It looked out of place. Gleaming in the setting sun, it was the only thing we saw that looked new and untouched by the flooding and looting.

'Looks like someone else has come for the notebook,' said Nessa.

'There's got to be a pilot inside,' I said. 'We can't give him much time to think, so we'll approach at the back, near the tail rotor.'

We crouched by the Best Mate enclosure, around fifty metres from the bird. The flood waters were up to our knees.

'I'll go first,' I said. 'Nessa, give me the gun.'

She handed me the weapon, saying: 'If you try to wade through the open water, whoever's in that helicopter will hear you splashing about.'

'You're right,' I said.

'Why not swim?' said David.

'What, in a couple of feet of water?'

'Backstroke,' he replied. 'You stay on the surface. I learned it at school.'

At that moment came a loud burst of artillery fire, then another and then a third in rapid succession, followed by explosions. We turned toward Cleeve Hill, above the racecourse. Turbs now stood on the top of the hill, bending, bobbing, hacking at the English positions. We could see a couple of our tanks coming down the hill in full retreat.

'It's now or never,' said Nessa.

'It's now,' I said, shoving the pistol under my belt.

I swam the backstroke, turning my head now and then to gauge how near I was to the helicopter. When I could see the tail rotor blade above me, I stood up, sopping wet. There, I thought, the pilot couldn't see me. But if he started the rotor, it would chop my head off in an instant.

The crackle of the chopper's radio reached my ears. I took a step toward the front of the bird, straining to make out what the voice on the radio was saying. Then I heard the reply from within the cockpit.

'I'm still waitin' on Phil Burnley.'

I *knew* that voice – it was Wayne. *He* was the pilot. I realised at once he could only have been there because Phil had told him to come – for the notebook.

Just at moment the side door slid open. Wayne emerged and plopped his legs into the water.

'Shit!' he said.

I crouched under the chopper, wondering what he was up to. Then I heard the sound of water. He was having a pee. I saw my chance.

'Don't move,' I called out, raising my gun.

'Who's there – ?' said the American, turning his bulk toward me.

'Who the fuck are you?' he said, quickly taking in the gun in my hand.

'I'm the man who's going to borrow your helicopter,' I said.

'The hell you are,' he snorted, making for the open cockpit door.

I threw myself against his body, but the impact against so massive an object was slight. He managed to get an arm inside the door and grab a weapon. A hideous instrument of death, it looked like a cross between a rifle and a pistol, with a long snout ending in two deadly nostrils and what looked like vision-enhancing antenna fixed to its sight, above a double cartridge clip.

He held it aloft in one hand as I tried, with one arm, to push his arm back and, with the other, to bring my pistol into his gut. But with his free hand he swatted the pistol away and it slid from my fingers into the water.

I changed tack, grabbing the snout of his weapon with both hands and diving into the water. This pulled him down with me, as he held fast to his gun. Now, we were both under water, but I was quicker to get back on my feet. I jumped on his stomach – a wide target – and felt his arms on my ankles as he tried to roll to throw me off. That did the trick – he let go of the weapon and I sprang off him and turned, grabbing it and pointing it at his chest.

'Now,' I said, breathing deeply. 'You're going to tell me what you're doing here.'

He heaved himself up out of the water.

'I'm not going to tell you anything,' he growled. 'I'm an agent of the United States government and I don't have to explain anything to anyone. It's you who's going to talk. Where's Phil Burnley?'

Then a look of recognition crossed his face.

'I've met you – you're Jack Mason,' he said. 'Well let me tell you, boy, you're in way over your head.'

'I would say you're the one in deep water,' I said. 'I've got your gun. And you're alone – Phil's not coming.'

'The gun's called an M36, and it's US Government property, by the way,' he replied. 'Like the notebook I came here to get. I paid Phil for it. Now you'd better give me that gun *and* the notebook. Fast. My patience is liable to wear thin.'

He leaned back against the chopper and folded his arms across his chest. He was obviously what the Americans call a 'tough cookie' and I could not help feeling a little nervous.

'I'm going to count to ten,' he went on, as if he were pointing the gun at me, and not the other way round.

'Better yet,' he said, 'I'll have a smoke, and if you haven't seen the light by the time I'm finished, well...'

He reached into a pocket but instead of cigarettes out came a 9mm pistol. Instantly I squeezed the trigger of the M36 – and nothing happened.

'It's kind of a special weapon,' he laughed. 'You have to know where the safety is.'

As he raised his pistol, my fingers raced frantically over every knob and switch on the M36. I only just saw his finger on the trigger of his pistol when the thing suddenly spat out a stream of bullets. Like a jackhammer out of control, it sprayed everything in sight. My finger felt glued to the firing knob and it took a conscious mental effort to relax it. The fusillade stopped as smoke eased from the barrel and I looked up.

The American lay in a couple of feet of water, and the side of the helicopter was peppered with bullet holes.

'I guess I found the safety,' I said to myself.

22

ISLAND

I bent over the body. There was no need to feel for his pulse. He was dead. I thought to rifle his pockets, but I was in a hurry to get Nessa and David.

'Nessa!' I called out between the booms of artillery that continued to sound from Cleeve Hill. 'Come on, we've got to get out of here.'

Suddenly came a loud bang and I looked round for our tanks or artillery, but it was a turb that had crashed through the roof of the grandstand. Bang! Came a second turb's blade, piercing the stand. These were clearly monster-sized turbs, and they were close.

'David won't come,' she yelled.

'I'm afraid,' David screamed. 'The turbs!'

I waded back to the enclosure and grabbed him, lifting him onto my shoulders. By the stand, we were safe within the radius of the turbs' blades – safe, that is, unless a chunk of falling debris should hit us. To reach the helicopter we would have to go outside the radius, but it was the only chance of escape.

I prayed the noise the turbs themselves were making would cover the sound of our splashing through the water and not attract their attention.

'Walk,' I said to Nessa. 'With small, quick steps.'

I turned my head as we walked, eyeing the turbs. They continued to peck at the grandstand.

Then one of the giant turbs straightened up. Its nacelle turned this way and that. Nessa saw it, too.

'Jack, it's looking for us,' she said.

'Keep moving,' I said.

We were perhaps twenty metres from the chopper.

The big turb moved out of line with the others and lumbered around the grandstand.

'It sensed us!' she said.

'It's coming for us!' said David.

The turb lurched out onto the racecourse as we reached the chopper.

'Get in, quickly,' I said.

I calculated the chopper was just about at the radius of the turb's blades – it could hit us.

But then it stopped. I watched it.

'Jack, get in,' cried Nessa.

'Wait, it's – ' I said. What was it doing? It was obviously trying to move – I could see the wheels spinning. It looked like – a car stuck in the mud! It hit me – the turbs' wheels were stuck in the mud that the flooded racecourse had become. I laughed. It was so simple.

'We have a new anti-turb weapon,' I said. 'Mud.'

'Jack,' said Nessa, popping her head out of the chopper. 'We're still near the radius – the thing can stab us from where it is.'

'Shit, you're right!' I said, clambering into the cockpit.

I looked at the gauges and controls. This was no training helicopter. It was a Royal Navy Manx Mk16. It was equipped, I knew, with missiles – but which were the knobs and switches for launching them?

Still, I said to myself, a helicopter was a helicopter. I located the starter button and punched it. The engine whirred to life and the main rotor began to turn.

'Stick, collective, pedals,' I said to myself.

Thump! The mud-stuck turb had slammed a blade into the earth not ten metres from the chopper, shaking it and splattering us with water and mud.

'Nessa, shut the door,' I said.

'Jack, it's going to try again,' she said. 'Look!'

The blade wrested itself free and rose out of sight.

The rotor was turning faster now. I pulled up the collective, slowly.

Nothing happened.

'Jack, maybe we're stuck in the mud, too,' said David.

He was right – the pylons had undoubtedly sunk into the layer of mud covering the heli-pad.

'Here goes,' I said, pulling the collective further upwards.

The chopper began to shake violently, as the lift force of the rotor battled to raise the weight of the bird out of the mud.

Thump! The blade hit the earth again, not five metres from us, covering the chopper with another mud shower.

This time the blade didn't pull up. We watched in horror as it began slicing sideways through the mud, like the fin of an approaching shark.

'Jack, it's going to slice us in two!' Nessa shouted above the engine noise.

I yanked the collective now with all my strength and – finally – the rotor prevailed and the chopper shot straight up into the sky, missing the turb blade by a margin too close for comfort.

I pushed the collective down to slow the upward thrust, at the same time playing with the stick, making small movements to get a feel for how to fly the bird. Even the smallest movements produced immediate changes in the attitude and roll of the aircraft.

'Jack, can you fly this thing? Keep it steady,' Nessa shouted in my ear.

'The stick is very responsive,' I replied nonchalantly, wiping sweat off my brow.

Slowly, I became more comfortable with the bird. I pressed the pedal to turn around, and we gazed down on what was left of Cheltenham racecourse. The turbs had destroyed the grandstand and a fire had broken out somewhere inside the ruins. That drove them away, toward the centre of town. There, we could see a rag-tag unit of tanks and artillery organising a last-ditch defence.

'Won't be long before they reach the Doughnut,' I said.

I turned the helicopter due south, using only the compass for navigation.

There, below us, the Doughnut came into view. We could see that the flood waters had risen considerably, submerging part of the ground floor.

'Somewhere in there is what is left of the English government,' I said. 'I'll put her down in the centre of the Doughnut. Looks dry enough.'

'Wait, Jack, there are anti-aircraft guns on the roof – they might shoot at us!' said Nessa.

'Can't,' I replied. 'This chopper is surely sending out the right signal. They know were friendly.'

'Let's see if we can't help those defenders in the town before we set down,' I said.

I pressed the pedal to turn the chopper around and face towards the centre of Cheltenham.

'Now we're just going to hover for a moment,' I said, actually for me one of hardest things to do in a helicopter – I didn't have the patience for the countless tiny movements which a pilot is required to execute to keep a chopper still.

'Nessa, help me,' I said. 'Flip that cover open. Look for anything marked "target" or "missile".'

'There's a screen here showing moving shapes,' she said. 'Ah, there are the turbs. I can tell. Now, there's something here called "auto-acquire".'

'That sounds about right,' I said. 'Give it a punch, will you?'

She thrust her thumb down on the button. A red light flashed the word 'locked.'

'Right, is it a turb you've locked onto?' I asked.

'Looks like it,' she said.

'Are you sure?' I asked.

'Yes, I'm sure,' she shouted.

'Here goes,' I said. I flipped open a cover and pulled up a toggle marked 'fire.'

There was a *whoosh* and the chopper jerked back sharply with the recoil of the missile's release. Nessa screamed as a flash of white sped away from us. And then came a blast as the missile struck one of the turb leaders, blowing its head off.

'Let's try that again,' I said, exhilarated.

We fired a second missile, and again the recoil pushed the chopper back like it had been hit by a fly swatter. The missile's trail sped away, ending in another huge explosion, this time at the base of a massive turb that wobbled and then keeled over with bang as its blades hit the earth.

'Great fun,' I said. 'But we can't fight the turbs this way. We'll be out of missiles in a minute. I'll take her down.'

I manoeuvred the chopper into the centre of the Doughnut and pushed the collective down. The bird began to drop.

'Not so fast, Jack!' Nessa shouted.

The bird was dropping like a rock. I pulled up the collective, and she steadied.

'Once more,' I said, letting the collective down gradually, keeping the stick steady. Everything was fine, until we suddenly began to spin clockwise. I must have pressed a pedal, so I pressed the other one to counteract the spin, but instead of stopping it, the whole chopper began to shake violently. I released both pedals and the bird hit the ground with a sharp jolt.

'Everyone all right?' I said.

I looked around. My passengers were fine.

'Smooth landing, Jack,' said Nessa, slapping me on the shoulder.

Patel and others were outside, waving their arms and pointing, but not coming closer.

'Blast!' I said.

I had forgotten to switch the rotor blades off. I shut the engine down.

Patel came up and pulled open the chopper's door.

'Have you got the notebook?' he asked.

'Yes, it's here,' I said, patting a bulge in my anorak.

'Good,' he said. 'Let's not waste any time.'

We hurried behind him to the Doughnut's nerve centre. For Nessa and I this meant another period of waiting, which I could hardly stand after the adrenalin rush of firing missiles from the Mk16 chopper.

'Tell Lang I want to see him,' I said to Patel. He made a call and gestured me to follow him. I took Nessa's hand and led her and David with me.

He led us back to the same conference room on the top floor, only this time Lang wasn't there. The room was empty. We gazed out at the approaching turb herd.

'They're holding back,' said Nessa. 'Looks like our lucky missile shots took out two of the leaders.'

'They won't hold back for long,' I said. 'See over there? That one looks like another leader.'

A door opened and in walked a woman with an instantly recognisable face. It wasn't Lang. It was the prime minister.

'Are you Jack Mason?' she asked.

'Yes,' I said. 'This is Nessa Chao. Where's Toby Lang?'

'I sacked him,' she replied. 'Sit down, please.'

'I understand you've given our technical experts information that may help us get control over the turbs,' she said. 'We'll know soon enough whether it will work.'

'I think it will, prime minister,' I said.

She stood and began to speak to me and Nessa and David, and to the aides, advisors, civil servants and military officers who'd filed into the room after her.

She spoke slowly at first, but her eloquence grew.

'We can deal with the flooding. It's not easy but we can,' she said. 'But we haven't got one threat, we've got two. The turbs are without doubt a more serious threat.'

'The whole secret of the deviation factor is incredible,' she went on. 'But it's true. I've had it verified. I've talked to Professor Gordon at Oxford and to others. The turb computer networks haven't been hacked by another country or by terrorists, as we had thought. The technology has simply run amok, and run straight into nature's force, one of the oldest forms of life on our planet: plants. They have become our competitor for domination of this planet, and it looks like they're winning.'

'The question is how the secret of the deviation factor is going to be used,' she continued. 'It may lead to a war *among* the nations using "turbzilla nukes" – as the Americans have proposed. This path I have decisively rejected. Or it may lead to a war *by* the nations against the turbs. That is the course I have set. Either way, the future of our species hangs in the balance.'

'If it's the first, and man makes war against man, using the turbs as nuclear weapons,' she said, 'the *neodymium* will surely cause more mutations in the plant genetics. Flourishing in a post-war radioactive world, there's no telling what kind of new, deadlier plant species may emerge, with millions and millions of turbs at their command.'

'And even in such a war, millions of turbs in neutral nations would *not* be used as weapons – the millions of them in South America, Africa and Southeast Asia, for example – and the foul, radioactive wind born of war would carry the spores of new, more deadly plants around the planet. They would find their way into the turb heads, and there blossom and control the turbs. A new danger would threaten all who survived such a war.'

'But if our species can unite against the turbs, we can perhaps stop them from usurping our planet. We can reverse climate change, and make our world sustainable,' the prime minister continued.

'If we can't, there will be a long road of research and study before the day when we or our children or grandchildren, or generations in the distant future, can drive the turbs back off our island.'

'If that happens, maybe there won't be an England. Maybe our island will break up into small, primitive kingdoms, barely worthy of the name, as it was a thousand years ago.'

When she finished the room was silent.

Colonel Napier entered and whispered into the prime minister's ear.

'It's working,' she said simply. 'Thank God, it's working.'

She went over to the window and beckoned for us to follow. Soon, everyone in the room was standing before the window, staring intently at the turbs.

It was true. They had begun to pull back, and the herd was breaking up. People began to clap and cheer. Napier, the stuffy officer, put his arm around me.

'It will take some time to sort this out,' I said to the prime minister. 'We'll have to figure out which turb came from where, and somehow instruct them to return to their original location. That will take time. Then we'll have to re-connect the tethers. There will be a lot of manual labour involved. Only after that will be have electricity from them again.'

'I gather we won't have Sir Philip Burnley to lead such an effort,' she said, eyeing me closely. Her look told me she knew what had happened at the racecourse. 'That's why I've decided to name you as his successor.'

I didn't know what to say.

'Could I have a day off first, prime minister?' I asked.

'Whatever for?' she said. 'As you explained, there's a lot to do.'

'I'd like to get married,' I said. 'To Nessa here. Today is our anniversary.'

The prime minister looked at Nessa and Nessa looked at me.

'Oh, Jack,' she said. 'Yes!'

She threw her arms around me and kissed me, and I kissed her back.

'You've got it,' said the prime minister. 'Take two days.'

'One other thing, prime minister,' I said. 'Can I borrow a Royal Navy helicopter?'

'I think you already have,' she replied.

*

'Jack,' asked Nessa, after we'd taken off. 'Where are we going?'

'Why, the Isle of Wight, of course. When we reach the south

coast, I'll fly east. It makes sense. It's the only place in England that is free of turbs. And they can't invade – we saw that in Cheltenham – their wheels won't be able to carry them across the Solent.'

'Perfect place for a honeymoon,' I added.

'I have no idea where the Isle of Wight is,' said Nessa. 'I only want to know if you can land this helicopter.'

'Don't worry,' I said. 'I know how to land a helicopter.'